Vermilion Harvest

Playtime at the Bagh

Reenita M. Hora

Vermilion Harvest

Reenita M. Hora

ISBN 978-1-953278-51-7 Hard Back
ISBN 978-1-953278-52-4 Soft Back
ISBN 978-1-953278-53-1 E-Book

Published by

INDIGNOR
— HOUSE —

Chesapeake, VA 23322
www.indignorhouse.com

Cover Design: Indignor House

Note from the Publisher

This novel is a work of pure fiction. A story of young love surrounded by an actual event during 1919 in India, the Jallianwala Bagh massacre. Although historical names do appear throughout this novel, no account should be labeled as fact. Fiction and our ability to transcribe tragic events into a meaningful dialogue is a critical aspect of our acceptance and forgiveness. Every great story ever told is somehow entwined on actual events. However, the words written or spoken are not always based on truth, but on the heart. As many would say, 'truth is stranger than fiction.'

Please enjoy the romance of two teens during a turbulent time of India's past, present, and future. Although technology may have broadened our world, our people and their emotions will forever remain the same.

"Set against the backdrop of the Indian freedom struggle, *Playtime at the Bagh* is a novel about identity and love, in equal measure. While a country struggles to break free, all that a young Aruna seeks is an anchor in her life. On one hand the peaceful city of Amritsar suddenly starts simmering, on the other, two lovers try to find and forge a life together amidst this uneasy calm. Reenita Hora creates a stunning love story in troubled times, amidst one of the darkest events in modern Indian history. Read it!"

Saugata Mukherjee
Head of Content – Entertainment, India
WarnerMedia

Dedicated to my late grandfather, Gopal Krishan Vij, who sparked in me the art of storytelling, inspiring the character of little Gopal. And to the undying spirits of Amritsar, forever marked by the tragedy of the Jallianwala Bagh massacre.

HAPTER 1

January 1919

Ayaz Peermohammed - a man of gray eminence

Ayaz's choices certainly put him at risk of being ratted on. But the day that we met, it was he who was doing the ratting. Of course, I didn't see the irony.

It was five o'clock on a wet January afternoon. A fitful, undecided rain spat across the streets of Amritsar, winding its way through an aggressive outburst of a thistly wind. I stepped into Pritam Da Dhaba, just past the city's boundary, somewhat discombobulated. A down and dirty *truck stop* roadside diner was not my destination of choice, but I'd been caught unaware by the showers. Tired, hungry, and disheveled, I stepped into the no-frills eatery with about thirty bare tables balanced precariously on an uneven, earthen floor.

A multitude of individuals seeking comfort from the downpour sat at tilted tables, ordering the lachha parathas and dal fry – a signature dish – at the dhaba. The restaurant's din saturated the air with loud jokes and colloquial obscenities filtering through the room entwined with the uncouth laughter of male voices. In Amritsar, rarely did one find women at a dhaba and rarely did anyone ever go hungry. Both were against the norms of the Punjabi mind-set. At the heart of the robust food culture, the city's legendary dhabas were a belt-loosening exercise in culinary excess. From offal addicts to staunch vegetarians, mustache-twirling truck drivers to dapper fat cats, food lovers of all stripes found salvation in these tatty, soot-stained eateries. That particular afternoon was no different from any other, other than a female had just stepped into a male frequented eatery.

I was too focused on searching for my book I had misplaced to notice how, within moments, the clatter died to a deathly silence. *Had I left it on the end table of my favorite armchair in the school staffroom? Or was it under my nose, lost among my untidy collection of files and papers?* Why was it, I could never quite master the art of organizational skills? Clearly, I wasn't the only one. Looking up from rummaging through my bag, I noticed a band of dhaba customers frozen in stance and gaping at the spectacle of my disorderly state. Was I really that much of a mess? Or had they never seen an Anglo-Indian woman grace this shrine of local succulence?

Before I could begin to question the rationale behind my insecurity, as I usually did in similar situations, my eyes caught this dashing fellow staring at me. All I could see at first were dimples barely discernible at the corners of his mouth. Then his enchanting smile. Then those dark brown coffee-colored eyes. I had never been one for romantic fairy stories and love at first sight, but there was something about him that was infatuating. I was immediately pulled into his gaze. But before I had a chance to make sense of it all, the scene transformed into utter chaos.

The dashing dimpled fellow raised his finger to his lips and pointed at my feet. As if following his signal, a gigantic, brown rat with a tail the length of a ruler stared up at me through a pair of massive, black, beady eyes.

A loud scream rushed from my lips, piercing through the hushed silence. I jumped onto the nearest chair with a deft, feline grace. Within moments, others had joined me – mostly younger men – a few perching precariously on the tables.

Perturbed by the commotion, the rat scurried across the floor, darting under tables, over feet, and around chair legs. Men, young and old, scattered as it ran the gauntlet. It pranced back and forth across the restaurant, ensuring no corner of the room remained untouched by its presence.

The dimpled fellow, trailed by a motley crew of kitchen hands, dish-washers and chefs, grabbed whatever they could – knives, serving spoons, dish clothes, mops. One clever chap brandished an oversized broom. It was live-action dramatization of Pied Piper with his entourage, kitchen style.

The impromptu task force, ably assisted by plucky customers, stormed through the restaurant in a dovetailed effort to corner the rat. Tables and chairs overturned, guests shrieked, and customers hurried out the front, presumably without paying.

Several burly kitchen staff picked up an overturned table, and with great coordination and with the assistance of the remaining staff and braver customers, they managed to trap the rat behind the table against a far corner. The dimpled fellow, who was clearly a server, threw a dishcloth over the critter, trapping it. He picked up the cloth – rat and all – and triumphantly paraded the length of the restaurant, disappearing out the front door.

A stunned silence enveloped the dhaba as I surveyed the chaos – overturned tables and chairs, customers perched on tables, and numerous thalis of food upturned and strewn across the floor.

The dimpled fellow returned, issuing a series of instructions to his co-workers who had already taken it upon themselves to clean up the mess. Offering his rather large hand, he helped me down from the chair and poured me a cup of chai from a teapot that had been forgotten in all the excitement.

"I suppose you wouldn't care for a portion of ratatouille?" he asked with a twinkle in his eye.

My puzzlement must have been overtly apparent as the left side of his mouth curled up – just a little.

"It's a stewed vegetable dish from the Provence," he added.

"Province?" I asked, repeating what I thought I heard.

"Indeed, a province too," he replied. His amused expression accentuated his dimples. "A region in France known for its sunny weather, colorful countryside, and traditional wine and food."

Of course, Provence! Good heavens, what a complete dolt I must have appeared to be. As an English instructor, it was customary to know a bit of French. Not to speak it fully but to understand the roots of certain words. Here was an opportunity to make up for my idiocy.

"Ratouiller is an expressive form of the verb touiller meaning *to stir up*," I said.

"Indeed." His grin, once again, emphasized his dimples. "Under normal circumstances, we aim to stir up vegetables … rather than trouble caused by rodents."

My heart warmed to this dashing young man's weak attempt at humor. Embarrassed about my disheveled state, I sat on the chair behind me and smoothed out my kameez.

"Rain showers in January are quite atypical, don't you think?" he asked, pulling up a chair.

I looked at him, feeling perplexed, trying to pat down my rain-dampened hair.

"As is a young schoolteacher memsahib visiting a dhaba like this."

"How do you know I'm a schoolteacher?"

"Pride & Prejudice doesn't make the popular reading list for the local Punjabis," he added. He reached over and picked up my book. It had been there all along, just fallen from my grasp on my way in. "I don't suppose Elizabeth Bennet made it to too many dhabas on the outskirts … or whatever the equivalent is in rural England."

"Don't you start," I said, organizing my thoughts. "I already get flack about this kind of stuff."

"Oh?" He seemed amused. "What are you given flack for?"

"That I run off on my own without friends and frequent undesirable corners of the city."

"I don't think anyone in Amritsar would say Pritam Da Dhaba is undesirable."

"It's not the dhaba or the area of town," I replied, glancing around. "Just the fact that I'm here on my own … continuing to underscore the definition of what society deems to be unladylike."

He appeared to be resisting another smile, which made him look even more dashing. "It's true. I wouldn't expect to see young girls here. Not on their own. But how disappointing to hear you talk about *all* women as if they are fine ladies instead of rational creatures."

I tilted my head at the familiar words of Jane Austen. Seemed as if this young man had tuned in to my aura. *Was this a sign?* Or merely an opportunity to quote my favorite author? "Quite right, sir. 'None of us want to be in calm waters all our lives.'"

"Ayaz!" someone called out from the kitchen.

He waved his hand in acknowledgement before breaking into another smile, and there were those dimples. "I'm Ayaz, by the way." He glanced back at the kitchen, his dark brown eyes glowing with a hint of mischief.

"Ayaz?" I repeated.

"Ayaz Peermohammed," he said. "I just started here." He glanced over at the main floor of the dhaba. "Fortuitously." He winked with a naughty grin. He was clearly having a bit of fun.

And I was going for it. "Well, Mr. Peermohammed," I replied. I cleared my throat as I thought about what to say. "You do realize that in some parts of this world, that, er, gesture, may be considered offensive or … a little forward."

"Ma'am, my actions are never intended to offend. Although oftentimes, I end up doing just that. In our case, I was taking a calculated risk."

Something from inside softened. I don't know what or where, but it was definitely something.

"And though Ms. Austen would no doubt consider it appropriate that her protagonist refer to Mr. Darcy by his formal name, might I suggest that we stray from Austen-like propriety?"

What on Earth was this fellow talking about? He must have been some sort of mind reader. Either that or he could read my face like a book.

"That is to say, you can call me Ayaz."

"Ayaz?!"

"Is that a question or a statement?"

"It's an exclamation. Warranted by the rather forward suggestion that we stray from Austen-like propriety."

"Indeed." He broke into a coy smile that lit the entire room – and a glimmer of something, awakening a something deep inside me. "Now as far as being forward, I figured I wasn't running much of a risk considering I don't even know your name."

I didn't quite know how to respond.

Ayaz seemed to sense my hesitation and shot me a self-assured grin. He clasped his hands and brought his elbows up to the table. He tilted his head to one side. I responded by twisting the tassels at the end of my dupatta.

"Aruna Duggal," I said finally, smiling. "I teach English at Saint Mary's School."

"An English schoolteacher?" he replied with a slight smirk. "Very befitting for a young Amritsari."

How was I to respond to that? I decided to laugh it off. "Yes and no."

"Meaning?"

"Meaning, yes, it's a befitting profession for a young Amritsari, but what's not so befitting is that these positions are typically reserved for Britishers."

"Exactly my point. A perfect example of staying the course."

Like a well-trained racehorse. What was this fellow alluding to? "Unfortunately, not as perfect as what meets the eyes." I sighed. "The school granted me a teaching position because ... my biological father is British."

"Biological?"

I hesitated. I already revealed too much. "He doesn't live with us."

"Your family?"

"It's just my mother and me. Siblings were not a part of their life plans." I twisted my dupatta, three tassels at a time.

"I see," Ayaz said, tapping his fingers against the knuckles on the other hand.

I waited for it, for the judgment that would no doubt come now that I had revealed my Anglo-Indian identity. I eyed him carefully for the telltale signs, but nothing.

"I'm an only child," he said. "The Nizari Isma'ili Shias do not believe in big families."

"Oh? That's quite unlike most Muslims."

"Indeed. We have a different perspective, one that believes in education. But big families raise educational overheads. And my family's big on education. My father is a retired professor of mathematics in Murree, in the outskirts of the Rawalpindi district of Punjab. He is keen for me to complete my studies."

"And yet here you are, serving tea in a dhaba rather than poring over books?" I asked. I was quite unaware of how condescending that must have sounded.

"And yet here you are, drinking tea in a dhaba rather than poring over your books?" he added.

I felt stumped.

He laughed, attempting to break the tension before it fully set in. "Actually, I'm a lawyer." He sat up straighter as a voice yelled out for him again. Removing his arms from the table, he sighed. "Almost."

An almost-lawyer who worked in a dhaba? This conversation was hardly becoming easier to decipher. "Let's see," I said, wrinkling my 'brows. "Ms. Austen would say it isn't what we say or think that defines us, but what we do."

"Indeed, Ms. Austen would also say every savage can dance."

Referring to Mr. Darcy of course. Ayaz Peermohammed was fixated on the hero of Pride & Prejudice. It was his time now to twist things. For him it was his beard. Was that a sign of nervous anxiety? Or was it just a habit? I couldn't tell.

"It's actually not that complicated," Ayaz added. "Truth be told, I'm a lawyer-in-training. I'm actually a student ... in Lahore, technically ... when I finish, I will qualify for a barrister position in the Superior Court of Punjab. Ideally in Lahore. That said, having just arrived in Amritsar and gauging the political state, I see there's much more to learn outside the classroom. And Amritsar seems to be the ideal place to immerse myself in a little service-learning."

I raised my 'brows again, intrigued by the mention of service-learning. "Then, you're a political activist?"

"Merely a member and servant of the Indian National Congress," he replied.

"Merely? There's nothing *merely* about being a member of the only political party that represents the economic and social upliftment of Indians."

Ayaz's eyes twinkled. "'You pierce my soul. I am half agony, half hope.'" He laughed.

By quoting Jane Austen yet again, was this fellow trivializing what I had said or was he trying to get to know me better? I suspected it was the latter. However, I was pleased with the opportunity to connect on a level of literature and politics.

The Congress Party's Swadeshi movement for self-sufficiency by boycotting British goods and its move toward Home Rule were ideals extremely close to my heart, and secularism, of course. I seized the opportunity to play along. "In other words, Mr. Peermohammed ..." I untwisted the tassels on my dupatta.

"Ayaz," he stated.

Vermilion Harvest

"Ayaz," I repeated, "*merely* is the furthest thing from my mind when it comes to judging others by their affiliation to Congress. I'd much rather replace the notion of *mere* with *merit worthy.*"

Mere was not even remotely what came to mind when I looked at this dark-skinned man sitting across from me with his arms folded across his chest. His kurta sleeves tightened around his flexed muscles, and his face glowed with a flame of intent.

My dupatta tassels were back to their original state, except for the tell-tale creases that signaled my anxiety. I had begun to relax into the conversation and was already thinking of all the places it could lead. Whether it was a good idea to think about venturing down a path that led to those places, the thought entailed straying from the resolve I'd taken just a few months ago when I was appointed to my teaching position. I decided then that there was no room for outsiders. Becoming involved with an Anglo-Indian schoolteacher would only frustrate a local gentleman because I straddled two worlds – one that over the last several months had been underscored as that of the enemy. Clearly frustration for a potential suitor was only likely to frustrate me. But there was no room for frustration in my life, especially when it was likely to be permanent. No, public scrutiny and wagging tongues would definitely keep a local gent and me from truly sharing our lives.

Without further adieu, I reigned in my wandering mind. Studying Ayaz, my instincts warned me that entanglement was a bad idea. Yet there was something about him –

physically, politically, magnetically – that made me want to dig deeper.

I abandoned the dupatta twisting and turned to rubbing the base of my neck. It was an attempt to rid the tension that was building.

"How long will you be here?" I asked, trying to sound casual.

"Not sure." Ayaz sighed, looking into the distance.

There was something wistful about his gaze but whether he was homesick or adamant to stay, who could say?

"There's talk of the administration turning DORA into a formal act. A British judge by the name of Sidney Rowlatt already created a proposal. Apparently, he's working on drafting a bill to introduce next month. We shall have to see how things go."

DORA or the Defence of India Regulations Act was an emergency criminal law enacted by the Governor-General of India in 1915. Its aim was to curtail the revolutionary activities in the aftermath of the Great War. Per the new bill, the wartime emergency measures stood to be extended for an indefinite period, giving a legal stamp to such actions as indeterminate preventive detention, internment of suspects without trial, and trying certain political cases in the absence of juries. But why dwell on this? The war was over. Ayaz could apparently read minds in addition to reading books, or maybe it was just mine.

"It gives authorities an excuse to deal with so-called revolutionary activities," he said. "And terrorism."

Terrorism? I scratched my chin.

Vermilion Harvest

Ayaz curled his lips and responded as though he'd read my thoughts, again. "The Britishers are calling Swadeshi a revolutionary movement. They've already tried to ascribe a number of terrorism charges to those involved in it." He sighed and fixed his eyes on the outside view. He leaned forward, his body language conveying a sense of purpose. "The local chapter is extremely active in advocating against this bill. They need help in organizing their political activities. They've asked me to volunteer. I think that's a little more important than studying the theory of law."

As he talked, his face grew increasingly expressive. His eyes ignited like fireworks on a dark Diwali night. You could see the strong conviction in what he said. He spoke from the heart and wasn't afraid of being judged for his beliefs. The flame that kindled inside me flickered. It was hard not to be caught up by his sense of fervor.

Like many young people in India, I was intrigued by politics and the rising power of the dynamic Mahatma Gandhi. For the first time, here was someone who really showed signs of guiding us to the path of freedom. Had I the courage, I would have joined his cause. But fear of losing my position at the school kept me from being an outright activist.

Not that I had anything against other activists, and not that I didn't wholeheartedly admire their actions. Ayaz seemed more attractive now than ten minutes ago. Not just in the physical sense, but his passion and emotion exuded a certain sex appeal that I found captivating. Not one to be driven by physical desires, I couldn't help thinking about how attractive he was and how complicated it could be if this by-chance encounter moved beyond this conversation.

"Back to that issue of receiving flack for going off alone. I wouldn't want that to happen," he said. "May I safely escort you home?"

I had to physically hold myself back to keep from spitting out my chai. That would have been most unladylike. But wait a minute – had I really just heard him ask?

"Mr. Peermohammed …" I stopped and corrected myself before he could. "Ayaz, I live just outside the cantonment walls. You really think I wouldn't receive flack for showing up with a strange, young man?"

"A young man or a young Muslim man?" There it was, the other elephant in the room. If it wasn't bad enough that I was a half, and an Anglo-Indian at that, it certainly would not help the Hindu half to be seen with a Muslim. We had only just met yet were long acquainted by the taint of Indian social norms. Ayaz eyed me for the truth. It was a test perhaps to validate whether I was indeed the kind of woman that was not afraid to shirk societal norms by walking fearlessly into a male-frequented dhaba.

"Well … both." I shuddered. "Man and Muslim that is. But to be quite honest, that's not a reflection of me …" I could feel my cheeks turning red.

"I understand, Miss Duggal." He twisted his beard in the opposite directions and smiled.

"Miss Duggal?" I returned the smile. "I thought we had ditched Austen-ism in favor of first names?"

"We did. It was a test to see which of us you were more comfortable with escorting you home … Mr. Peermohammed or Ayaz."

Ayaz – what a beautiful name – erudite and lyrical at the same time. Shouldn't this distinguished lawyer-in-training know that Indians living in the cantonment area were granted homes because of their loyal service, be that service forced or otherwise? And that visitors like Ayaz, who did not have obvious ties of loyalty, were unwanted and unwelcomed.

What Ayaz didn't know was that the reason we lived there was because my father, a British army officer, had taken pity on my mother and granted her a modest home outside the Amritsar cantonment, after her first husband had thrown her out following an assault that ultimately led to my birth. Eighteen years and that was all I knew about my father. That and the fact that he lived somewhere in the country. Who he was, what led him to be in Amritsar the week I was conceived, what circumstances led to the assault, or what eventually became of him – all remained a mystery. Over the years, I had pressed my mother for details, but each time, she simply froze and refused to communicate. I learned to live with the stigma of being a fatherless child born with a kind of evil that I never understood. In our world, all happiness was laced with the sadness resulting from a truth.

Ayaz was just a year older than me, nineteen, but he seemed wiser beyond his years. Maybe he sensed more than I had revealed in words. "I'm sure they'd understand the positives of a safe escort," he replied. "Your mother isn't wrong in looking out for the safety of her daughter."

I smiled through the flush of embarrassment. There was something about him that was spelling out 'take me now.' Even if I was incorrectly interpreting it, which I wasn't, and why I relinquished the chance of extending this encounter.

The rain had subsided, and we decided to walk rather than take a tonga. It seemed like an ideal opportunity to get to know each other, and for Ayaz to demonstrate his chivalry by carrying my books and papers. I made sure to maintain an appropriate distance, and the perfect gentleman that he was, Ayaz adhered to the protocol. Looking back on it now, I realize what an act of patience that was for us, and how popular literature was integral to those first precious moments. Neither of us wanted the other to leave, yet the awkwardness of finding suitable topics of conversation lent itself perfectly to bonding through Jane Austen-speak.

"Speaking of Pride & Prejudice," he said, "much like Mr. Darcy, I certainly have not the talent of conversing easily with those I've never met. I cannot catch their tone or appear interested in their concerns."

I smiled. This had to be a message from the divine. "Have a little compassion on my nerves, Mr. Darcy. You tear them to pieces."

I felt the touch of his fingers against the back of my hand. A conditioned reflex, resulting from an old-fashioned upbringing, made me pull away. Yet, it sent a shiver down my spine. And although we exchanged no more than words during that journey, it opened a floodgate of silent passion. Thank goodness, for the next time he would make a move, I would not be so quick to retreat.

Vermilion Harvest

When we arrived at the edge of my street, I ushered Ayaz to stand back, allowing me to walk the rest of the way on my own. He understood and acknowledged, but even so, I imagined him watching me all the way with protective eyes. Maybe it was only what I wanted to believe.

The moment I stepped onto the landing and closed the door behind me, I remembered my mother's constant refrain about how there were no chance encounters, and that our entire lives were a puzzle planned by Shiva's subconscious dream-state. And that to weave our way through this maze we called life, we were aided by the laws of karma, which guided us to different doorways. Yet it was up to each to take the chance to open a single door to reveal the world that lay within.

My mind wandered back to my earlier supposition. If I chose to open this particular door to the world of Ayaz Peermohammed, it could lead to complications of unthinkable dimensions. But then my life had never been simple. Be it destiny or a planned puzzle, I was convinced Shiva's dream-state intentionally landed me into this intricate maze of circumstances, much more intricate and harder to figure out than the life-maze of most people I knew.

Whatever decision I made, I would be judged by one ethnic community or the other, by one religious community or the other. Therefore, the truth freed me from the shackles of society.

I needed to allow my risk-averse nature to sit on the backburner. I needed to take this chance and open this door to Ayaz. Or at least try. I had to have him, and it was much more than just a physical attraction.

CHAPTER 2

February 1919

Dhaba - no room for harmony

It took a few days of visiting the dhaba, under the guise of wanting a quiet place to work, to figure out his routine. Ayaz was serving chai and pakoras to customers in the same verandah where I'd met him that first day.

I was attracted to a waiter …

Feeling my cheeks flush, partly by the romance, partly by the forbidden nature, I sat at my customary table – a rickety-wooden old-thing that remained aloof in the corner of the same verandah. Each day, Ayaz would jam a paper napkin under one of the legs to stabilize the thing, a ritual just for me. And then with a polite *thank you*, I'd settle into my books and student papers without exchanging another glance for the next several hours. I'd look up to sneak a peek only to discover that he was already eyeing me – his dimples a little more prominent than his smile that melted my insides. The thought of where that forbidden entry could lead was enough to keep me determined.

I frequently visited the dhaba, taking a tonga after the closing school bell. Ayaz would finish his afternoon shift, and we'd take a stroll at the Rambagh Palace gardens. It was during those walks where we'd explore each other's past and future, catching up on details, sharing ideals or having silly little talks. It soon became clear that our future was meant to be together. We didn't actually talk about the details – we would just have to figure it out.

Ayaz always walked me home. My safe escort. But as we neared the outskirts of the cantonment, I would feel the scrutiny of disapproving eyes. It would be only a matter of time before the neighbors would gossip, and their tales would reach my mother.

"What you don't seem to understand, Aruna, is that all your highfalutin views don't work in our society." My mother always scolded with a level of high authority. "As it is, I do not like you out on your own. I say a hundred times."

Her statement was true for she had said this on numerous occasions. Ma lived in the shadows of her experiences. She was barely a few years older than me when on that fateful day my father forced himself on her. She now lived in fear of history repeating itself. I could hardly blame my mother for her paranoia given the circumstances. However, I was not about to allow her experience to cast a shadow over mine. I was different. I was living in a different time. I wanted a different life. Nothing would stop me from charting my own course.

But Ma refused to let up. Her face would crease, resembling deep grooves on the bark of an old banyan tree. "Educated girls do not cavort with strange men on the street!" She pulled her pallu, the edge of her saree.

"Strange men?" I repeated, trying to look skeptical. "Ayaz is hardly strange. Might I remind you that is the purpose of getting to know him. In *cavorting*, as you call it, Ma." I clasped my hands, interlacing my fingers.

Ma lowered her gaze, agony written across her face. However, my eighteen-year-old self refused to accept that I was the reason for her shame. Or should I say, her newest episode of shame. Being disgraced in society had become part of my mother's DNA. She refused to admit that her marriage had failed because she had illicitly bedded with a British army officer. Or so the world believed. They never knew the truth. The lie was bad enough.

"It is not right, Aruna," my mother whispered. "A Hindu girl —"

"A Hindu girl with a full-time career," I replied, blocking her words and freeing my hands.

"Doesn't matter, my daughter," she replied. "It does not give *you* a license to do whatever *you* want. And ... with a Mussalmaan!"

There it was, the proverbial elephant in the room. My mother's double standard over people. "Ma, how dare you? So hypocritical."

My mother's eyes overflowed with a pained expression, her pupils shrinking and her hands shaking. "I'm anything but!"

I had hit a nerve.

"I have only wanted you to have an ordinary and safe life as every other Khatri Punjabi girl."

My heart pounded. I was not like every other girl. I was different. My birth made me different. "Ma ... look at me. You are used to this face ... my skin color. Others don't see me the same as you do ... I'm an *outcast!*"

Ma sighed, shaking her head. "Your heritage is not obvious to everyone. You *could* be a fair-skinned Punjabi girl."

"I could ..." I laughed. "But why pretend to be someone I'm not?"

Ma wrapped her pallu around her wrist, her signature action indicating stress. More prominent than the wrinkles on her forehead or the salt-and-pepper locks around her temples. The stress had aged her over the last several years. The vermilion maang tika she placed carefully where her hair parted above her brow each day to indicate to the world that she was still a married woman, despite being ostracized by her husband.

"Aruna, you say how others label you. Why give them more to talk about?"

Ma wasn't the only one who was stressed. "You're right. I don't know if there is an upside to constant humiliation, but if I don't care what they think, the labeling will stop. No entertainment. Perhaps they would ignore my choices ... whether it's a tonga ride or meeting a *Mussalmaan* friend for chai."

Ma released her pallu. "People will *never* stop talking, regardless what you do."

"If that's the case, then I might as well carry on, ignore them all the more."

"What you don't understand, my daughter, is that you are not the only member of this family. People are also judging me based on your actions."

"Actions for what? Raising me to be a coquettish girl who does not exemplify Hindu values?"

"Aruna … I just want you to be happy."

"I am happy, Ma!" I took a step closer and touched her arm "Can't you see? Ever since Ayaz entered my life, things have changed. I have a new happiness I never knew existed. We want to plan a future together. And when we get there, we will be even happier than we are today."

How far in the future, I wondered. I clasped and unclasped my hands over and over again. Challenging a mother was not something a daughter should do.

"You are naive, my child." Ma plopped down on the sofa. "*Puppy love* does not last forever. It will not work with a Mussalmaan … I promise. Society will not allow it."

"Oh, but society will bless my life with a Hindu man?" I sneered. "Look at how that worked for you."

Her chin trembled as she turned away.

Later when I would think back, I'd often bury my head in my hands, knowing how much my words had hurt my mother. But at that moment, I was too brazen to see it.

"That was not a pre-meditated state of affairs," she whispered. "Bhagavan-ji only knows what I did in a past life, but in this one … I fell prey to extremely unfortunate circumstances."

She grabbed her pallu, and with the ferocity of a weaver sitting at a loom, she wrapped it around and around her wrist. Try as she might, Ma could not help from bringing God into every conversation. She truly believed in karma, and in all fairness, it wasn't as if she wallowed in the misery of her past circumstances. When we actually brought them up, I knew we had reached a breaking point.

"Sorry, Ma." I stared at my sandals. "I don't mean to stress you out."

Ma sighed and pulled her pallu from her wrist. "You ask Amrita. Sometimes your friends can give a better perspective on things."

Not a bad idea. Amrita was two years older than me, and as a working, married woman with a young child, she did not typify the average *Ambarsari kudi*, as they say in Punjabi — the average young Amritsari girl. Who better to offer a valuable perspective than Amrita?

"Long time no see." Amrita waved. "How did you manage to lose your way to our shop?"

It was close to four in the afternoon. Too early for the daily evening to begin. Shopkeepers were just re-opening after their afternoon siesta. The occasional bird chirping broke the silence for a few short seconds. The quietness slowly returning. This was one of the busiest streets of Amritsar, but it wasn't apparent at this time of day. Ram, the tonga driver, always made it here from the school in no time. With most of the shops still closed, only a handful of people were on the sidewalk. No real activity save for a few vendors with their handcarts.

Amrita was a typical Punjabi young woman – undeniably attractive in her pastel-colored, salwar kameez outfits with her dupatta covering her head – flawless, northern complexion, accentuated by a set of jhumka earrings. She was unquestionably mu phat. If she didn't like you, she'd let you know right away with a raised 'brow. A fabulous cook and the ultimate multi-tasker, she handled everything from their shop, to running a home, and taking care of her four-year-old son, Gopal, with ease.

As a child, I was a loner. Ma never allowed me to play outside with the other children. Mostly because there were no other children for me to play with. The British children in the cantonment refused to play with a half-blood, and given that we were ostracized from our Hindu community, there was no chance of making friends there either. But there was more to it than that. Ma had some kind of aversion to the idea of *play*. It was yet another mystery emotion that she chose not to share. As a young child, I sensed how the mention of playtime seemed to irk her.

Finding a friend in Amrita during my sixteenth year came as a blessing. We had much in common – our life, our ideals, our shared Punjabi culture. Yet our set of circumstances were different. I had found an extraordinary level of comfort from our first exchange. The day she brought Gopal into Saint Mary's compound for a song-and-dance show for the families in the community. We were drawn to each other, intrigued by the details of our different lives. I frequented her shop in the bazaar after that, and through our many conversations, we became good friends. Our lives, polar apart in experiences, were bound by a common thread of being young adults. I respected her. Over the last few years, she had become my personal confidant.

Her husband, Gurcharan Singh, was also a typical Sikh adult – tall, well built, turbaned in an orange dastar. He was kind at heart, good-natured, but when he discovered the truth about my identity through Amrita, I couldn't help but sense an air of uncertainty.

"Not true at all," Amrita would say. "You know Jeeo-ji is always aloof and questions a lot, politically. These things impact his personal demeanor."

Aloof – he definitely was aloof. Most of the time he was absent, or at best, present for just a few minutes. The shop itself was a family business, started by Gurcharan Singh as an excuse to escape from the drudgery of rural Punjab. He hailed from an agricultural family, but farming wasn't his *thing*. Shortly after their marriage, he whisked his young bride from the family homestead in the lands around the Upper Beas River and journeyed downstream to Amritsar where they set up a fruit and nuts shop in the city's famous Hall Bazaar. They now lived in an apartment right above the shop. He could add value for the family by selling the produce from the farm, but he also wanted to explore the life of an intellectual at Khalsa College – the historic educational institution that Amritsar was known for. Gurcharan Singh's true pursuit was the study of world history, but he was actually an administrator. Like Ayaz, the academic world had exposed him to a social and political movement he had only heard about as a youth in rural Punjab. Gurcharan Singh had become increasingly involved, supporting the Swadeshi movement, and the call for Home Rule. The shop was simply a means to an end. He occupied himself with movement activities, leaving Amrita to mind the shop along with Gopal.

Amrita was busy uncovering her array of fresh fruits and nuts to sell during the afternoon traffic. Gopal, still dozy from his afternoon nap, was sipping a glass of lassi. Nothing like cool, fermented buttermilk on a warm spring afternoon.

"Your regular visits are down from three a week to just one," she mused.

"I didn't realize you were counting." Greed ran through me as I eyed her scrumptious mangoes.

"Counting your visits is more fun than tabulating the expenditure of this shop," she replied. She picked up a mango and polished it with a dust cloth. "I miss our afternoon talks. The price a girl has to pay for her best friend falling in love."

"I'm sorry. I miss you too." It was true. I did miss her. But I suspected that with Ayaz's political commitments heating up, it would be a matter of time before our regular friendship took a dive. "These last few weeks have been a heated whirlwind like I've never seen." I ran my fingers over the mango, caressing its outer skin as though it were human.

"Heat as in the onset of spring?" Amrita asked with the innocence of her four-year-old still sipping lassi.

"Noooo!" I whined, wondering whether I really needed to further vocalize my thoughts.

Amrita slapped my hand away from her precious mango. "That kind of heat … mangoes are a heating fruit, but thank you, not in my shop young lady."

Amrita's attempt at humor made me smile. I pictured Ayaz eating one of these mangoes.

"Remember those moments when you fell in love with Gurcharan Singh?" I asked. "Where were you? In Jullundur?"

"We first met outside there, yes. It was when he and his parents came to my home for a proposed matrimonial visit." Amrita blushed like a shy bride on her wedding morning. "I'll never forget how he looked that day. So handsome in that white kurta pajama set and that perfectly tied saffron pagdi ... and his talwar tucked neatly into his sash."

"Is that when you first fell in love?" I sighed.

"Waheguru, no!" Amrita laughed. She measured out a series of dried almonds on a double pan weighing scale and caressed them in her hands before piling them in an empty space in the first row. "I was too shy, and too focused on doing what was expected. Falling in love happened *after* we were married, when I moved in as his wife. But even then, we barely spent time together. The family was always around, and there were chores on the farm."

It hardly sounded romantic. But I still wanted details. "How did you get to know each other? How did you discover your passion?"

"In a Punjabi household, there is focus on giving a newly married couple their privacy at night. Obvious reasons ..." She laughed. "We spent nights talking and that was more important than anything else. He would tell me about his dreams of studying history. I barely knew a thing and soaked up everything he said. It wasn't long before Jeeo-ji and I escaped to Amritsar. That's where we fell in love."

They had fallen in love, yet Amrita still acknowledged him as her superior, always referring to him with a traditional terminology of respect. How different it was to Ayaz's more casual sobriquet, endearing though it was, *jaan*.

"Escape to Amritsar!" I said dreamily. "It sounds like the title of a romance novel."

"In many ways, it was." Amrita laughed, pointing to the picture-perfect fruit display, flicking off an interfering fly and twirling to indicate her environs. "This is where it all happened. We built this little world and fell in love."

Gopal had finished his lassi. He sat the glass down and walked over to his mother, burying his face in her dupatta.

"My good baba," she said, planting a kiss on his forehead. "Run along and play with your friends. Stay near the shops where I can see you."

"Don't forget to give your Aunty Aruna a hug," I said, smothering the little boy in kisses before he jumped off the shop's platform.

Gopal was my special joy. I had watched him grow. And when Amrita would let me, I stole him away to the school library, transporting him to another world through the power of storytelling. His English was much better than that of the average Punjabi child.

In many ways, I envied the life that Amrita and Gurcharan Singh had built. It was simple but complete. A home away from the extended family, a livelihood, and a child. And for Gurcharan – the ability to pursue his passions. Along with Gopal, the shop's business had taken on at a fairly rapid pace. With Amrita running it fulltime and Gurcharan Singh so deeply entrenched in his academic and political life, they had less and less time to spend together. How unromantic was that?

"You built a world, yet for all intents and purposes, you live separate lives. A case of absence makes the heart grow fonder?"

Amrita shrugged. "As a marriage matures, you find that it's less about sparks and more about keeping a steady current." She often felt the need to impart sisterly advice. And I was always ready to receive it. I valued her perspective and take on the world.

The activity on the street had picked up. A couple of housewives had stopped to buy fruit. As Amrita tended to their needs, I thought about her electricity metaphor. It made sense, I suppose. But I wasn't sure about her choice of words, *steady current* – was she referring to a steady stream of physical passion, or the more mundane interpretation of a regular functioning life and household?

"We live in separate worlds," I said once the customers left. "Ma insists that marrying a Mussalmaan will never work."

"I see her point." Amrita nodded. "Our society doesn't permit inter-caste unions, let alone interracial ones."

"Then maybe it'll work. I'm the posterchild for interracial unions." I shrugged.

Amrita looked the other way. "Don't talk like that. You are a different example. You were raised Hindu and most think of you as a Khatri Punjabi girl. It's not just about you. It's unlikely that Ayaz's parents would accept a Hindu girl."

I tilted my head and leaned in. "They're Nizari Isma'ilis, more progressive than other Muslim sects."

"None of that matters when it comes to the basics of religion and family," she insisted. "Progressivism is just an ideal."

"Indeed, he is ideal," I whispered. "He takes me to places I've never been before."

Amrita squinted. "Do you mean …?"

"Physically, emotionally, intellectually …" I zoned-off into a dreamlike state.

I imagined Ayaz holding me under our tree at Rambagh, his open kurta buttons revealing the carved, lean, muscular physique of his upper body. As he drew a picture of our future together in a free India, my hands found their way beneath his kurta, and my fingers explored his chest. The image was exhilarating, but too graphic to reveal to Amrita. I needed to corral my emotions.

But Amrita understood. "Steady yourself, Aruna. Some fantasies are better for the privacy of a bedroom with a closed door."

A bedroom with a closed door? Where would we find that kind of privacy? With Ayaz staying at his friend's as a paying guest, and with my mother and everyone else watching, the evening shadows of a public garden were all the privacy we could afford.

"He is a very good man from what Jeeo-ji tells me," Amrita said, changing the subject. It was an honest attempt to snap me out of my lusty daydream. "He has met with him a few times at Congress meetings at Khalsa College. Jeeo-ji said his intentions are noble and ideals are bold. And that he's a follower of Gandhi-ji's cause."

"It's just one reason why I'm so enchanted."

"Then follow your passion," she replied. "Just be vigilant of society's wagging tongues."

Amrita was the one with whom I had shared the details of my past. She was aware of the dark secrets that clouded my existence and my mother's. She was the one who knew about the pain my mother had experienced over the last nineteen years of her – my – life.

"If this union is truly meant to be, then Babaji will give you the support you need to cement it. Until then, you must be careful. Your mother already has the deck stacked against her."

It was true. Although I was more than ready to take my chances, I hadn't really thought about how my actions would impact my mother, and how my free-spirited intentions could backfire and de-spirit her. She had moved into her home in the outskirts of the cantonment months before I was born. Even though it was filled with interfering gossipers who annoyed the very daylights out of me, these gossipers were her friends. They had accepted her for whatever it was worth, and I could argue the reasons they disapproved of me and my wanton ways were out of a sense of protection for her. Ma had plenty of arguments standing in my defense, even if it meant teetering on the edge of so-called reason. After everything she'd done for me, I couldn't just sell her down the river. Not now, not ever. I'd have to think through how I would handle my new life. How I could separate church from state as they said in Britishers' parlance.

HAPTER 3

Mid March 1919

Amritsar - a romantic interlude

Sitting on a bench under the bushy-green jujube tree at the Rambagh with Ayaz, my hands refused to remain still. My fingers clasped and rubbed before releasing, only to beg to be together again. The gardens surrounding Baradari with the twelve-doored pavilion now filled my view. The huge, summer palace of Maharaja Ranjit Singh with the domed corners gave me reason to pause. The ancient beauty had long since given way to dilapidation and weeds, but its lush green gardens seemed to be the choice for morning and evening walks.

It was also *our* secret place. A secluded bench far from prying eyes of nosy onlookers. The wide-open expanse of the inner lawns only a few feet away created a new perspective on life for me, and the aroma of freshly cut grass added to the overall mystery of the moment.

Vermilion Harvest

Three of Amritsar's gentlemen clubs, frequented by the British army and civil officers, were within the boundaries of the gardens. But the thick leaves of the jujube tree cast deep shadows hiding us within the safety of its branches. The disappearing evening sun lingered, pushing the club-goers indoors and providing us our much desired privacy. The Rambagh filled with sounds of crickets created the ideal place for young love to blossom.

"Ironic, isn't it?" I glanced up at Ayaz. "We espouse the concept of freedom, yet we ourselves must escape dismissive eyes to see each other?"

It was the perfect Jane Austen moment, and Ayaz started with, "'You must, therefore, pardon the freedom with which I demand your attention; your feelings, I know, will bestow it unwillingly, but I demand it of your justice.'" His hand slowly found its way onto mine.

My fingers barely wrapped around his thicker hands. The difference made it hard to believe we were just a year apart. I eighteen, and he just recently celebrating his nineteenth birthday.

It wasn't only the size of our hands that set us apart. Ayaz was a large man with bushy 'brows and a thick, black beard. His dark coloring against my fair complexion made me pale in comparison. Two souls plucked from the same matter – spirited, passionate, and idealistic.

How could I fall in love with someone so different? He a Muslim, I, a young Anglo-Indian schoolteacher. He, so fearless and daring. As for me, naturally drawn to keeping up my guard. *Opposites do attract.* Were it not true, this moment would never be. What a feeling, signified by our longing touch contrasted by his hand caressing my trembling fingers. His warm grasp made my heart pound.

"As I said ... isn't it ironic?" I sighed. "We ask for freedom from the British ... to be pardoned, yet you yourself have no freedom to even speak of it." I glanced out at the dark lawns and frowned. My words conveying a tease or taunt.

Ayaz remained quiet, perhaps too quiet. As he had said before, molehills were meant to remain as molehills. He pulled me closer, his chin rubbing gently across the top of my head. Something that calmed me down. Not that I was hyper or anything like that, but Ayaz often sensed my agitation layered behind the irony.

"Perhaps," he whispered. "Freedom may be a concept, but it's also a choice."

But it wasn't a choice. We were not truly free. If we were, we would not need to hide to steal a kiss. Could we ever be daring enough to kiss without stealing?

Most of my daily routine was considered daring. At first, I decided it was just my mother's personal opinions. However, as the days passed, I had to accept that her views simply mirrored those of our society, which was ironic since we were repeatedly victimized by its so-called rules. My mother spoke of feeling like an outsider who yearned to be on the inside. As for me, I swung either way – just an internal desire swelling like a deep-rooted toxin. However, most times, I didn't care what others thought. Perhaps a self-defense mechanism to allow me to overcome societal norms that would never hold me back regardless of Ma's intentions.

Vermilion Harvest

"Genteel ladies don't steal away from home on their own, especially when the sunlight is waning!" my mother would say – her constant refrain.

I, however, was less concerned about *fitting* in. I simply disregarded her words, which over time became a significant source of tension between us.

With my naivety of eighteen years, it was just best to respond to her controversial comments when her attention was diverted elsewhere. Therefore, I would only pipe up while we were wringing out wet clothes to hang on the clothesline.

"Perhaps I am daring, Ma. Maybe more so than the average Hindu girl. But then again, I'm not your regular Hindu girl, am I?"

She stopped hanging and glared with her dagger eyes. "Let me be perfectly clear about one thing ... there is nothing *irregular* about you. You are as Hindu as anyone else."

I slapped a wet towel over my shoulder sending a spray of droplets into my mother's face. "Fair enough." I used my dupatta to wipe her dry. "Something of a regular irregularity, maybe?"

"Meaning what?" she asked.

"Meaning ... I'm not the kind of Hindu that's regularly acceptable."

Ma snorted emphatically and grabbed another shirt from the basket. She shook it out before slapping it over the slender rope. "You don't look *any* different to our Pahadi hill tribes. You're just minus the silver jewelry."

She was right, of course. My father did not share his British, blonde hair, blue eyes, or defined features with me. Most assumed that my pale skin simply classified me as a descendent of the northwestern tribes of Punjab, which were known to have mixed blood from Asia and Arabia. From the way I donned a traditional salwar kameez with conservatively wide paunchas to ensure no leg exposure and an endless black plait that swung around my hips, most assumed I was a regular Punjabi Hindu kudi.

Ma sighed, gazing wistfully at her long bare fingers. "It would be nice to see you wear your grandmother's ring or a pair of the meenakshi earrings she left you."

I cringed, slapping another wet towel over my shoulder.

My refusal to wear a parandi hair braid or bangles went a long way, convincing the genteel ladies of Amritsar that I'd become somewhat westernized. I had even mastered the English language enough to be granted a government schoolteacher appointment. Although, government school-teaching positions were typically reserved for English women – or an Anglo-Indian, like me.

"I think not, Ma," I stated. "My half-blood status might give my employers a reason not to welcome me into their social circles, but it does give them the opportunity to offer me my position. These government jobs are hard to come by for pure-blooded locals."

Ma ran her fingers through her silver locks before stringing a towel over the clothesline with unruly aggression. "Think before you speak girl," she whispered. "When did you last see a woman working in the post office or telegraph exchange … or the railways?"

"There's got to be a first, right? What about Emma Nutt?"

"And who is Emma Nutt?" Ma's curiosity was undeniably absent.

"Just the world's first female telephone operator. American women have been working in the telegraph industry since the middle of the last century."

"This is not America!" she countered. "We are not as forward."

"You mean progressive?"

"Excuse me?"

"I think you meant to say *progressive*, not forward." I grinned.

My mother grabbed another shirt. "A matter of semantics."

"Not just semantics," I replied. "Unfortunately, to other Hindu girls, I'm different. The school administrators know I'm a half-blood. That some of *their* kind runs through my veins. Not a bad thing, actually. Gives me a privilege."

"Privilege?"

"They honestly do not care if I wander into town on my own. Or that I stay out a little late. My actions are not any different from other British schoolteachers. Why not milk the opportunity?"

We generally spoke in Punjabi, but when we argued, it was almost invariably in English. The fact that I enjoyed a British education, and she had not often kept my mother from understanding simple basics.

"Milk? What are you talking about?"

"Milk it, Ma. Like you milk a cow? Figure of speech."

She looked confused as if I was speaking another language, and maybe I was.

"I don't understand your *figures of speech*, or why you have to try and be so daring just because you work with the Britishers."

Regardless of what it seemed like to Ma or others, I didn't think of myself as daring. I wanted to live by my own standards but there was also a little place for daring in life. Given that we desperately needed my income, there was no way I would risk losing my position. Contrary to my mother's opinion, I considered myself somewhat risk-averse.

Ayaz delved into our Jane Austen-speak, pulling me from my thoughts. "Were Mr. Darcy to ask 'penny for your thoughts,' he might be accused of feeling the danger of paying Elizabeth too much attention."

I played with the tassels on the ends of my dupatta as though that would help me with a timely repartee. "I ... er ... my thoughts and reflections are habitually my best companions."

"Mansfield Park," he replied with a twinkle in his eyes. He caressed my hand, bringing it to his lips, my body responded. I had just been brushed by fairy wings.

Growing up as a Muslim youth in a predominantly Hindu and Sikh locality, Ayaz saw himself as more righteous than fearless or perhaps adventurous. Even during his youthful years, he tried to live by his own rules. Rules that would bend the world closer to his visions. Maybe not the entire world, just the world that constricted his freedoms.

We faced each other, and I shied from making eye contact. But he lifted my chin, forcing my eyes to meet his. He paused for only a moment. "If we were truly free, we wouldn't hide our opinions about Home Rule." He sighed.

I cocked my head to one side, trying to make sense of his words. "So we should live life and risk imprisonment?"

"That's the whole point, Aruna," he whispered. "Our liberties have been stripped by immoral laws such as the Rowlatt Act. Therefore, freedom is nothing more than a concept. And that is only if we so choose. Perhaps, we can help freedom transcend to a more meaningful truth."

The Anarchical and Revolutionary Crimes Act of 1919, commonly known as the Rowlatt Act and referred to as the Black Act, had fueled protests throughout India. The law gave authorities complete power to imprison without a trial, and to shoot to kill without notice. As stated in sub-section 3 of section 26 – *'inquiry shall be conducted in such manner as the investigating authority considers best suited to elicit the facts of the case: and in making the inquiry, such authority shall not be bound to observe the rules of the law of evidence.'* Public opposition was strong against the law even though it was enacted across the Indian subcontinent.

Mahatma Gandhi of the Indian National Congress delivered a scathing condemnation, calling for protest to mark Indian disapproval, which his party deemed as *'a silencing measure designed expressly to suppress the Indian will and desire for civil liberties on their native soil.'* A member of the All-India Muslim League, Muhammad Ali Jinnah, resigned from the Imperial Legislative Council in protest. Both men were strong role models for Ayaz.

A hearty and heated subject Ayaz was truly passionate about. As the flame of his passion kindled the heat simmering inside me, I gently stroked the back of his fingers. His thick 'brows raised in response.

"Politically speaking?" I asked.

"Romantically too." He grinned.

The heaviness of his statement felt like a stone inside my chest. Why must his romantic ideals always line up with his political standards? Why couldn't he be more Jane Austen-ish and just enjoy the moment? I looked directly into his large, coffee-colored eyes, and suddenly, I felt lost.

"Romantically speaking, Ayaz? If that were true, then our love would never be legitimized without our freedom, and who knows when that day will come."

The overly quiet evening felt deafening. Everyone had left Rambagh except for us – and another couple in hiding under the shadow of a different tree. The occasional bird chirping was all that broke the silence but only for a few short seconds.

"My dearest jaan, did you read the story about Vasanti?"

Hearing him use the endearment jaan – the word for life – made my heart pump a little faster. Ayaz had hooked me on a monthly journal – The Indian Ladies' Magazine. Edited by a woman, Kamala Satthianadhan, it was targeted to a class of Indian women who'd been educated in English. Ayaz valued my interest in Jane Austen's romance and satire but insisted that I needed to understand the plight of love from the Indian woman's point of view. To me it was rare and extremely interesting that such a young man would be interested in the Indian woman's point of view, so much so as to make an academic study out of it.

But I was not about to relinquish his soft spot for Jane Austen-speak. And certainly not while I was lost in his gaze. "The person, Ayaz, be it gentleman or lady, who has not found pleasure in a good novel, must be intolerably stupid."

Ayaz grinned and played back perfectly. "Beware how you give your heart, my jaan. For Padmini shows us through her tale about Vasanti that love and pain are interlinked."

I sighed. Why did that have to be the case? Why couldn't all love just be like the kind I read about in a Jane Austen novel?

"Why do love and freedom have such a complicated relationship?" I asked, edging my face a little closer to his.

"That I do not know," Ayaz replied. "Karanveer said yesterday that he would walk barefoot to the rallies to register his protest. 'If my business suffers, then so be it. Motherland comes before money.'"

Karanveer was the owner of Pritam Da Dhaba where Ayaz worked, just one name amongst an increasing number joining local sit-ins, seemingly unaffected by financial losses and threats of repercussions at the hands of the government. A huge source of inspiration for this feisty young activist. His eyes glazed as he smiled.

He slowed his speech and continued, "But you are right, love and freedom have a complicated relationship. You could argue that love cannot exist without freedom, just as freedom cannot exist without love. And so, my jaan, we the people must protest this oppressive Rowlatt Act."

I completely failed to make any sense of the love-freedom analogy he was presenting, but somehow it didn't seem to matter. His deep brown eyes entranced me, becoming more pronounced as he focused his gaze. In that moment, I could see that he was strong, strapping, confident, and a drop-dead knockout.

"Forget about the Rowlatt Act, I'm in the mood for romance," I whispered.

But Ayaz was not feeling the same way, not at that moment. His glazed expression became less focused on me and more on his philosophy.

"No, jaan," he replied. "If our personal freedom is politically suppressed, then how can we ever be free to love each other?"

I looked out at the darkened lawn and sighed. When his political passion awoke, his romantic passion faded, and he'd speak in an idealistic way with lofty words and dreamy eyes. I found him incredibly desirable, but his attention was elsewhere. I sat up straighter and contemplated his words.

I wanted to believe Ayaz. But a nagging doubt inched into my soul like a virus. Yes, the current political impasse between the British government and us Indians called for quick action. The imbroglio needed to be sorted out in a judicious manner, if our freedom – economic, political, and otherwise – was to be honored. But even inside a free world, how could our relationship ever be not a secret? A Muslim man and an Anglo-Indian girl? His community had no place for an outsider like me. And when it came to my community, where would I belong? Most assumed I was a light-skinned, Hindu Punjabi like my mother. However, Hindu Punjabis would never accept a Muslim man. And when it came to the British, half my blood, well they would not accept an Indian woman, period. Not when it came to an open marriage. Our relationship had no place in our society. We had no choice but to nurture it within the darkening shadows.

Ayaz closed his eyes for a few moments before intensifying his gaze. Those coffee-colored eyes always melted my insecurities.

"Should we be bonded by the shackles of our society?" he asked. "Wouldn't you rather be bonded by shackles of our love?"

"It's not a choice, Ayaz."

"But it *is* a choice," he responded.

I focused on the opening of his kurta, revealing his broad chest.

"Freedom is a choice," he whispered. "Some relationships allow us the freedom to choose."

"A relationship like ours?" I kept my eyes on his chest.

"Maybe our relationship is like those that are chosen by the Great Divine."

Oh for goodness' sake! I shook my head. *The Great Divine* was more like *The Great Divide.* "Which Great Divine chose *our* relationship?" I asked. "I'm not seeing support from either the Hindu or the Muslim gods."

Ayaz shifted his weight and sighed. "In time, Aruna. In time … when you really desire something … the universe will conspire to help you achieve it." He chuckled. "Isn't that why we are here now … together?"

"Meaning what, exactly?" I held my dupatta, fidgeting with the end. At this exact moment, it seemed to be the only thing that made any sense. Why? I didn't know.

Ayaz took my hands and drew them close to his beating heart. "Meaning, that despite what your mother has experienced, the truth is she ended up with the one thing she truly desired ... you."

Ugh. If it were only that simple. All my life I wondered, when she looked at me was my mother reminded of what happened, of how I was conceived? Truth be told, *I* was the victim of her circumstance. Would the universe conspire to help an Anglo-Indian girl, who was already an outcast from two societies, achieve what she desired? A Nizari Isma'ili Shia Muslim man, even if he was on his way to graduating from Government College, Lahore?

"If you and I were chosen by the Great Divine, then why are we keeping our love for each other a secret? Why not just accept the consequences?"

Ayaz caressed my cheek with the back of his hand. "Your colleagues might look the other way as you wander through town on your own, however, you have not considered what they might say if you are seen to be cavorting with a young Mussalmaan."

I raised my 'brows.

"On a regular basis, I mean," he said.

I had not considered that. A classic example where *daring* met at the crossroads of *risk-averse*. My natural, free spirit would definitely be confronted by our societal impropriety.

"We will one day come out with our secret, Aruna," he whispered. "And we will have to deal with the consequences.

But for now and with so many obstacles to overcome, we must choose our battles one at a time. But this I will promise ... when things have settled and I finish college, I will take you away from here. Bombay? Perhaps there I can find a legal position and continue my work with Gandhi-ji. You and I can escape the disapproval of others. Until then ... we must wait and save our money."

"Will the people of Bombay not judge us too?" I wiped away a tear.

"Bombay?" He laughed. "Where the educated meet ... and talk ... and hold salons?"

His statement was true. The Indian Ladies Magazine portrayed Bombay as a Mecca of progressive cultures. It was a primary meeting ground for discussing literature, education, and social causes.

"Who knows, jaan? Perhaps Bombay is not as forthcoming as we'd like to believe. But at least we'll have a chance to be anonymous. Where we can celebrate our love openly, despite our separate religions. No one will ever need to know that you come from a Hindu background."

Part Hindu ... and part ... who knows what!

Ayaz unfastened the clip binding my hair. My long, black curls fell loosely around my shoulders, disordering the neat folds of my dupatta. He gently pulled the scarf down to my lap. My hand he placed on his lips and to the ends of my fingers each in turn. I felt his body tense as he leaned in to kiss me. A strange thrill spread through my body. I glided my hand up his arm, relinquishing any preconceived notions of what others might think. In one deft athletic move, Ayaz lifted me onto his lap. I was now straddling his legs, breathless as my dupatta fell to the bench.

There we lingered for only a moment. His lips locked onto mine in a deep heated exchange of passion. His fingers found their way to my bare cleavage, exposed by my fallen scarf.

Even though I had wanted this, yearned for this, a strange force compelled me to push away. I placed my hands on his chest and leaned back.

"Ayaz, no ... I'm afraid ..."

"Afraid of what?" he asked, caressing my cheek.

I sighed, trying to escape the response of my body reacting to his. Strong and gentle fingers found their way to my breasts, and my nipples responded. Each stroke pushed them harder against the material of my kurta. I wanted his fingers to stay there forever. The desire startled me.

"Of ... myself ..." I whispered.

"Resist the urge, Aruna," he whispered. "Relax and listen to your heart."

Control was one of my weaknesses. Actually, the only thing that kept me safe. But it also held me captive. A victim of my own life, partitioning me from that place of supreme physical bliss.

A familiar tension was growing, and Ayaz sensed it. He slowed down ever so cautiously. With rhythmic, gentle motions, his fingertips moved down to my hips. And I was powerless from his tense desires.

A vision of my neighbors appeared, casting a disapproving look. My mother glared at me from deeper inside the shadows, and I scanned her despairingly for a clue as to what to do.

Relax, Aruna! It was just my conscience playing tricks. A habit of walking the same path over and over again. This was a place of supreme bliss, beckoning me to enter. But only if I could escape my self doubt. If I refused now, a door would close and shut me out. A door I would never find a key for. I pushed the visions away and relaxed into his essence, enjoying this brief moment of exotic freedom.

During these sensuous interludes at Rambagh, we explored each other's bodies, minds, and souls. Inside the darkening shadows of our jujube tree, our love grew as did our bond. An unmarried woman making out with a man was frowned upon in our society. But for me, it was new, exciting, and daring. Our passion grew each time we met, but Ayaz refused to cross that invisible line. He was, after all, a gentleman. For me, it was so new and refreshing. I trusted him implicitly. He always scanned the area, choosing a spot away from prying eyes. He kept my position hidden, protecting my identity.

Inside his embrace, I was safe. As the days passed, I became more and more entrenched, caring less and less. *So what if we were discovered by people we knew?* This was the man I wanted to be with forever. A bold statement for a Hindu woman in Punjab during 1919. But hardly a compromise for I had already closed the doors on *risk-averse* and acquiesced to *daring.*

ℰHAPTER 4

March 30, 1919

Amritsar - prepare for the hartal

Mahatma Gandhi called for Satyagraha, non-violent opposition to the Rowlatt Act. He honestly believed that a peaceful resistance would change the minds of our colonial masters while keeping us locals out of physical harm. The current administration was concerned, rumors of a revolution was taking root spreading like wildfire.

Gandhi-ji called for a number of cities in India to unite in the first all-India united protest. Local residents suspended their business activities, spending the day fasting, praying, and holding peaceful public meetings against the Black Act. In colloquial terms, it was known as a hartal. Shopkeepers and traders would remain closed as a sign of their opposition.

The civil disobedience to protest the Black Act was known as *Rowlatt Satyagraha.* A deliberate intention to disturb the daily life and affairs of the city. Specifically, the British residents. It was imperative that the British administration woke up and took notice. The exercise appeared to have achieved its desired effect. British housewives had to strategize on how to stock their kitchens.

"Can you pick up a few extra mangoes when you visit the bazaar?" Mrs. Simeon had asked my mother somewhat out of breath, scurrying over to us, holding her hat to her head.

We were laden with shopping bags on our way home from the market. It appeared to be a chance encounter, but I had the feeling that she'd been waiting for the opportunity to corner us.

"With talk of the hartal and all, shopkeepers may not be receptive of me." Her voice sounded somewhat patronizing.

Mrs. Simeon, the proverbial gossip, always made it her business to keep an eye on me. She was aware that my friend's shop was well stocked with mangoes.

Ma sat down her shopping bags, smoothing out the folds of her bright, blue saree and moved a wisp of grey hair from her eyes. She cocked her head to one side. "The shopkeepers will not receive anyone during the hartal." She smiled. "They will close their shops to everyone."

"Yes ... yes, of course." Mrs. Simeon nodded. "I just thought that perhaps they might ... sell to you, being a local and all."

I held back a laugh since Ma's gaze seemed dumbfounded. She fidgeted with the edge of her saree. Something I often did with my dupatta. Obviously, I subconsciously picked up the habit from her. A sign that neither of us knew how to respond. Even though she kept her distance from the British memsahibs, Ma made it a point to maintain good relations with them. Given our history and that we'd been given our home by a British officer, Ma insisted that we show *extra gratitude*. However, often she went overboard, to the point of appearing obsequious.

"Perhaps, I can make a special request to the local fruit-sellers," she whispered.

"Not much of a point in doing that," I stated. "The hartals are to close *all* business activities and to everyone."

Why wouldn't Ma stick to her principles? Making life difficult for the Britishers was the whole purpose of the hartal. She looked at me with a pleading gaze.

"Maybe we can ask our friends for help," she suggested. "Like Amrita Singh."

I shook my head. "Ma, no. Amrita already said her shop will not be selling to anyone."

"It's just a few mangoes," Mrs. Simeon said, harshly as if to satisfy her imperious vanity. "It *is* the season. What will they do with them? Let them rot? Or send the fruit to other cities?"

"All the cities of the Punjab will participate in the hartal movement." I raised my 'brows. "They'll sync up with Mahatma Gandhi's objectives, and Amritsar will be no different. That means *no* mangoes for anyone, season or no season."

"Oh, that Gandhi!" Her face took on a darker tone and she frowned. "Sod it then. I've had enough." Mrs. Simeon pursed her lips and took leave with a staccato nod of the head.

Ma remained silent. It was clear she was torn between the principle of the Rowlatt Satyagraha and keeping up her self-professed dutiful relations with her British neighbors.

On March 30th, a group of several thousand Hindus, Muslims, and Sikhs gathered in Jallianwala Bagh to discuss the state of affairs, all under the guidance of Indian National Congress leaders, Dr. Saifuddin Kitchlew and Dr. Satyapal. I attended the event as did Ayaz. It was interesting to watch the visible change in his body language. His political activist persona took over the amorous Ayaz that I had fallen in love with from our interludes at Rambagh.

"I don't know how Dr. Satyapal will manage to address this crowd," he said.

We eyed the men preparing to speak from a makeshift stage.

"Manage what?" I asked. "You mean in terms of what he says?"

"No, in terms of saying anything at all," Ayaz whispered. "The British administration of Punjab has prohibited him from speaking to the public."

"But he did so two days ago," I replied. "Near the Hall Gate when I was riding home from school."

"It happened yesterday," Ayaz said. "They're concerned about his influence over the local Amritsaris."

Dr. Kitchlew stepped forward. His mid-parted hair smooth with pomade and neatly tucked behind his white shirted high collar, juxtaposed with the quivering ends of his perfectly waxed mustache.

"Will we ever be prepared to sacrifice personal over national interests?" Dr. Kitchlew asked. "You were read the message of Mahatma Gandhi. Countrymen ... come prepared for resistance! No blood or death. The resistance will be a passive one. Be prepared to act ... be prepared for jail!"

The crowd cheered. "Satyapal-ji ki jai! Kitchlew sahib ki jai!" Their shouts filled the air.

The two Congress political leaders were successful in uniting the crowd, however, the British administration didn't like what they were watching. Newspaper headlines and radio anchor's reported against the unison. Regardless, violent or passive, Indians should not sacrifice themselves for a national interest. The idea was horrifying. To shake the British rule was more dangerous than violence.

Following the meeting, Dr. Kitchlew was ordered to refrain from further public speaking. A huge disappointment as it disrupted the flow of political meetings, curbing the influence of our local heroes proved to not be the answer. There had to be a better way to calming the woes of the British administration. The meetings were broken into smaller groups, each facilitated by a designated member of the local Congress Party. Despite the efforts of the British administration, the people of Amritsar remained resolute. The hartal would continue as planned.

HAPTER 5

April 5, 1919

Amritsar - Rowlatt Satyagraha

It had been just three months since Ayaz and I first met, but it seemed like we'd known each other forever. Even though I didn't have as much time with Ayaz as I would have liked, I was learning to respect how he divided his time between work, political activities, and me.

His work was the least important but was necessary to make ends meet. We were saving for our future, to one day be together in Bombay.

Since the enactment of the Rowlatt Act, Ayaz's focus on his political activities took priority. I never questioned his passion for wanting to follow his views for that passion was what attracted me to him. Unfortunately for me, the more he became involved in Gandhi-ji's cause, the fewer hours we spent together. And when we were together, they were laced with conversations on his growing loyalty to Gandhi-ji – who was elevated from an obscure politician to the ranks of a national leader overnight. Any incidence of romance in Rambagh or Jane Austen-speak was becoming fewer and farther between.

Ayaz's politically-charged outbursts were underscored by ideas from the revolutionary media like Ghadar, a newspaper founded in San Francisco by the feisty Punjabi immigrant Lala Har Dayal Mathur. The paper's purpose was to foment a revolution against the British Raj. Lala Har Dayal Mathur, having emigrated to the Pacific Coast of America along with thousands of other Indians in search of a new and better life, had made sure that copies of his prized newspaper widely circulated in America and ultimately smuggled into India in sizable quantities. His goal was to influence political idealists like Ayaz who was tasked with organizing, gathering, and presiding over political meetings during the hartal. Facilitating hartal operations was not part of Ayaz previous experience, yet managing came to him naturally. Perhaps because it was a natural extension of his purpose for being in Amritsar. Fortunately or unfortunately, it was an event that meant as much to Ayaz as his relationship with me. Something that became obvious during our dates at the dhaba.

I sipped slowly on my elaichi chai, eyeing Ayaz as he settled accounts at another table. His white outfit was not that white anymore, a telltale sign that the dhaba had not been his first stop. His furrowed brow indicated there was something serious on his mind. As he walked toward me, I dusted off an imaginary *something* to ensure I was presentable. His eyes pierced through mine with a booming silence before he moved his lips to echo Gandhi-ji's Satyagraha – or *soul force* oath.

"I will never forsake our mission to observe the truth without a single act of violence," he whispered. His expression glowed with a moral purpose. "Even as we oppose this duly unjust Black Act, we will do so through Rowlatt Satyagraha."

"Rowlatt Satyagraha?" I closed my fingers around the wet glass. "What does that mean?"

Ayaz's look was somewhat distant. He seemed surprised by my question as though the answer was obvious.

"Gandhi-ji has called to set up Satyagraha Sabhas all over India … tomorrow." Ayaz smiled. "Mini factions to discuss the cause of a passive resistance. To unify the country in showing opposition to the Rowlatt Act."

"What?" I asked. "Is it safe?"

With a nibble of a grin, he softened at my amateur question. He caressed my cheek with his fingers before pulling away, remembering where we were. "Gandhi-ji's supporters will meet to discuss the cause of passive resistance." He straightened and sat back in the chair.

"Revolutionists?!" I formed a mental picture of men fighting as I sipped on my chai.

"Supporters," he replied, but no smile. "Either way –"

I banged my glass on the table, spilling the chai. "Either way, what? You'll be labeled for partaking in the revolutionary crimes. You are not a criminal." I wanted to support his cause, but I was also against any risks on our chance of being together.

Ayaz stared at me. Maybe I sounded a little insane.

"The Rowlatt Act is a game changer, Aruna. The executive has the power to restrict our liberties ... in writing, in speech, and in movement. How does the Indian government have the right to intern a person without a proper trial!?"

"They do not," I replied. "Nobody has that right." As I said the words, I flinched, understanding they were anything but the truth.

The local police were indiscriminately arresting shopkeepers in the Hall Bazaar, insisting on searches without warrants. I witnessed the dishonorable acts on my way home from school. As I stepped out of the school compound, my tonga ride was obstructed by unruly men protesting outside the kotwali *(police station)*, the Government House, and the cantonment. But the day it happened outside Saint Mary's School was when I grasped the hardened truth that my employer, a stronghold of progressive education, had somehow become a symbol of oppression by the British Raj.

No sooner had I climbed aboard Ram's tonga when an angry crowd charged the school's gates. Their hostile body language startled me.

"Why are they waving their fists in the air like that?" I asked Ram.

"The police detained suspects without a trial," he replied. "Trying people in courts with no jury and no right of appeal."

"But why come here? To the school?" My fingers crawled to the ends of my dupatta.

Ram's breathing hardened. He seemed nervous. I didn't push for an answer. But I didn't have to either. The school's headmaster, Colonel Lewis, appeared at the window. The retired colonel was friends with Mr. Plomer, the Deputy Superintendent of Police. Apparently, they played bridge together at the Gymkhana Club. His grim visage glared out at the commotion. I could actually feel the tension rising. Voices coalesced into a unified cry, "No vakil, no daleel, no appeal." *No lawyer, no argument, no appeal.* The slogan was becoming Amritsar's war cry. With Colonel Lewis added to the mix, it was only a matter of time before we'd be required to make harsh choices.

The following morning, I was greeted by Rakesh, the school hamaal, who customarily started his porter duty before the teachers arrived.

"The colonel would like to see you, memsahib," he said.

"Oh?" I whispered. "I'll head there after I drop my things off at the staff room."

"No, memsahib, he would like you to go directly to his office without stopping at the staff room. He asked me to let you know first thing."

"Did he say what it was about?" I asked, tilting my head. What matter of life or death prompted a meeting with the head of the school this early in the day?

"No, memsahib."

"I see." I bit my lip not understanding what was so urgent. I had never been summoned by Colonel Lewis before. Therefore, it couldn't be anything good.

The colonel was seated behind his wooden desk, pouring over ledgers filled with loose papers. He looked up, giving me a critical eye through his horn-rimmed spectacles. "Miss Duggal. I'm glad you came."

I nodded. It was not like I had a choice. "Good morning, Colonel Lewis." I added a fake but polite smile.

"I suppose you're wondering why I summoned you. I see no upside in dilly-dallying, therefore, I'll get straight to the point." He let out a long sigh. "It's come to my attention, through several sources, that you have been seen cavorting with a local Muslim chap."

His words struck me like an arrow to my chest. Did I just hear what I had just heard? Without a sound, I grabbed the ends of my dupatta.

"Miss Duggal, I understand this might come as a surprise, but I must warn you that as a representative of Saint Mary, we cannot have you doing such things."

I twisted my dupatta with passive aggression, feeling dumbstruck. I grappled for words to fit the emotions rushing through my head. The colonel looked at me with a measured pause. Was he gauging my reaction?

"We take our position as progressive educators quite seriously."

I dropped my dupatta. "Did you just say *progressive?* Is progressive education defined by a headmaster's attempt to deprive his staff of civil liberties? Just because he is ex-military?"

"Miss Duggal!" The colonel gasped. "Is that a finger you're waving at me?"

His question made me aware of my unconscious movement. I forced my hands into a clasp. "Colonel Lewis, if

I may … it's an abuse of power ordering me who to befriend and who not to … don't you think?"

The colonel pushed his chair so strongly that it hit the wall. He pursed his lips. "I appreciate your feisty qualities, Miss Duggal. Stands you apart from the more droll instructors. The main reason I like having you here. But with that said, we must all do our part in adhering to social norms … or else."

"Or else what, Colonel?" I unclasped my hands and re-clasped them.

"Like I said, Miss Duggal. I like having you here. I wouldn't want to lose you."

There it was. The words I had silently dreaded were hitting me right between the eyes. Why had I given in to falling in love with a local when I knew that nothing good would come of it? Someday our love would come home to roost. Not wanting to hear it, I stood fixed in front of the colonel.

"Carry on, Miss Duggal. Before you go, you should know something."

What more could I possibly need to learn?

"They're making a list of revolutionaries. Your friend's name is on it."

"My friend?" I asked.

"Mr. Ayaz Peermohammed," the colonel replied.

My hands desperately clasped to keep my gestures calm. For the first time in months, years maybe, tears welled in my eyes. Amrita would always remark on my inability to cry. *Were she to see me now?* I forced the tears not to fall.

A list? They were watching Ayaz, looking for an opportunity to arrest him.

"I found out this morning … through Dr. Kitchlew and Dr. Satyapal." He twisted his beard in that characteristically Ayaz manner.

Dr. Kitchlew, the lady-killing sportsman, was one of the undisputed champions of the Amritsari people. The other, slightly more reserved, was Dr. Satyapal. He believed in peaceful and constitutional methods to obtain political freedom.

Both were in their mid-thirties and equally forceful public speakers. They first came into the limelight by leading a local protest over the decision of the railway authorities to stop issuing platform tickets to Indians. They protested stating it was an act of racial discrimination. And rightly so, despite the authorities claims that it was a move to prevent over-congestion of the trains.

I swelled with pride each time I thought about how this Muslim-Hindu pair constantly kept the Britishers on their toes. Dr. Satyapal believed their religious beliefs would keep them as loggerheads – the main plank in the British argument as to why we Indians would never be able to govern ourselves. Yet our local Congress heroes dismissed this as part of the Raj's *divide-and-rule policy*.

Although I admired them for shaking the foundation of Amritsar's political will, the fact that I, we, Ayaz, became directly involved in their activities, made me grapple with the idea of providing support. However, I needed to build strength within myself first.

"What does this mean, Ayaz?" My voice quivered as I imagined the possibilities.

He leaned in and closed his hands together.

"I'm a *political* suspect ... that's what they call me. Which means, I can be imprisoned at any time and without a trial."

I sat speechless, trying to grasp the truth behind what he was saying. Just yesterday, jail was nothing more than a notion – a distant place for other people and other things. Today, it was a reality. How could any of this be happening? How could the Rowlatt Act have changed things overnight? The Rowlatt Committee was appointed to report on revolutionary crimes in India and recommend measures to cope with it. Not incarcerate people.

Ayaz took my hands in his. This time he scanned the room to see who might be looking. "My dearest jaan," he whispered. "The law allows anyone to be imprisoned for up to two years for possessing a so called *seditious* document. What is a seditious document? According to the committee, anything. A copy of Karl Marx's, Das Capital. A flyer circulated by that American socialist, Charles Schenk, outlining his views against the country's espionage act. The letter I wrote to you last week."

The letter he wrote to me last week? The sweetest, most romantic words outlining how we should run away, just like Heer and Ranjha, Romeo and Juliet – to build a life together in the face of the oppressive societal restrictions. Ayaz poured a glass of water from the jug in front of him. He took a few sips.

"To you and me, these are curiosities of literature. Proclamations of love. But to the executives, they could be rendered acts of sedition."

A feeling of tightness took form in my chest. Nothing about the world made any sense. "Sedition? Something that instigates the use of criminal force against the King ... or the government? How can a love letter do that?"

"The very use of the word *oppressive* could render a letter as a seditious document. I could be labeled as guilty. Because here in India, if you are Indian, you are guilty until proven innocent. Negating the first principle of British justice, which presumes a man to be innocent unless proven guilty."

I pulled back from Ayaz, feeling horrified. How could such a double standard exist? One set of rules for the British and another for the Indian locals. How could it possibly be?

"Guilty by virtue of a love letter?" I whispered.

Ayaz took a deep breath, running his fingers through the tapered dark locks on the front of his head. "When does a love letter become an ordinary thing? If I'm not guilty of a revolutionary crime, then I'm guilty of loving an out-of-caste woman, am I not?"

That was our reality. Verbalizing it was making it only harder to accept. I hadn't said anything about my job and our relationship. As much as I was afraid of being fired, I was equally afraid of losing him. My hands flipped into nervous mode - clasp, unclasp, clasp again.

"But I'm content with my guilt and my decisions," Ayaz said. "Truly content. Why should I live in a constant state of fear? All for a society where they want to control my thoughts?"

I bit my lip.

Ayaz touched his fingers to my mouth, gently releasing my lip from my teeth. His fingers felt like velvet, I wanted to rub them all over my body.

"In a society where I'm not allowed to speak freely about my political ideals or about the woman I love," he whispered.

An innate bolt of desire hit, and I wanted to leap into his lap and bite his lip. Not out of stress. Quite the opposite. I wanted to press my lips into the nape of his neck and nuzzle my face against his. If only we were alone and not in public – surrounded by disapproving eyes.

"Ayaz, I don't know what to say ..."

Unlike me, Ayaz was not afraid of the world. He touched my forehead, running his finger down the outline of my nose. "Say this, my jaan, that you love me and will be with me as we sit in the hartal tomorrow."

"I love you, Ayaz," I whispered. My voice quivered as I listened, my words speaking the truth. "What will we do tomorrow?"

He smiled. "Just rally ... as Gandhi-ji asked us to do. We will close our shops and this dhaba. We will halt our business activities and deal with the consequences later."

"Rowlatt Satyagraha."

"That's what it entails. We'll play our role from here in Amritsar as part of the first unified all-India non-violent struggle against the British. Jai Hind!"

My heart pounded at the sound of the victory slogan, *Long Live India*. A non-violent struggle that loomed ahead, large and real. To be a part of the revolution was to be part of history. Nothing could be more exciting. To *hell* with

Colonel Lewis and his threats. I unclasped my hands and stared deeply into my lover's eyes. My heart filled with hope for a new tomorrow. A tomorrow that underscored a permanent picture of me and Ayaz.

"Jai Hind ..." I repeated.

CHAPTER 6

April 6, 1919

Amritsar - seditious documents

Today was different from most days. It was calm, yet not peaceful. The morning breeze was a tad feisty for April, and the birds sounded panic-stricken. Perhaps it was an unconscious foreboding of a coming storm.

The aggressive breeze wound its way outside the cantonment, rustling through the leaves of the hundred-year-old neem tree that guarded the corner. A group of men standing within its shade were whispering.

"What do you think will happen?" questioned one. He tugged at the end of his loosened turban. The same question was on the tip of most people's tongues. Life was suddenly moving quickly and no one had any answers or predictions.

"Let's see how things unfold," another answered, his eyes cautiously patrolling the area. "The Britishers aren't Bhagavan-ji." He opened up a paper packet and offered a samosa to the other men, but they didn't appear to be interested in a bite.

"Not today," one replied. "There'll be time for samosas tomorrow."

The hartal was to be a massive shutdown throughout the country. A day of fasting, prayer, and abstention from physical labor in protest of the repressive new law. The response was overwhelming.

On that one frightful day, millions of Indians simply refused to work. For twenty-four hours, twenty-four agonizing hours for the British administration, the country grounded to a halt. People refrained from working and spent the day holding meetings against the Black Act.

The Rowlatt Act provoked indignation across the length and breadth of India. However, the indignation was more prominent in Amritsar. Amritsar grounded to a halt that day. Deeper down, there was a feeling of discontent. I simply saw it as the usual Punjabi hotheadedness reacting to the rules of constriction.

At the Golden Temple, the day seemed normal, peaceful and serene. Pilgrims still visited, chanting hymns and verses from the Guru Granth Sahib as they barefooted through the cleansing troughs of water surrounding the holy precincts.

The activity at Hall Bazaar and in town had come to a complete standstill. The labyrinth of narrow streets lined with booth-sized shops, normally teemed with bazaar-goers, were clear – open walkways for the housewives who'd decided to see what was happening – or not happening. An old sacred cow wandered the city on its own as if to claim back the right of the streets. Shops and businesses were quiet and dark. The usual cry of traders, silenced. The typical jostle of the rickshaw and tongawala was absent of passengers, persuaded to walk instead. None of today were easy. Many of the housewives swishing their long parandi-tied plaits around their gaily colored salwar kameez clad, magnanimous Punjabi hips had clear misgivings and tried to bully their way into transactions, only to be met with staunch refusal.

A dark cloud loomed on the horizon. No one knew what the next few hours would bring, but the clock continued to tick, one hour ominously giving way to another as the people of Amritsar waited.

The afternoon papers cited that Deputy Commissioner Miles Irving had sent Mr. AJW Kitchen, the Commissioner for the Lahore Division, to monitor the activities. He apparently described it as *'a day that London policemen would have described as panic.'* Why they all looked upon a passive resistance with such concern was a matter of mystery. However, one thing was clear, it threatened the foundation of the British Raj like never before. And in Amritsar, our activities that day rested at the core of that threat.

Even though the strike was announced only twelve hours previously, nobody could buy as much as a glass of chai from their local teashop. A treat I looked forward to each day on my way home from school.

I knew better than to try and visit the dhaba. On principle, Ayaz would not allow anything to be served. Not to mention, he would not actually be there. Instead, he would be roaming the streets of the Hall Bazaar, maintaining solidarity with the striking shopkeepers.

My dear friend, Amrita – she and Gurcharan Singh would surely open the doors of their establishment to me – hartal or no hartal.

Amrita greeted me with a feather duster in one hand and a broom in the other. Gopal played quietly in the corner with a set of two small dinky cars. The moment he saw me, he ran to me ready with a huge bear hug. I swooped him up and planted kisses all over his adorable milk-stained cheeks.

"Aruna Aunty, are you here for chai?"

"I'm here to see you, my favorite boy," I said, my insides ridden with guilt. I had just been caught by a four-year-old.

"That's good because there's no chai," he replied.

"No chai?" I asked.

"No chai during a hartal," he chimed in a sing-song voice.

Taking just one look at my downcast expression, Amrita decided to interject. "Hey, hartal da puttar," she said with loving sternness. "Time to play with your dinky cars. Aruna Aunty and I have things to talk about."

Gopal happily disappeared behind the gaudy curtain hanging near the back.

"I'm sorry, Amrita." I sat cross-legged on the shop's platform. "I know you're officially closed."

Amrita flashed a wicked grin. "Closed for customers."

"I thought I *was* your best customer." My teasing was intentional, yet innocent.

Amrita set her broom aside and wiped the sweat from her forehead. "You *are* my best customer." Amrita lit the stove under her saucepan. "But if we're going to talk about customs, then why shy away from offering our friends a cup of chai?"

"And a paratha?" I licked my lips at the thought of delving into her scrumptious flatbreads.

"Gobi or aloo?" It was always a tough call – her cauliflower and potato stuffings were equally enticing.

"Gobi, please." I was already salivating at the thought. "And as far as the tea goes, I am changing things. I'll take just one cube rather than my regular two."

"Dieting again?" Amrita asked, raising her 'brows as she cast a disapproving tone. "I don't know about this thing of living on love and fresh air. As it is, you're way too skinny. Why be afraid of a little pudge around the edges?"

I laughed at my friend's candid sincerity. "It's not the pudge I'm afraid of. It's the blood sugar that rears its ugly head when all you do is eat ghee-laden parathas."

I assumed the discussion was over when she dusted off a small table occupying the corner of the shop. "And why are you afraid of that?" She took a break from wiping to draw total attention to me, as though I was a child resisting the bitter taste of medicine.

"Because it could kill me." Logic was my only weapon.

Amrita threw her feather duster on the floor and thumped the heel of her hand against her forehead. "Such a western thing to say. Arrey, we are all going to die one day, Aruna. Some of us perhaps sooner than later. Why let that destroy the simple pleasure of food and flavor? Besides you're way too young to worry about diabetes."

Amrita had a point, still it was not valid enough to make me change my mind. She glanced behind the curtain to check on Gopal.

"I suppose that's one way of looking at it." I pinched a layer of skin around my waist to measure how much sugar to add. "For the present, I'll stick to just one cube."

Amrita shook her head and shrugged. She placed her copper-lined tea kettle on the burner.

I watched as she prepared the tea, noticing that she had removed the sugar cube from a piece of paper with blue ink scribbled on one side. I could not make out the writing but my attention woke up.

"What is that?" I asked, pointing.

Amrita looked up from what she was doing. "What is what?"

"That piece of paper … in your hand," I said.

She looked to see what I was talking about. "This waste paper wrapping the sugar cubes? The rationwala who delivers us sugar and other rations uses it to wrap his wares."

The rationwala. Indeed, it was customary to wrap rations in paper, but typically they used the local newspaper. This was different. I snatched the paper from Amrita and held it up to the light. I gasped. Were she to be caught with this, who knows what could happen. Was someone intentionally trying to charge her husband with treason?

"How could you not notice this, Amrita? Look at this lettering."

Looking puzzled, Amrita tucked back a tress of hair that had fallen over her eyes. "What does it say? You know I can't read English."

I cowered as I read the words. "Prepare to die and kill others." I glared at the words, my heart pounding. I felt a familiar tightness in my chest. My mind raced with everything that Ayaz had said about seditious documents. The newspaper reported stories of recent arrests of those who had apparently been in possession of purported seditious documents. Documents they believed were part of a conspiracy to develop a plan to overthrow the Raj or threaten its stability. What did these documents mean? And why did this one have these ominous words? More importantly, how had this paper made its way to Amrita's shop? Or could it be that it was somehow planted? And if so, then by whom?

My head pounded with the myriad of questions that were racing through it. In a flash, I was shadowed by overwhelming darkness that stripped me of my ability to act or think straight. I felt like I was being squeezed through a tight rubber tube. I couldn't hear. I couldn't breathe. I couldn't see. I felt myself struggling to break free and to see the light.

Amrita's voice jolted me. "My goodness! Why would it say that? What does it mean?"

I wasn't sure, but I knew it couldn't be anything good. Amrita's lips pouted. A momentary sign of worry, but her innocent eyes widened telling me she was feeling the stress pounding in my chest.

"Is somebody trying to threaten us?" Amrita asked. She shot a concerned glance over to the curtain. "My goodness, I must show this to Jeeo-ji."

That's when it occurred to me that Gurcharan Singh wasn't here. Seized by a sense of vexation, I stood and paced the floor. "Where is he? Where is Gurcharan Singh sahib?"

The panic in my voice must have been obvious. Amrita looked deeply into my eyes.

"You are a bag of nerves, Aruna!" she said. "Jeeo-ji is out, of course, meeting with people. You know that's what they're doing at the hartal. Maybe he is with your ... Ayaz Peermohammed sahib." She picked up a bartan, a saucepan, and began to polish showing not the least bit of concern. Then she went back to making the tea.

Ayaz! My heart fluttered at the mention of his name, but the excitement lasted for only a fleeting moment. It never occurred to me that Gurcharan Singh would be meeting with him today. Not that Ayaz ever gave me details about where he was going or who he was seeing. But he knew that Amrita and I were good friends. We had just talked about their shop the previous day. Therefore, it was a surprise that he hadn't mentioned it.

"What are they meeting about?" I asked.

"I have no idea. But this morning, Ayaz sahib was here. I overheard him say something about speaking to the public on Baisakhi day."

Suddenly, it all made sense. Ayaz had asked me where Amrita and Gurcharan Singh's shop was located. But he hadn't said anything about speaking to the public with Gurcharan Singh, and nothing about Baisakhi day. I thought his duty began and ended with hartal operations.

Amrita passed me a cup of tea. I clasped my hands around it passively as I speculated on what they wanted to talk to the public about.

"They want to show that the Sikhs and the Muslims are united in their support of the Home Rule Movement," she stated.

Ayaz?! Why did he have to be amongst the most active of activists? "Ayaz and Gurcharan Singh? I mean … could they not leave this kind of thing to others who clearly have the same intentions?"

Amrita pursed her lips. "Aruna, the Congress speakers have been prohibited from speaking in public. Dr. Satyapal received a restriction order before the March 30th hartal." Amrita sighed, awkwardly. "And yesterday, so did others … Dr. Kitchlew, Dina Nath, and Swami Anubhav. Luckily, the restriction order doesn't prevent others from speaking. So … Dr. Satyapal and Dr. Kitchlew are urging supporters to take up the cause in public."

It was true. Dr. Satyapal and Dr. Kitchlew had spawned the rise of new local Congress leaders who they believed would agree to their cause and not be influenced by Deputy Commissioner Miles Irving or the local administration. To me, it sounded like Ayaz could possibly be well on his way to becoming one of those local leaders. Perhaps he was taking Gurcharan Singh along for the ride. I didn't like the idea, and I rejected the logic of her words, which were clearly empowered by a sense of belief.

"Singh sahib now wants to hop on the bandwagon?" I asked. By now I had unclasped my hands and was fidgeting with my neck. I could feel the heat rising under my collar.

Amrita clenched her jaw. I couldn't tell if she was confused or dispassionate. She could probably have said the same for me.

"Why are you so hyped up about this?" she asked. It seemed as if she was shifting her emphasis from her husband's purpose. "He's a well-respected administrator. Don't you think he could make a difference?"

Yes, he could, but the thought of him doing so annoyed me. Why couldn't he focus on his family instead? And the thought of Ayaz becoming wrapped inside this movement also bothered me. Why couldn't he just focus on making a difference to me? I sighed. "He could make a difference to your lives by being absent from all this nonsense."

Amrita was obviously displeased with my remark. "That's a negative thing to say, Aruna."

Ayaz's example of our love letter came to mind. Amrita clearly did not recognize the potential of the problem. I bit my lip, clasping my hands. "Why is it that these academics want to be some sort of activist involved in the political movement? Why do they think they can make a difference?"

"Why do you think they *cannot* make a difference?" Amrita placed her hands on her hips.

Really? Amrita was my confidante, and I respected her views, but sometimes she was so besotted by her duty as a wife that she just couldn't see the forest for the trees. I could feel my anxiety dial ticking up toward midnight.

"Come on Amrita, every single newspaper is crammed with stories of those arrested for no apparent reason. Citing the euphemistic headlines for the Rowlatt Act *Na Daleel, Na Vakil, Na Appeal.* The clarion call of the current wave of ongoing protests. Gossip-mongering. Did you know that down in the Hall Bazaar, people are talking about how a policeman is coveting another man's wife? And to get the husband out of the way, he uses the Black Act? Are you aware that the government is extorting the parents of newlyweds for money equal to what they spent on the wedding?"

But Amrita shook her head and shrugged. She picked up a cloth and continued polishing her bartan. "What does that have to do with anything?"

I couldn't believe what I was hearing. I glared at her, watching her viciously polishing her bartan as if to rub away the topmost layer of varnish. Why on Earth was she in denial?

"Amrita, whether this is a highly elevated rumor or whether it has shades of truth is a matter of speculation. But this I know … rumors don't start out of nothing." I unclasped my hands and waved them in the space in front of me.

"You talking with your hands like that …" – Amrita looked into her saucepan – "… maybe it makes sense for you, but I cannot understand what you are talking about." She intentionally avoided looking me in the eyes.

All she could understand was my over-excitement. "What I mean, Amrita, is that the Black Act has changed everything. Life is in the crosshairs, and of course, everyone is in a mood for a fight. I'm not against taking Gandhi-ji's satyagraha oath against the Black Act, but I am convinced that as responsible people in society, we Amritsaris must pick and choose our battles. What good could come from us joining the agitation?"

Amrita watched as my hands waved through the air before she vocalized her thoughts. A growing volume of voices behind me grabbed my attention. People were streaming through the narrow street. Their tell-tale uniform of khadi kurta pajamas, homespun tunics, and pants donned by Gandhi-style caps, openly announced they were unmistakably supporters of the Indian National Congress. At least a hundred marched toward us. Maybe two hundred, with a cohort of protestors leading the charge, brandishing the symbolic artifact of Gandhi-ji's swadeshi movement - the Khadi charkha flag, its center depicting a native spinning wheel superimposed over three bands of white, red, and green. The visual symbol of self-sufficiency was the most powerful emblem of public self-expression.

The tightness in my chest was even more pronounced than before. But disregarding it, I jumped back onto the shop's platform as they approached the front of the shop. The protest leader glanced over at us.

"The hartal will be tomorrow!" he proclaimed. "Shutter your windows, shutter your doors. Reclaim Punjab ... this is the revolution of our time!"

The crowd following him echoed his sentiment with the familiar gesticulation of waving fists. Their voices unified in the clarion call of the moment.

"Na daleel, na vakil, na appeal."

Even though the Indian National Congress was not officially a part of the protest, individual members in Amritsar were supporting it. All would have a busy agenda conveying the message of Gandhi-ji's call. These men were proceeding from shop to shop and business to business, asking owners to halt activities in favor of fasting, public meetings, and prayers.

No sooner had they moved passed, we were accosted by police officers brandishing lathis and bamboo sticks. "Take no heed!" they warned. "Shuttering your businesses will do nothing but negatively affect your livelihood. What will you achieve by having food taken from the table or halting transport in the city?"

The idea of the hartal irked the Punjab government. Addressing radio audiences earlier that day, Lieutenant Governor O'Dwyer had asked, "What exactly is it that you want to reclaim? What do you want to restore Punjab to?" Indeed the word *revolution* rankled the British Raj and hence they resorted to what was in their power. In other words, to create a counter retaliation. Any fool could see that the British Raj was petrified of the possible outcome of a successful hartal.

I was once again fidgeting with the tasseled ends of my dupatta. And the dark color of Amrita's face made it clear that she was petrified. She didn't say it in so many words, but her eyes and the vicious polishing of her bartan revealed her stress. Now, I was irritated with Gurcharan Singh. It irked me that he would leave his wife and young child to mind the home and shop while he protested. It seemed irresponsible. If people had wives and young children, should they not avoid the risk of jail?

I didn't voice my concerns, partly because it troubled me that Amrita never questioned his actions. She was ready to stay home and be the housewife-cum-mother-cum-shopkeeper he expected her to be. Essentially, the wheel that kept their life churning while he was out and doing his thing. I loved Amrita and respected her home life, but I also detested the way she took on her husband's emotions, ideals, and sensibilities to define her own. Even though I knew it wasn't true, it was as though she wasn't capable of thinking for herself. Deep down inside, I knew that Amrita wished Gurcharan Singh would spend more time at home with her and Gopal. But I wished she would assert herself and verbalize this to her husband rather than relenting to a "Yes, Jeeo-ji" and continuing to be the good and silent wife.

Pulling at my dupatta tassels in my usual manner, I allowed the details to roll through my mind, this piece of so-called waste paper threatening to kill others. Even if it ended up here by accident, which I really hoped was the case, it could cause harm if someone else discovered it. Especially given that Gurcharan Singh had decided to support the political agitation.

Amrita's statement broke me from my thoughts. "If you keep biting your lip like that, you'll be spilling blood all over my mangoes."

I wasn't conscious that I was biting my lip. But I needed to be more specific to help Amrita comprehend. "This piece of paper ..." I said, shaking it in the air, "... could be construed as a seditious document."

Amrita stared at me. "This piece of paper ..." she replied, equally slow, "... is nothing but a piece of waste paper to wrap sugar cubes."

I felt helpless. Amrita had clearly missed the recent news stories about innocent people being locked behind bars for possessing so called documents with language taken out of context. How I wished Ayaz were here. He did a much better job of explaining this. I took a gulp and tried again.

"The government is on the lookout for evidence that could incite a revolution. Like the Ghadar movement."

Har Dayal's efforts and those of his Ghadar movement led to a series of terrorist campaigns marked by bombings, shootings, acts of arsons, and dacoits running riot throughout the Punjab. Lieutenant Governor Michael O'Dwyer went out of his way to crush the attempted revolution, and luckily for him, most Indians remained loyal. The few that didn't were sent to the gallows and some to penal settlements in the Andaman Islands.

Gurcharan Singh came from an interesting place. He understood the high-strung emotions of the Punjabi people and how their passion could rapidly morph into violence. Having witnessed violence during his youth, he grew to detest his native environment and yearned to leave, which drove him to move to Amritsar. When he learned of Mahatma Gandhi and his call for a peaceful revolution, Gurcharan Singh was an immediate fan. I heard him often refer to this particular movement. While he didn't have respect for the violence it ultimately led to, he openly applauded Lala Har Dayal Mathur's ability to influence the thinking of his Punjabi brethren from abroad.

As a dutiful Punjabi wife, Amrita's opinions were shaped by those of her husband. I didn't particularly respect this, wishing instead she would think for herself. But this was the way of most Punjabi women. I had very little to work with. I knew that citing the example of the Ghadar movement would hit home, and that Amrita would understand the dimensions of my fear.

"Do you know what they could do if they find this?" Again, I waved the incriminating paper in her face.

"What?" she responded in a feeble voice, my words somewhat hitting home.

"They could send Singh sahib to the gallows. Or ... to the Andamans!"

She stared at me too stunned to move. I, on the other hand, fixed my gaze on my friend. Amrita's face darkened. My mention of the Andaman Islands had perhaps struck a nerve. She paused, trying to process this information.

"Amrita, please say something!" I begged.

She placed her hand on her chest as if freeing a blockage in her throat. "I should stop buying sugar for my chai?" she asked.

I folded my hands in a prayer position, bringing them to my face. Did she not understand after all my explanations? *Oh, Amrita, were it that simple.*

"Relax, Aruna. I was just making a joke." She shot me a wan smile. "I know you think of me as a country bumpkin who doesn't think much and only follows the way of her husband. And while that may be true to a large extent, I do understand the seriousness of this. I was just trying to lighten things up."

"I'm sorry, Amrita. You're not a country bumpkin. I know you listen to your husband's views and frankly, who am I to question that. It's not like I have a husband."

"I could argue against that with the way things are looking these days." A glint of mischief landed in her eyes.

"Amrita, that is a whole other story."

"By the way ..." she said, changing the topic, "... you're doing that lip-biting thing again, and those hand movements have become a natural expression of your feelings."

I smiled weakly, forcing myself into a controlled clasp. I thought about how I had yet to tell my friend about my meeting at the school with Colonel Lewis, which was the main purpose of my visit. Now just wasn't the time. From somewhere behind me, female voices asking about mangoes grabbed my attention. A group of women were standing on the pathway outside the shop, complaining about the hartal.

"I'm out of fruit ..." she whined, "... how will I feed my family?"

"Can't you just transact on the side?" another asked. "I promise we won't tell."

My mind flew to Mrs. Simeon. Had she somehow sent these two here on a mission? In some ways it was a ridiculous thought, these were probably just innocent wives who had nothing to do with Mrs. Simeon. But my mind wasn't making much sense, it was completely filled with conspiracy theories.

Amrita wouldn't have any of it. She knew better than to get into useless conversations. She shrugged and placed her hands in a humble namaste. The women became fed up and moved farther down the pathway to another part of the bazaar. Amrita turned to me after the group had passed. "So, where do we go from here?"

I took a deep breath, hoping the added oxygen would force me out of my dejection. I needed to be back in a state of relatively higher spirits to think clearly and come up with the right solution.

"To start, we get this paper out of your shop. Then we look for Ayaz and Singh sahib to figure out what it is and what it means."

CHAPTER 7

April 6, 1919

Amritsar - handbill on the clock tower

Finding Ayaz Peermohammed and Gurcharan Singh was easier said than done. I thought they would be somewhere in the market, but Hall Bazaar was a large maze with many intricate corners and alleyways. Getting lost would mean taking forever to escape. Not to mention that finding them would be tantamount to searching for a needle in a haystack.

A hartal had been observed in many towns on March 30th. In Delhi, the police did not allow free movement to the demonstrators, which led to shots fired by the officers, causing a number of casualties – civilians and police. It was considered to be successful despite tensions running high. In Amritsar, a hartal was observed that day, but it wasn't like when the city came to a standstill. If anything, it seemed to whirl, a carnival of bodies and busyness – busy with the activity of non-activity. Shops closed, businesses ground to a standstill, and about forty-five thousand individuals gathered in Jallianwala Bagh for a meeting presided over by the articulate Dr. Kitchlew who echoed Gandhi-ji's message. "We will ever be prepared to sacrifice personal over national interests. This does not mean that this sacred town should be flooded by blood. The resistance would be a passive one."

The March 30th hartal was a success. Rumor throughout the cantonment was that although Amritsar's deputy commissioner was relieved that there had been no incidents, Mr. Miles Irving was petrified about what another hartal in Amritsar might lead to.

What could it lead to? I too was unnerved by Irving's attempts to silence the protestors. For the first time, I was bothered by the sight of British officers as I walked from place to place. *Would there be blood on the streets? Would they use physical means to suppress the protesters? Would the locals be willing to seek a peaceful resolution?* Questions upon questions ran through my mind, but only time could answer them.

"He fears this is merely the calm before the storm," Mrs. Wintertree, the woman who lived next door to us, had said. "It's a matter of time before the underlying unrest provokes some kind of tempestuous action."

She should know, considering her husband Commander Wintertree, was one of Mr. Irving's closest aides. He was one of the members of Colonel Lewis and Mr. Irving's regular bridge table. All three had lived in the cantonment long enough to understand that Punjab hot-blooded temperament underscored a certain mentality that often resulted in unplanned violence. He feared a situation where he might be forced to fight the lion in its own den. He gave orders to the local police to do everything they could to prevent another hartal from taking place on April 6th but to no avail. The people of Amritsar remained steadfast in their goal. Such was the power of Gandhi-ji's call for satyagraha.

I was all for satyagraha, yet I was irked by the politics of it, the fact that *politics* gave people the right to cross boundaries and breach parameters. Anything could be completed with *politics* as the underlying reason. Like how Congress leaders not silenced by the banning orders kept open the lines of communication. Given their experience with the administration's lack of openness, they knew it was the only way to understand what they were planning next. When Mr. Irving appealed to them in the days preceding the hartal, they promised it would be canceled. A ploy to allow the planning to continue without disruption. Dr. Satyapal and Dr. Kitchlew may have been prevented from speaking in public, but in private meetings, they urged its continuance.

Both Gurcharan Singh and Ayaz were participants in those meetings. Even as British garrisons lined the streets, picketing specific spots on the way to the church visited by the Europeans, the two satyagrahis took it upon themselves to travel from business to business, educating people about the morally damning nature of the Rowlatt Act. My words might fall on deaf ears, however, I needed them to know that they were playing with fire.

I finally found them at the central chowk, an open crossroad in the marketplace. The atmosphere was particularly warming with Muslims and Hindus standing together in harmony. Ayaz was not easy to spot. Attired in his white kurta pajama, black waistcoat, and black prayer cap, he could have been any of the Muslim men in the crowd.

Gurcharan Singh, on the other hand, was distinctly recognizable. All six and a half feet of him, attired in a khadi kurta pajama and freshly starched orange turban. He towered above everyone else.

A crowd had gathered to meditate and pray in the absence of commercial responsibilities. Hindus observed fasting rituals in advance of the Rama Navami festival, Muslims offered namaz on personal prayer rugs, and Sikhs recited verses from the Guru Granth sahib.

Together, Ayaz and Gurcharan Singh were speaking to a group of about ten to fifteen locals. The fervor in their speech, passing to the crowds through their perfectly expressive elocution skills. Their audience listened intently, acknowledging every so often with a nod or a clap.

I bit my lip, consciously this time. Private in my prayers with the Divine, partly because my Hindu background observed prayer as something one did in the inner sanctum of the home, and partly because my Anglo-Indian ethnicity caused me to privately wonder what god I was actually born to pray to. Religious gatherings always put me on edge, and the larger the group, the more uneasy I felt. Not that this was a planned religious gathering per se, but with everyone focusing on a unique conversation with a god different to that of their neighbor, it made me wonder whether they had actually come to pray or were trying to outdo the other. North India's religious communities got along from a social or political perspective, but one never saw them praying together. This particular gathering seemed almost artificial. To me, it was more about religious competitiveness rather than secularism. With mostly men around me, I was even more uncomfortable. The sheer numbers felt overwhelming.

Standing several yards from the small gathering, I wasn't sure if it was a good idea to confront them. My feet slowed even as my mind raced. I was tempted to shy away and run home, but something told me that succumbing to timidness would serve no purpose. I took a deep breath, forcing my way into the gathering, making a beeline for the two I came to find.

"Ayaz sahib, Singh sahib!" I tried to get their attention.

The moment Ayaz saw me, he broke into a natural-Ayaz smile, relinquishing his outward public persona for the intimate man that I knew and loved. But within a moment it was gone, the natural-Ayaz smile replaced with a formal one - one that was polite and fake. I knew what he was thinking. In public, I was not the vulnerable girl he held hands with but rather a confident schoolteacher who spoke English. I wanted to throw myself into his arms, but under the watchful eye of the community, I distanced myself, referring to him respectfully as Ayaz sahib. Ayaz read me like a scholar reads a book. Under his public persona, he took pride in knowing that I was his indefensible Aruna, warming his heart.

Conscious of several male eyes centered on this one female at the edge of the crowd, he responded with equal regard. "Aruna-ji!" he replied. His hand gesturing in an adab sign of honorable respect. "I'm glad you are here. We were just speaking about last week's hartal in Delhi."

"Not a good subject to talk about," I said. "These things are far too dangerous." My tone was less respectful than his.

A murmur of whispers spread as everyone looked in my direction with disapproving eyes.

Why had a woman arrived in this crowd of men? I took a deep breath reminding myself that I didn't know anyone, so none would know me. Why should they expect anything of me? I could be with whomever I chose, go wherever I wanted, and could speak my mind.

Ayaz didn't seem concerned. He cocked his head. "What are you referring to, Aruna-ji?"

"The railway station incident in Delhi, and the violence that ensued."

Ayaz acknowledged my concern with a deferential nod. "Case in point, Aruna-ji." Making an example, he turned to address the rest of the gathering. "Take heed of Aruna-ji's words," he yelled. "Violence is not an option. If our hartals are to be successful, they must be peaceful!"

Maintaining calm when you are itching to say something was not easy to control. "Ayaz sahib ..." I shouted, "... if I may, the hartals are not peaceful. Violence is lurking. Perhaps at every corner of Amritsar."

The crowd clearly discerned how rattled I felt. I could sense Gurcharan Singh's suspicious stare penetrating through my thoughts. Though he knew I was a good friend of his wife, he couldn't help being a little judgmental.

Deep down, it was always about my identity. Ayaz knew my views and insisted that I had a habit of overreacting. I knew better. Being an Anglo-Indian lowered my worth in the eyes of Gurcharan Singh. Therefore, I didn't blame him. It wasn't his fault that he was conditioned to think in the same way as everyone else in our community. I was more than aware of it and forgave him.

The others stared at me. Their doubts arose not so much by virtue of frowning upon my identity but because they were skeptical about a woman, and a Punjabi woman at that, speaking in such an audacious manner to a gathering of men.

"No violence here in Amritsar," Gurcharan Singh said, supporting his friend. "We've had nothing but peace, and we intend to keep it that way."

"And how long do you suppose that will last when rationwalas are delivering documents like this to our households?" I asked. I pushed the paper into his hands.

Ayaz looked over his shoulder with a furrowed brow, scrutinizing the contents. "What is this, Aruna-ji?"

"I ... don't know. It appears to be some sort of threat to us all."

Gurcharan Singh had a grave look on his face. He clearly had an idea about this. "Is it an advertisement from Waqt?"

The mention of Amritsar's local newspaper pushed the crowd into chattering. Gurcharan Singh's question didn't make any sense. Why would the newspaper publish an advertisement with such threatening language?

Ayaz seemed like he was in the know. His hands moved to his chin, twisting his beard. "No, alas," he whispered.

"Alas, what?" I repeated.

"It's a copy of the handbill," he said. He shifted his expression as we talked. Whatever it was, it surely had not come as good news.

"What handbill?"

Ayaz sighed, a thought once again weighing his brow. "There was a group of khilafatis who prepared this yesterday."

Khilafatis? A group of Muslim nationalists, pressuring the British government to preserve the authority of the Ottoman Sultan as Caliph of Islam following the breakup of the Ottoman Empire at the end of the war. I knew Ayaz supported them, he had said so many times. But what could they possibly have to do with this? Judging by the suspicious faces gathering around me, I could see I wasn't the only one brimming with questions.

"Why would khilafatis prepare something like this?" someone asked.

"To post for public view," Ayaz replied with a faraway look in his eyes.

"Where?" someone else asked.

"On the clock tower."

"On the clock tower? Where everyone could see?" another asked.

"As I said, for public view." Ayaz shook his head.

His eyes filled me with a strange compassion even though I was disappointed that he so readily recognized the origin of the fiery words. My fingers found their way to my dupatta tassels.

Gurcharan Singh looked at Ayaz with equal surprise.

"You knew about this?" he asked. I could see the disapproval in his eyes.

Ayaz nodded.

I was right. We all were. A murmur spread through the crowd. Violence was lurking, and Ayaz did know about it. What about his oath of satyagraha? Wasn't knowing about violence and not saying anything the same as being a part of it? I wanted to scream. Public demeanor be damned.

"Ayaz sahib, you support the khilafatis? Were you part of this?" a man asked.

I, too, wanted answers, the Aruna that had fallen in love with him and trusted him. I wanted answers now.

"Are you involved?" I asked, my voice trembling.

Visibly taken aback, Ayaz furrowed his 'brows. But he didn't rise to the bait. He was not about to lose his guard in the face of the crowd even as he attempted to shed light on the matter.

"Aruna-ji, as I said when you came in, Gandhi-ji states that violence is not an option."

But his answer was not satisfactory. Not to me nor anyone else. My fingers, dupatta in hand, trembled to match my voice.

"What exactly do the words on this paper mean?" another man said.

"People are incensed, some more than others," Ayaz spoke his convictions. "The Black Act has kindled flames of passion all over the country, including right here in Amritsar."

I felt the need to dig deeper. "Ayaz sahib, with all due respect, flames of passion have not served in a positive manner for our political stance. Given the winds of change, these flames can quickly be fanned into a fire."

He sensed my anxiety and presented his argument to pacify me as best as he could in a public setting. "No doubt, Aruna-ji, you are right to be concerned. But take heed in Gandhi-ji's soul force. If we are successful in teaching our people about the importance of satyagraha, we can avert the fire. That's exactly our purpose here today."

Gurcharan Singh took a step toward me. "Where did you find this paper, Aruna-ji?"

"In your shop, Singh sahib," I replied. "Discovered it when Amrita was making tea."

The surprise was written across his face. Clearly, this was not what he expected to hear. "My shop?"

"Exactly ... Amrita said the rationwala delivered the sugar wrapped in this so-called waste paper. But I must ask, was it actually waste paper or a planned message?" I wanted to let go of my dupatta but was unable to trust my hands.

Gurcharan Singh dismissed the idea without giving it a chance. "Cannot be a planned message."

Ayaz sensed that I was trying to bring an unknown conspiracy to light. "Wait a minute, Singh sahib," he stated. "Aruna-ji has a point."

"What do you mean?" one of the men in the crowd asked.

"Yes, what exactly *do* you mean?" Gurcharan Singh repeated.

"The tongawalas outside Hall Bazaar and those near the railway station," Ayaz replied. He gazed into the distance, tilting his head.

"What about them?" Gurcharan Singh asked. He obviously was taking Ayaz's words more seriously than he took mine. Although, this wasn't the time for egos.

I wanted them to understand the danger I sensed.

"They've been refusing to take Britishers to the church," Ayaz added. "Your local rationwala's father is a part of the tonga-driving community."

Gurcharan Singh looked even more confused. "Why do you know about my rationwala's family, and what does that have to do with anything? It doesn't mean this was a strategically planned message."

"But it doesn't mean that it wasn't either," Ayaz said. He twisted his beard, a sure sign that he was feeling tense.

Gurcharan Singh refused to accept that something was wrong. He looked away from the crowd, voicing his thoughts, "Why would anyone wish to send me a message of *'Be prepared to die and kill people?'*"

Ayaz stared at me with a silent acknowledgment of what we had discussed earlier before glancing back at Gurcharan Singh. "Only because it's incriminating." Ayaz's voice seemed deeply layered with innuendos.

I was confused by now. I thought about Ram, my regular tongawala. Such a lovely man whom I had known and trusted for months. Surely his community could not be a part of this nonsense.

"But why would they want to incriminate Singh sahib, a well-respected administrator at Khalsa College?" I asked.

Ayaz it seemed had worked it all out. "Because of his brother."

The conversation was rising above my head. I could not grasp the concept, so I kept my mouth shut and just listened.

Gurcharan Singh, following Ayaz's example, stroked his beard. "Prithvijeet? No."

"Unfortunately, yes," Ayaz said slowly, perhaps guessing that Gurcharan Singh would not like what he was about to say. "As an ex-soldier, you know he was an informant to the Lieutenant Governor of Punjab, Mr. Michael O'Dwyer."

"That may be, but what's there to inform about me?" Gurcharan Singh asked.

Ayaz's words were not making any sense to us.

"That you're a revolutionist," Ayaz replied. "That you're in possession of seditious documents."

I gasped, gradually understanding what Ayaz was trying to say.

"What revolutionist?" somebody asked from the crowd. "Gurcharan Singh is a well-respected faculty at Khalsa college."

"Bilkul bakwaas!" huffed another voice.

I couldn't tell whether his words of dismissal referred to Gurcharan Singh or his brother. Gurcharan Singh, for his own part, was stunned by the suggestion. It took him a few moments to respond.

"My brother?" he repeated. "Nonsense. He would never do such a thing."

"Do you not remember how your family opposed him when he wanted to become a soldier? And how you were so much a part of that?" Ayaz asked.

"That was a family matter," Gurcharan Singh replied, his stance darkening. "Nothing at all to do with this."

My gaze shifted from Ayaz to Gurcharan Singh and back to Ayaz who scrunched his hands into fists. His fingers rolling around his thumb. He too used his hand gestures to convey stress.

"I disagree, Singh sahib," he stated. "To the contrary, it might have everything to do with this. Think about it. Your brother still resents you for your lack of support. Does he not?"

Vermilion Harvest

Gurcharan Singh scrunched his face. "Look, I didn't want my only brother, my baby brother, to risk dying. That is all."

"He didn't see it that way," Ayaz replied. He raised his 'brows. "He wanted to enlist and hated you for stopping him."

It was my turn to be confused. Ayaz had met the Singhs barely a few weeks ago, and yet he knew all about Gurcharan Singh? Just how much time had they actually spent together? And did Amrita even know about his family's history? I had not heard about any of this from her.

"For stopping him from possibly dying in a war that was not ours to fight," Gurcharan Singh stated, his eyes casting down.

I could sense the pain behind his words.

"He was wet behind the ears. Didn't know any better. It was my duty to advise him."

Ayaz placed his hand on Gurcharan Singh's shoulder as if to console him. "And so you did. But it fell on deaf ears. He considered it to be *our* war. But enough of your brother and the ugly truth that it conjures. The point is that it's highly likely this document was intentionally planted. From now on, you better not accept anything inside your shop or home."

Gurcharan Singh continued stroking his beard as he continued to stretch the cogitation of his mind. "You're suggesting that somehow my brother wanted to set me up by planting this incriminating message in my shop? How does this make sense?"

"Singh sahib, I'm only outlining a possibility. Over-theorizing perhaps. I hope so, but better to be safe than sorry, don't you think?"

Gurcharan Singh walked around as he brooded over the matter. "Then how do I buy rations for my business?"

"Open the wrappings outside the shop. Have Amrita-ji check everything carefully. If you come across anything daring, burn it ... immediately."

"Immediately?" Gurcharan Singh repeated, looking surprised.

"Immediately."

The chatter had picked up around Ayaz, Gurcharan Singh, and myself. Silent members were alarmed by what they had heard and whispered among themselves. Ayaz once again turned his attention to them.

"When the war was in full swing," Ayaz stated, "my friend Kasturbai, a well-to-do accountant, was found with a copy of Das Kapital. It was seized and he was imprisoned. But Das Kapital is a historical work, a curiosity of literature, you could say. Tell me how Karl Marx's views on the working class are likely to instill criminal force against the government?"

"These Britishers will *create* a crime out of anything," said a young Sikh man.

"Indeed," Ayaz replied. "These are fictional crimes. When Kasturbai was released from jail after two years, they brought him in again on the grounds that his previous conviction could be used against him."

I stood back, taking in the information. It was all new to me, and I didn't quite know what to make of it except that Amritsar was going through some kind of change, a deep seated one at that. That had to be the case if you couldn't even trust your brethren or fellow citizens. What did this mean for us? For Ayaz? For me? For Ma? For the Singhs? And what would happen next?

My thoughts were interrupted by another voice, this time an older one. The man was in his late fifties or early sixties. Clean shaven with cropped hair, wearing a white kurta pajama, he could not be identified by his faith, nor his political affiliation. To me, he represented the face of Amritsar – or maybe all of Punjab on that fateful Spring day of 1919.

"Where in British law is that written?" he asked.

"Nowhere," Ayaz responded, his fists again clenching. "I'm a student of the law and this I can guarantee you in blood."

I could see the fervor building in eyes. When he embarked on an episode of storytelling, he used more than just his voice to make his point.

"Kasturbai was shunned by his guild of colleagues … they wanted to have nothing to do with him because *they* feared any association could be used against them. He was ordered to report to the police on a regular basis, and one day he was late because his mother fell ill. They arrested him again. That was within days of releasing him the first time."

I was going over what Ayaz had said earlier. While the conversation moved on, I could not pull the image of the clock tower out of my head, and what a violent notice posted on it might mean. Were the walls of a peaceful Amritsar about to come crashing down? I needed to speak up.

"Ayaz sahib, what about the matter of the handbill on the clock tower? Are we to expect violence soon?"

Ayaz turned to me with a grave expression. He cast his eyes at my lips, indicating that once again I was unconsciously biting them. "There's no saying what anyone can or will do, but as satyagrahis, we must stand firm. If violence ensues, we will not continue with the hartals."

"But who is this group of khilafatis? Shouldn't we try to convince them of the dangers?" I asked.

"Of course, I already have," he replied. "We talked this morning, and we'll continue to talk throughout the day. What ultimately happens though is in God's hands."

But I couldn't let it go. I scrunched up the end of my dupatta and spoke, "Why are they thinking of being violent in the first place?"

I sounded like a little girl coaxing her parent to say something false to mitigate her fears. But I was not a little girl, and Ayaz was not my parent. He would stick with the truth.

"Because they are exasperated. In the eyes of the administration, even a peaceful protest is looked upon as a criminal act. Our freedom has been stolen. You tell me, Aruna-ji, who is the criminal? He who speaks, or he who suppresses that natural right?"

"Naturally, those goras!" someone shouted.

"Yes, those Britishers," someone else yelled.

"Swatantrata ki jai!" cheered a third.

That was enough to get the rest of the group chiming in to champion the cause of liberty.

Somehow, with the underlying threat of violence, it didn't sound so glorious. Neither did Ayaz's formal tone. I tried my best to ignore his conscious politeness, referring to me as *Aruna-ji* in place of his usual terms of endearment. I knew it was a cover in front of the others, but I couldn't stand it. Besides, the whole thing underscored our ability to be free. I sighed as Ayaz tried to appeal to the crowd.

"Don't worry," he said. "We'll stand firm. Resorting to violence is not the answer, and we meet today to impress this truth among the people. As Gandhi-ji has said repeatedly, violence is not an option."

As I watched them shaking their heads, I hoped that they had truly accepted Ayaz's words from the heart.

The threatening handbill pasted to the clock tower turned out to be an empty threat. Nothing ever came from the copy that made it to the Singhs' shop as a ration's wrapper either. We could only thank God for small mercies.

The hartal in and of itself was successful. Aside from the handbill and verbal intimidations of Indian loyalists, nothing untoward happened that day. But the success of the hartal scared the living daylights out of the British administration. It was the second time in barely a week where they witnessed a peaceful disobedience rally from the people of Amritsar. They saw it as a conspiracy and could simply not wrap their heads around the legality of it all.

The Legal Remembrancer to the Punjab Government reported at the Legislative Council meeting in Lahore the next day that *'Even in its purest form, the Passive Resistance Movement, which preaches disobedience to certain laws as a means of procuring repeal of a particular law is in my opinion, a conspiracy to do a legal act by illegal means.'*

Deputy Commissioner Irving called it a *triumph of organization.* Even though the inhabitants of the city stayed true to the Gandhian principle of peaceful resistance, with not a stone thrown or a person hurt, Irving still referred to them as *mobs.* Truth be told, Irving was afraid. For him, the underlying tension was quickly becoming a nightmare. He saw Dr. Satyapal and Dr. Kitchlew as representatives of a deeper conspiracy that he couldn't quite understand or control.

CHAPTER 8

April 8, 1919

Amritsar - Anglo versus Indian

I arrived at school to find the staff in a fury. Mrs. Blackwood, the history teacher, Mr. Linchfield, the science teacher, and Miss James, the Form I English teacher, had their feathers ruffled about a current newspaper article. I took a quick peek over their shoulders. The article was on the front page of The Tribune of Lahore, describing Sir Michael O'Dwyer's speech as a *blazing indiscretion.*

At last evening's meeting of the Legislative Council in Lahore, Lieutenant Governor Sir Michael O'Dwyer delivered a scathing attack on those who opposed the Rowlatt Act, including the Indian Members of the Legislative Council. "A day of reckoning is in store for those openly endeavoring to rouse public opinions against the government," he threatened. "Standing back, rather than attending the public meetings at the hartal is a missed opportunity for the Indian members to help the rest of us exert restraint on the agitators."

Unfortunately, the Indian members had not taken well to this written attack, neither had the vernacular press who labelled his remarks as insulting and inflammatory. Just another example of O'Dwyer riding his favorite hobby horse. In other words, attempting to denigrate the educated Indian.

Preposterous!

Since when were the Indian members responsible for encouraging their brethren to continue to be servile to the British rulers? The thought set my nerves on edge.

"As if standing back and letting all these people conspire against us is not an indiscretion!" Mrs. Blackwood placed her hands on her hips, ready to take up more space, foisting her opinion on us whether it was welcomed or not.

"Indeed," Mr. Linchfield added. He lifted his head and thrust his chin forward as if to join Mrs. Blackwood in her crusade of aggression. "These puerile demonstrations against the Rowlatt Act just shows how ignorant and credulous people can be misled."

Misled?

I could not believe what I was hearing, and felt my insides steaming. But as much as I wanted to lash out, I couldn't. How was I to stand up to a room full of British schoolteachers who clearly echoed the views of the British government? Yes, I'd been given this position because I was Anglo-Indian. But under these circumstances, anything I said would be construed as conspiring. Rather than reaching for the tassels, I settled my dupatta and looked for a place to sit.

Vermilion Harvest

"I'll bet there is not one in a thousand of those demonstrators who knows the first thing about the act," Miss James stated.

Discrimination of any kind made me see red. "What exactly do you believe the demonstrators do not understand about the act, Miss James?" I tried to control my anger. "That these laws can be used to issue warrants for crimes that have not been committed?"

All three glared at me with an icy gaze. Two teachers looked up from marking papers with narrowed eyes. No one expected to hear the words I just spoke.

"The demonstrators are ignorant people." Miss James was now breathing heavily as if a bull ready to charge. "Shopkeepers … traders … all easily misled … simple-minded people."

I pursed my lips, considering a response. "Miss James, there is nothing misleading about protesting laws that strips one of their civil rights." I shook my head. "They are not ignorant or misled. This is simply a matter of asserting their freewill to demand justice."

Perhaps I had not chosen the correct phrase. The moment the words escaped my lips, I understood my error. My colleagues stared at me with daggers. They didn't need to foam at the mouth. Their message was clear about the classic differences between the English's stiff upper lip and the Punjabi's firebrand emotions.

I, on the other hand, couldn't stop there. The feisty Punjabi blood within my Anglo-Indian veins took control. Not to mention that I was a lone native warrior surrounded by an army of foreigners.

"And on your point, Mrs. Blackwood, how does any of this smell like a conspiracy?"

Maintaining her *hand-on-hips* position, Mrs. Blackwood continued her dagger-glare as if to size up the competition. She actually broke the British silence without jumping off the deep end like me.

"Isn't it a conspiracy?" she asked. "The Indian members of LegCo just stood back and did nothing when the government was threatened. History just might label that as treason."

Ayaz's technique to demonstrate passion without succumbing to stress gave me reason to pause. I clenched my fists to keep from shaking. However, I did not wrap my thumbs over my fingers. Clenched fists were decidedly better than a clenched jaw.

"You're a history teacher, Mrs. Blackwood," I said, reaching for my dupatta. "Isn't treason defined as crimes of betraying one's country? The Indian members did nothing wrong ... even if they supported the demonstrators. When does supporting justice and civil rights equate to treason?"

"I could tell you a thing or two about treason!" Miss James stated loudly. "Treason can be defined as betraying your colleagues by cavorting with local rag-headed rebels! And ... you are still here even after that warning ..."

Rag-headed rebels?

My Ayaz was just reduced to a rag-head?

How dare she!

Miss James was perpetually high-strung – *common knowledge* – but she never used derogatory insults before. My meeting with Colonel Lewis was obviously common knowledge, although, behind my back. I stood silent, unable to think of a proper response.

"Come, come, Miss James," Mrs. Blackwood whined. "We are still working together for the common cause of British education. We must stay *calm* … go about our business."

Miss James crossed her arms, retreating to a sulk.

Calm!

The same response – detached stoicism – *appropriate* British manner. A series of 'brows raised with heads turning the other way. These very people – my colleagues – were disturbed over what a newspaper had published about O'Dwyer, yet when I tried to argue my point, they seemed quite unflappable. And what about Mrs. Blackwood's statement of *still here?* Was my job in jeopardy? What *were* the rumors about me?

Quiet and reserved – the ability not to express emotion were considered a strength in British culture. I knew this from being raised near the cantonment where my emotions flared over things large and small. 'It's that Indian blood running through her veins,' I often heard from the Britishers. 'She has much to learn about self-control. God willing, one day she will.'

In a misogynistic manner, expressing one's feelings was considered by the Britishers to be effeminate and weak. The Victorian stereotype of hard-working, silent, self-sacrificing, and emotionless was a positive characteristic where one believed they were better than the rest of the world. A belief rooted firmly into the British psyche, thriving to this very day.

I made my point or so I hoped. Our discussion ended, and I gathered my books, heading to my next class. My colleagues would now hand me the cold shoulder for the rest of the day. And unfortunately, my prediction would prove to be undeniably accurate. An inner voice of reason told me that I should consider the repercussions of the staffroom conversation. But a counter-voice of passion advised me to hold my head high, standing for my ideals. There was no upside, pleasing my colleagues. It wasn't as if I had ever fit in.

I entered the classroom, forgetting about the morning. My students' curiosity was a welcome therapy from the Anglo-Indian double standards that existed in the real world.

Irving's newly found fear of the so-called *mobs* led to his attempts to control civil administration. The British garrison took no risks since the day of the hartal. They paraded through the city with rifles, picketing the streets that led to the church used by the Europeans, and so it continued for the next few days. Irving's actions turned into verbal intimidation of Indian loyalists, the tongawalas, who controlled the horse-drawn, two-wheeled vehicles. Incensed by his threats, they decided to take matters into their own hands by refusing business to British residents.

Although the definition of *Indian loyalist* had become a gray area, loyalists such as the tongawalas began to make judgment calls on others as to how deep their loyalty actually ran. An argument I was not prepared to defend.

Vermilion Harvest

Amrita arrived to pickup Gopal from school. Three days a week, I would meet them outside the main gate just after the closing bell. We would share a tonga home. I would drop them off at the Hall Bazaar and continue down the mall to the outskirts of the city, before making my way to the dhaba to see Ayaz.

No crowds were charging the school gates today. A great opportunity for us to make it home quickly. Ram, our regular tongawala, was waiting outside as usual in his yellow and green tonga, toting his gaily-attired brown mare, Lakshmi. It was customary for tongawalas to give their horses auspicious names, one honoring the Hindu Goddess of Wealth. Lakshmi and his tonga were Ram's primary means of income. To honor her, Ram adorned his horse with a colorful bridle – belts at the neck and a bright blue and shocking pink feather set at the nape. It looked more like a feather duster, the kind you'd clean your home with, but Ram insisted that it was an outfit fit for the Goddess of Wealth.

Amrita climbed into the tonga, hoisting up Gopal to sit next to her. After settling the overhead canopy to shade the afternoon sun, she motioned for me to join them. I prepared to hitch myself up when Ram's words hit me like a bullet.

"Step down, please, memsahib," he stated with disingenuous politeness.

His words cast me into a state of disorientation. I'd never heard anything like this from Ram before.

Avoiding eye contact, he continued speaking in an unusual, clipped tone. "My tonga is not in service today."

I furrowed my brow.

What?

Ram's refusal made it clear he was resisting a debate. The sting of his words gave me a head rush. I glanced at Amrita, who twisted her hands in a gesture that characteristically asked what was going on. I glanced back at the tongawala, my foot perched on the step.

"Are you not here to pick us up, Ram?" she asked.

"Who do you mean by *us*?" he asked. "What's regular for *them* doesn't have to be regular for *us*."

My ears rang as his words echoed. I knew what Ram was saying but didn't want to believe it. I held back in silence. Amrita seemed to be flustered.

"What is this *us-them* talk? Who do you mean by *them*?'"

"Britishers!" he stated. "Given the events of the last seventy-two hours and how they try to control us since the hartal, we have decided that they cannot ride our tongas. We will no longer provide Britishers with our service."

What was I to do now? Twist my dupatta? Clench my hands? Cover my ears to avoid hearing this venomous drivel?

Amrita was more decisive. She furrowed her 'brows in an attempt to process his words. "Well and good. This *is* a British school, but *I* do not see any Britishers."

Ram glared at her for a few long moments before shifting his eyes to me.

That's when something hit deep inside the pit of my stomach. He had confirmed my suspicions with a single glance. He knew I wasn't the Punjabi kudi I purported to be. And here I was, marginalized by my tonga driver. Someone I knew and trusted and chatted with every day.

"Really, Ram? Since when did I become a Britisher?" I asked.

But unlike me or Amrita, Ram didn't care. "Since the very first moment that a *gora* impregnated your mother," he replied.

My mind raced to the image of Ayaz at the chow a few days ago. He was discussing the plight of the tongawalas and their new hatred for the establishment. I didn't want to believe that Ram was a part it. However, it was now apparent that Ayaz had been spot on with his analysis. Amrita and I held back in uncomfortable silence. We were gobsmacked by the insolence of his words.

Gopal looked at me and frowned.

The Anglo-Indian shadow monster had just reared its ugly head. I typically expected it from Britishers in the cantonment or the discerning friends of my mother, but never from a local who was a friend.

Even the horse, Lakshmi, appeared perturbed by his owner's words. She let out a nervous whinny and shook her head.

Amrita broke the silence. "Ram! That's not fair!"

But she was instantly interrupted by the tongawala. "No, memsahib, it isn't." He frowned as if there were no tomorrow. "But we live as servants to foreigners on our *own* land. That's not fair either, is it?"

I was pulled back to the similar, though different, experience in the staff room just that morning, and previously in Colonel Lewis' office. I was bursting to retaliate. Therefore, why did I feel so stunned?

"This is disgusting!" Amrita threw up her hands. She stepped down from the tonga. "Come, Gopal. We are *not* riding on this tonga today."

"Why not, Mama?"

Ram was quick to jump in. He pulled on the reins attempting to control his impatient horse. "I didn't say anything to stop *you* from riding, memsahib. Only white-skinned people."

Disgusted as I was by his double standards, I was more frightened by the idea he was just one of many service providers who might be thinking the same way. My legs felt numb as though my heart had suddenly stopped.

"You expect *me* to leave Aruna-ji on her own?" she shouted, waving her hands.

"That's your decision, memsahib," Ram replied.

"I'm *not* going to do that!" Amrita was almost screaming.

"As I said ... it's your decision."

His answer felt like a slap against my face.

Amrita held tightly to Gopal's hand. "Besharam! I'd rather walk than ride in your stupid tonga. Come, Gopal."

"But I like riding with Lakshmi!" Gopal eyes teared.

Amrita held him by the waist, pulling him off the two-wheeler.

I bit my lip, wishing Ayaz were here to help me without creating more drama. I gestured to Amrita to go back to the tonga. "It's okay," I said. "You and Gopal go home." I clutched my bag, wondering how *I* would make it home.

She refused. "Are you mad?" She glared at me. "Nothing about his words are okay. He cannot act like this. You are not a Britisher."

Ram scowled, cracking his whip. His body language spoke volumes. "What difference, memsahib? If you have British blood, then you are a Britisher!"

A ball of heat ran up my spine. How dare this little chit of a man rebuke me like this? "I have Indian blood in my veins too!" I stated, indignantly. It wasn't much of a comeback, but at least it was the truth.

"Which makes *you* impure. More like a mongrel that wanders the streets. Even more of a sin." His eyes showed his disgust.

Another arrow that ran deep. I hated who I was – Anglo-Indian – insecure. Always an outsider in another's world. Would it ever change? People generally skirted around the word mongrel, mostly to protect my feelings. Now it was coming full circle.

"When the parents sin, it puts misfortune upon their children," Ram stated, continuing to insult me. "Why do you think we want things to change in India? Because we want a better India for our children. I am a loyalist, memsahib. There is no longer room for Europeans in *my* vehicle."

Did he even know what that meant? If he did, he would understand he was disrespecting the term. He was speaking like a sadhu attempting to bring the wrongdoers on the right path but only to fill his pockets. Just like the Imam who preached peace but fueled rage in his subordinates, or a priest failing to live by the words of the bible.

My respect for the man vanished. Amrita was so angry she looked like she was ready to spit nails. Gopal stood next to me as his mother chased after Ram's tonga, spewing insults like a volcano spewing ash. Amrita removed the chappal from her foot and held it up ready to hurl it at him.

Ram *click-clicked* at the horse to move him along.

"I'm not European!" I stated, glancing around, although, there were no reasons for me to hide what I was saying.

Whether he thought I was talking to him or not, Ram took my words as a question. "What part of *no* do you not understand, memsahib? No means no."

With a crack of his whip, he allowed Lakshmi to trot in the direction of the Hall Bazaar.

I felt helpless and ashamed of who my parents were. Regardless of my circumstances, I could not change and become someone else.

HAPTER 9

April 8, 1919

Amritsar - Lahore sends reinforcements

We had no choice but to walk home. It wasn't far, but Amrita and I were still left speechless. Gopal had stopped crying, which made things a little easier. We didn't know what to say to each other. Frankly, whether to say anything at all. We made our way through the streets, my head spinning with his words. Ram, who had always welcomed me, now considered me his enemy. He verbalized exactly what so many silently thought, including Gurcharan Singh.

How everything had changed in just a few days. The sky was an orange canvas with swirls of radiant blue. The silence was deafening, my body hollow and stiff. The cracks in my soul would need to remain invisible to others.

The atmosphere on the street was tense. The civil administration had come to a standstill, but still no violence. We came across an empty tonga, and I lowered my head.

"Should we ...?" Amrita asked.

I held her arm and shook my head, remaining silent. I wanted to be as invisible as possible. Another discriminatory episode was not something I wanted to deal with.

We witnessed a few other tonga episodes on the way home, involving the refusal of service to British customers. Each time we passed, I squeezed Amrita's arm, indicating that we needed to keep moving. When we arrived at the outskirts of the Hall Bazaar, it was time to part ways.

"Come inside for chai?" Amrita asked.

I shook my head.

"He'll regret what he said, Aruna. He will learn ..." She looked deeply into my eyes, trying to infuse me with optimism.

I smiled to reassure her. Before she could speak her next sentence, I interrupted it with a hug. She hugged me back even tighter. I hugged Gopal before they disappeared into the inner gullies.

I pulled my dupatta over my head, wrapping it around my neck to keep the blaze of the afternoon sun at bay. I walked in the direction of the cantonment, my hands clasped under my bag.

"Jaan!" Ayaz's voice was both comforting and disturbing at the same time.

I wanted to see him but not in this state. My tears threatened to fall, but I controlled myself, pushing them back into those iron tear ducts. Ayaz must have sensed that all was not as it should be. He hurried his pace, gently placing his hands on my shoulders.

"What's wrong?" he asked.

Vermilion Harvest

His hands slid down my arms, forcing mine free. His fingers found mine, and I watched through misty eyes as he pressed our palms together, lacing his fingers with my smaller ones. Without looking at his face, I detected the alarm in his voice. He pulled me to him, and I collapsed into his arms.

"Hush, jaan." Ayaz softly stroked my hair.

The warmth of his voice and his tender touch were comforting. I felt safe, loved, and once again I entered my happy space.

"If I could only tell you," I whispered.

I was about to recount what had happened when Ayaz looked into the distance.

"What is it?" I asked. "Where is your attention?"

"I'm thinking of the preparations for tomorrow's Ram Navami parade," he said.

Ram Navami was a Hindu festival celebrating the birth of Lord Rama. What would a Muslim need to prepare? As always, all he needed was to take one look at my furrowed 'brows to read the pattern of thoughts racing through my mind.

"When the Hindus of Amritsar celebrate Ram Navami on the streets of Amritsar tomorrow, we Mussalmaans will march with them in solidarity. We will celebrate Ram Navami with gusto." He grinned. "I know it's not typically how the festival is celebrated, but Dr. Satyapal and Dr. Kitchlew are staunch supporters of Hindu-Muslim unity. Many of their followers have taken an oath to bury religious differences."

I shrugged. This was no time to bring him down with the woes of my day. Pulling away slightly, he used a finger to slide away an errant lock of hair that had fallen across my eyes. We were standing in the middle of the mall, so I pulled away. But Ayaz's grip was firm.

"Hush …" he whispered, "… it's alright. I'm going to walk you home." He lifted my chin, his eyes locking on mine with a glint of pure affection.

He loosened his grip and slid his hand into mine for a moment before separating it to maintain the decorum we needed to walk home. We wanted each other, but it was neither the time nor place for a romantic rendezvous. Exhausted after the day's tribulations, I simply needed to retreat.

Safely back in my room, my eyes caught the headline on the front page of the afternoon paper. I recalled Ayaz's words about Ram Navami. What was normally a Hindu celebration would now be shared by their Muslim brethren. How would Mr. Irving, with his fear of passive resistance, respond to this new measure of social unity? The newspaper alluded to his extreme uneasiness and his constant reference to the demonstrators as *mobs*. The article cited a report he'd sent to the Commissioner of Lahore, Mr. A.J.W. Kitchin.

'We could not go indefinitely with the policy of keeping out of the way and congratulating ourselves that the mob has not forced us to interfere. Every time we do this, the confidence of the mob increases; yet, with our present force, we have no alternative. I think we shall have to stand up for our authority sooner or later by

prohibiting some sort of strike or precision that interferes with the public peace. But for this, a really strong force shall have to be brought in, and we shall have to be ready to try conclusions to the end to see who governs Amritsar.'

I panicked as I read the bold print. My hands clenching into tight little balls. Was there a chance he could construe the Ram Navami festival to be something that it wasn't? Just another mob gathering? Could the Hindu-Muslim solidarity be perceived as anti-Colonial and increase the confidence of the so-called mob?

My mother's call interrupted my thoughts. "Aruna, come, darling. It's time for dinner."

I stretched out my fingers, pushing the thoughts from my mind, dismissing them as a function of my paranoia. What I needed was quiet time for dinner and perhaps meditation after. Enough with this political worry. Hindu-Muslim solidarity was a good thing – a great thing. What could possibly go wrong, and how could it be misinterpreted for anything but what it was – a show of faith between two religious communities to prove we were, and would always be, united.

What I didn't know, of course, was that while the inhabitants of Amritsar were preparing for the Ram Navami festival, Mr. Irving had asked Mr. Kitchin to send in reinforcements – increased forces – armored cars and machine guns. Also, a moveable column from Lahore to be available at six hours' notice, even though no violence had been reported.

What I also didn't know was that across the border of the city in Lahore, Mr. Kitchin was prepared to use force to reestablish control – and that he had taken it upon himself to help out.

☯HAPTER 10

April 9, 1919

Ram Navami - a Hindu festival

School was canceled. Crowds were expected to block traffic all over the city. I woke early to walk to the marketplace. I would not hail a tonga. No way after what happened the day before. However, I was not about to miss the Ram Navami processions.

I hoped to watch the procession with the Singhs, but I didn't want to impose upon their family time. As for Ayaz, he'd be caught up in the political aspect of the celebrations, and I would be the last on his list of priorities.

Amritsar's streets spilled over with people. Nearly every turn of road in the central part was filled with Hindus dancing to the beat of the dhol – the music of the street bands. Muslim men wearing Pathan suits and colorfully embroidered taqiyah marched alongside their Hindu companions bearing their garlanded deities on their shoulders as they chanted, "Hindu-Mussalmaan ki jai!"

Ram Navami was always a big occasion in Amritsar, but this year it marked a difference. The leaders of Amritsar's so called *revolutionary movement* decided there would be brotherhood of the Hindu and Muslim community.

In the front of the procession, a Muslim man took a sip from a wine cup and held it into the sky. He handed it over to a fellow Hindu who followed suit. It was unprecedented, underscored by the solidarity demonstrated by two local leaders from the Indian Nation Congress – a Kashmiri Muslim, Dr. Saifuddin Kitchlew, and Dr. Satyapal. They were watching from different locations.

The unity between the groups was apparent in every aspect of the celebrations. Ayaz would be the perfect spokesperson, but I couldn't find him anywhere. The activities were not well received by Deputy Commissioner Miles Irving, who observed from the balcony of the Allahabad Bank.

"Mahatma Gandhi ki jai!" the crowd chanted, their slogan growing louder and more fervent.

Irving looked visibly shaken, similar to a wild deer responding to the sound of bullets.

When the procession passed the balcony, the participants cheered, stopping to pay their respects to Mr. Irving. The bands switched their tune to play *God Save the King*.

Mr. Irving changed his stance. He smiled and waved at the crowds. For a moment, I thought he even caught my eye. But a group of Muslim students, dressed in Turkish uniforms, had halted below the balcony.

Where is Ayaz?

I turned my focus to the students who were clapping at Mr. Irving. In British terms, it was a mark of disrespect.

Mr. Irving cupped his fist, turning his back to the crowd. "Move along!" he yelled, staring at the superintendent of police standing by his side. "Immediately!" He glanced over at Dr. Satyapal and Dr. Kitchlew. Irving's pale face seemed to blend into the white wall behind him.

The dusty streets, overrun with paraders, created a subtle dig at Irving and the administration through the guise of the Hindu celebrations. Irving was not a fool, and he was definitely agitated by the events. Within hours of the festivities, Irving had arranged for the detention and deportation of Dr. Satyapal and Dr. Kitchlew to Dharamshala a few hundred miles away. I would hear about the news from a student at the mall the following morning.

"Rumor has it they were tricked into showing up at Irving's house this morning and arrested without notice," the student stated somewhat breathlessly to a group of people on the corner.

"Oh my god! Where are they now?" an onlooker asked.

"I'm not sure, but rumor has it they're on their way to Dharamshala."

Dharamshala? Why would they be taken to a meditative hill station? It sounded like they were being sent on a forced vacation.

"He had to get them out of the province. Everything out of the province. Even when he deported Gandhi-ji, he did so at Palwal, at the borders of the province," the student explained.

Regardless of Irving's motives, whisking them away proved not to be the best move. The news spread like wildfire and within another few days, people threatened more hartals and mass demonstrations, and not just in Amritsar, but also in Lahore, Kasur, and Gujranwala.

If that wasn't enough to unnerve the people, the administration's next move had an even worse reaction. Mahatma Gandhi was expected to arrive in Punjab to further lead the peaceful protest against the Rowlatt Act. However, O'Dwyer was not prepared to take chances. He had blacklisted those he believed could lead an uprising against the acts, including Mahatma Gandhi. He issued instructions banning Gandhi's entry into the state. When he arrived at the border of the province, Mahatma Gandhi was sent back to Bombay.

The deportations were massive mistakes that would have disastrous consequences. The events of the next twenty-four hours would actually prove more than that.

HAPTER 11

April 10, 1919

Amritsar - Dr. Satyapal and Dr. Kitchlew

The day following the Ram Navami festivities, I had hoped for some quiet time with Ayaz. I needed to tell him what had happened in the tonga and about the threat from Colonel Lewis. But given the events that unfolded that afternoon, it turned out that destiny was not on our side.

I was making my way over to meet him at Rambagh per our tentative plans but actually ran into him just outside the Hall Bazaar. He was waylaid by yet another overanxious member of the local Congress Party – Hans Raj, Dr. Kitchlew's attendant, who was twenty-three years old, incredibly good-looking, and was somewhat irresponsible.

The gossip in the cantonment circles was that Hans Raj was a *good-for-nothing* living off the earnings of others. Routinely accused of embezzlement, he had already lost jobs twice on account of the accusations – from the Northwestern Railway where he was a ticket collector and from the Union

Club. He enlisted in the party, and overnight, he emerged as a feisty and ardent supporter of the doctors. Like many others in the cantonment, I had my doubts. He applied to join the local Amritsar police force, but the superintendent rejected his application following the interview. Instead, he was placed on a waiting list. While he was waiting, he caught the attention of Dr. Kitchlew by joining the agitation over the issue of platform tickets. In the ten days that followed, he moved from applying to be a British-directed police officer to helping organize Congress meetings and planning the hartals. But how can one go from *wanting* to support the Angrez to *becoming* a supporter of Gandhi and the Congress? I failed to understand.

Hans Raj was appointed Joint Secretary of the Satyagraha Sabha responsible for keeping track of the members rapidly joining the movement. At the Ram Navami procession, he marched boldly through the streets, carrying a Home Rule banner and giving Deputy Commissioner Miles Irving the *evil eye.*

Dr. Satyapal, unlike Dr. Kitchlew, might have shared my concerns as with others in the cantonment, but Dr. Satyapal appeared to be more restrained in his public relations with Hans Raj, for he welcomed his support or so it appeared. But he did not openly encourage his company.

Ayaz and Hans Raj were exchanging animated, yet rational, words. Hans Raj paced, clutching a satchel in one hand while waving the other. Ayaz leaned against the wooden door of a closed shop, reviewing a sheet of paper. His dark eyes radiated a fierce, uncompromising intelligence.

Vermilion Harvest

Their strained expression demonstrated that the note was not a harbinger of pleasant things.

"Ayaz?" I called, trying to make eye contact. "What's wrong?"

Glancing in my direction, he broke into a powerful smile, and his eyes locked onto mine. For a moment, it seemed he had forgotten his worries, but his smile soon disappeared. He redirected his attention to the crumpled piece of paper in his hand.

Hans Raj turned to me, a fire raging in his dark, black eyes. "It's the Lieutenant Governor Michael O'Dwyer," he stated. "He wants to nip things in the bud by decisive action."

Hans Raj's tone triggered me. My adrenaline flowed although I had no idea what he was talking about. He cast a skeptical eye, peering suspiciously at the note.

"It's a letter from Dr. Satyapal to his father, describing what happened this morning," Hans Raj stated. "I made copies and will circulate them this afternoon."

A feeling of tightness took hold in my chest. Why would Hans Raj be circulating copies of private messages? There had to be a god-awful reason. I stared at the agitated man who slammed his fist into his palm over and over again. He was all but foaming at the mouth.

"Mr. Irving tricked Dr. Satyapal and Dr. Kitchlew into coming to his bungalow this morning ... on the pretext of *talking things over*," he continued. "I was with them, and the moment we arrived, the police superintendent was there in mufti – *plain clothes* – with a bunch of soldiers dressed as though they were going on a shikar. We knew immediately it was a political ploy and protested, but they said it was a waste of time, the orders had come directly from the Lieutenant-Governor."

I panicked as the gravity of the situation came to light.

"They escorted doctors Satyapal and Kitchlew to waiting cars with a military escort disguised as a hunting party. Both were arrested on a whim. No charges, no anything!"

Ayaz, equally fired up, piped in. "That man has stepped outside his boundaries."

By *that man*, did he mean the Lieutenant-Governor?

Ayaz twisted his beard in that all-too-familiar show of stress. "Not to mention, he stopped Gandhi-ji's entrance into Punjab!"

Hans Raj curled his lips. "The larger administration knows not to mess with the Mahatma. O'Dwyer already tried to persuade the Government of India to have him arrested, but they ruled that one out. Now he believes he can get around things by creating new rules that pertain only to him. He couldn't have Gandhi-ji arrested, so he forced him off the train when it stopped at Palwal Station. They escorted him back to Bombay."

"Why did O'Dwyer deport Gandhi-ji?" I asked.

"Some cock and bull rumor that we locals were planning to kill the Europeans in Amritsar on the 16th after Gandhi-ji's arrival." Hans Raj puffed out his chest and took in a deep breath.

His words hit me like an ice-cold wind from out of nowhere. My heart pounded louder, deeper, harder – thud-thud. I couldn't stop the pounding. Where were these rumors coming from? And who was responsible for spreading them? And what if they were *not* rumors? From the look in Hans

Raj's eyes, it was hard to believe that he would pass them off as *cock and bull*.

"I will take my leave, Peermohammed sahib," Hans Raj said, looking agitated. "I need to circulate these letters and get back to Irving's bungalow. Are you coming?"

Ayaz nodded. "Give me half an hour. I'll see you there."

Hans Raj clutched his satchel before spitting on the pavement. He stormed into the street of the Hall Bazaar, tripping into an untethered bullock cart.

My eyes grew moist, and I could feel the tears. "You're not going to Irving's house, are you?" I asked, my voice quivering. "Please, Ayaz, please tell me it isn't true."

Ayaz looked shaken. He reached out a trembling hand to caress my cheek but I drew back. This was not the time. He smoothed out the paper. "According to Hans Raj, several thousand have gathered at Irving's bungalow to demand the doctors' release."

"To peacefully demand their release, I hope, Ayaz?"

The answer was written across his face. He went back to twisting his beard. "Right now, the crowds are peaceful. Noisy, but peaceful. However, the people are incensed, and Irving is petrified that the crowds will get out of hand. He's ready to use force. Snake, that he is."

Snake?

But in India snakes were considered to be auspicious. Had Ayaz lost his sense of zeal? I could feel my pulse racing like a freight train. At that moment, I hated Ayaz for his involvement. I wanted to scream but what good could that do?

Enough was enough. I couldn't stand it anymore. His political views – they had transgressed the barrier of our romance. I was committed to braving all odds, but where was Ayaz's commitment to us? Politics were ruining everything, and I needed him to focus on me. I swallowed the lump growing in my throat, mustering the courage to tell him what I had come to say.

"Ayaz, there's something I need to tell you."

He leaned back against the arched wooden door with the large, steel hinges. A tall date tree was to one side and a banana tree on the other, it's blossoms flaring over his head. It was picture-perfect, like a postcard from paradise. Until I closed in on his expression, which was heavy with concern. Ayaz took a deep breath.

"I need to get to Irving's bungalow to see what's happening," he said.

I shuddered, and once again, my eyes welled with tears. There was little more I could say. Ayaz was preoccupied with the events of the afternoon. Was this selfishness? Or was I the selfish one? Oh, how I hated it all.

"What did you want to tell me?" he asked.

I clenched my jaw. It was all I could do to prevent myself from screaming about everything I felt. I couldn't stand the idea of injustice against us but more than that, I couldn't stand the idea of mob violence. I also couldn't stand the idea that if mob violence ensued, the locals would be to blame and not the Britishers.

Ayaz was involved and at the cost of our relationship. I hated his blinding passion for politics. But I loved him so much it twisted my insides. My fear grew with the thought of loss. More than anything, I wanted to support him. However, I couldn't handle the thought that his quest for freedom appeared to only exist at the cost of our own. The freedom to be a couple in peace without judgment or distraction. Not to mention that every moment I stood by him, I grew closer to losing my job. Unfortunately, now was not the time to share that tidbit.

"Nothing ..." I whispered, my eyes heavy with tears, "... just that, I'll come with you."

"No!" He held out his hand. "No ... I'm not comfortable with that."

"Why not?" I asked, salty tears rolling down my cheeks. "Is it because you can't be seen with a non-Muslim girl?"

Ayaz touched my shoulder. He looked at me as though I had just declared myself to be a flying purple cow or something.

"Wherever did you get such a ridiculous thought?"

Unable to look directly at him, I glanced at the ground. "From everyone, everywhere. No one believes our communities will ever allow inter-racial romances."

Ayaz held my chin. "I don't know why you're thinking that, jaan. I'll convince my family when I return to Lahore. No one will place obstacles in our way."

"Then why won't you let me come with you?"

"Safety. I cannot speak for the crowd, my jaan. Wearied patience can send eddies of emotion swirling through the streets. I'd prefer you go home."

Ugh! Wearied patience!

He could have made it easier to love him less by giving in to what the communities wanted. But Ayaz was not one to follow the herd. I wanted him more than ever. I stood there, holding my breath and clinging to his arm, desperately hoping he would change his mind. But he didn't.

"No, Ayaz," I stated. "If there's danger to you –"

"What are *you* going to do, Aruna?" he asked. "We have enough problems. At least one of us should stay safe."

We did have problems, and Ayaz did not know the extent of mine. I wanted to tell him. Even more than that, I was afraid of what it might mean. That Ayaz would take the noble path and suggest the two of us stay apart. I couldn't bear that.

Feeling weightless and anonymous, I pushed his hands away. "What is the point of one of us staying safe when the whole idea of *us* requires us both? This was supposed to be *our* afternoon in Rambagh … away from people and politics."

"I know, my jaan, but Rambagh is no longer a quiet meeting place for us."

"What do you mean?" I asked.

"A force of British infantry has apparently been sent there … to keep in reserve."

"In reserve of what?"

"In case there's trouble in the city."

I couldn't believe what I was hearing. Was Ayaz telling me that Rambagh, our oasis from the world, had become a paradise lost? A military fortress?

He squeezed gently, and a fuzzy feeling ran through me as his fingers inched to my waist. He pulled me closer, and I forgot about our time, our place, or how I felt just moments ago. I was wrapped in the sensation of being near him, contact with Ayaz, unable to resist the pressure of his lips as they pressed on mine. I drew him closer. I wanted to feel his bare skin on mine, but this was hardly the place. I clung to him desperately, not wanting the moment to end. But end it did.

As I broke off the kiss, Ayaz's coffee-colored eyes studied my body with a predator's unwavering attention. I knew that look. I'd seen it many times before, and it never failed to fuel my insides. I felt hot and increasingly bothered. His look told me that Ayaz was feeling the same – yet another reason we needed to stop. I forced myself to break away from his grasp – abruptly, before either of us did anything stupid.

Ayaz took my cue and loosened his hold, allowing me to pull away. "Jaan, we'll have our afternoon in the sun soon, I promise." He brought my hand to his lips, kissed my knuckles, and sighed. "I need to leave … already, several hundred are supposed to have gathered outside the bungalow. Promise me you'll go straight home."

I said nothing, my lungs burning.

"Promise me, Aruna!"

My ribs ached as I gathered the breath to speak. "Alright," I whispered. "I promise."

I watched with a painful agony, one that was part lust and part fear, as Ayaz walked away, heading to the British lines. His hands, shaking before clenching into fists. The classic Ayaz Peermohammed signature of stress.

CHAPTER 12

April 10, 1919

Amritsar - violence at the railway

Despite my promise to Ayaz, I didn't go home. I couldn't. I was haunted by his allusion of wearied patience. What if violence actually did break out? And what if something happened to him? I'd never be able to forgive myself for not being there. If I headed home, Ma would only usher me inside. I felt the urge to remain on the streets, ready to join Ayaz, should the need arise. If I went home, I'd be locked away from the outside world with only the radio for official news. I felt like I was waiting outside an operation theatre, not knowing what news the doctor would bring once he finally emerged through the door. Truth be told, the people on the streets had better, up-to-date news, especially those on the frontlines, like the crew that must have been gathering outside Irving's house. That was where the action was taking place, that was where I needed to be. So that was where I headed.

Vermilion Harvest

It was close to midday. The hour when April's sunshine morphed from a symbol of cheer to shadows of oppression before turning the city into a baker's oven. Late spring was always a punishing time in Amritsar. Intense heat from the noonday dulled the capacity for thinking city-dwellers who sought relief under the shade of a tree. Feeling exhausted, I wandered slowly through Hall Bazaar with dulled senses seeking a cooler spot for a five-minute rest. A punkah provided some refuge in Lakhani's tea stall. The clipped blades whirred like a slow-breathing yogi.

Conversation was not part of my agenda. It was hot and I felt irritated. The dual nature of sunshine reminded me of a metaphor with my relationship with Ayaz. Nothing brightened my mood – but with the brighter sky, the higher the heat. Sitting and feeling the calm around me, I watched, waited, and surveyed the scene.

A ruckus on the street grabbed my attention – a local subziwala. The man had parked his vegetable cart outside Lakhani's and started yelling. "There's trouble on the lines! They're not allowing anyone to cross."

By *lines*, he was referring to the railway tracks, exactly to where I was headed. In order to reach the cantonment area, the homes of the British administrative staff including Irving's bungalow, one had to cross the railway lines. For some strange reason, it was obvious that the administration was afraid of trouble breaking out.

He shifted his stance, spouting highly strung words between raspy breaths. "The people want to get to the Deputy Commissioner's house, but there are too many ... all shouting and protesting. They're being blocked!"

Those near the subziwala were visibly agitated. The louder their conversations, the less I could hear what they were saying. When resentment poisoned the air, then sanity naturally resisted order. Therefore, it was time for me to march into the fray. I gathered my things and left.

The railway was crowded with people resembling a stampede of wild-eyed cattle. Hundreds, maybe even thousands, rushed the crossing gates, shouting obscenities at the garrisons, threatening to charge. The mass was now obstructed by Captain Massey, Amritsar's commanding officer and a small troop of soldiers. Captain Massey, a burly man with a gruff manner, was used to throwing his weight around. He positioned a group of rifled men on the footbridge along with three British magistrates – the main crossing point of the railway lines. It was probably *his* way of making a point to the crowd.

"You must disperse ... now!" he yelled through a portable megaphone. "We are under order from the Deputy Commissioner. Our officers are in position with a mounted machine-gun! Move back!"

What kind of brutality was this? Clearly Captain Massey had taken steps to deal with just this type of trouble when the news of the Congress leaders' arrests leaked out.

My thoughts flew to Ayaz. Had he made it to the Deputy Commissioner's bungalow? Or was he stuck somewhere around here? I scanned the panicked faces for a glimpse. Where could he possibly be?

"Where are our Congress leaders?" the crowd demanded. "Gandhi-ji ki jai! Where is Dr. Satyapal! Free Dr. Kitchlew!"

Vermilion Harvest

Massey stood silent, brandishing his megaphone, refusing to answer. His burly self resembling more of an ogre as the minutes passed.

The crowd grew in size as I watched. The sheer momentum by which they advanced, forcing the mounted soldiers to retreat, gave me reason to pause. A few men near the foot bridge threw stones at the soldiers.

"Stop!" the captain shouted. "At *once!* I'll be forced to take action!"

My heart pounded as I watched. People continued to shout at the garrisons. A man removed his turban and brandished it under the nose of a horse causing it to rear. The soldiers pleaded with the crowds to withdraw. But they continued to yell louder and louder.

"Gandhi-ji ki jai. Hindu-Mussalmaan ki jai. Satyapal-Kitchlew ki jai." The slogans were probably heard for miles.

I was the only female I could see, and I was now standing in the middle of the angry mob. I desperately searched for Ayaz, but he was nowhere – actually, that wasn't completely true. He was here somewhere. At first, I only made out an amorphous blotch, then his head and his shoulders. It was definitely his face in the distance.

My presence here was inappropriate and sooner or later, I would receive my share of admonishment. However, *daring* had long since been replaced by the act of *risk-averse*. I inched through the angry men only to be blocked by demonstrators sitting on the road, cross-legged, and beating their chests. They howled and screamed.

A cane swiped through the air, hitting an army horse on its nose. The animal whined and reared up. The mob threw stones at the garrisons.

I lost sight of Ayaz and my mind fell blank. Was he in danger of being trampled? I strained for the amorphous blob I had recognized only moments ago. The feeling of urgency in finding him now controlled me. Panic-stricken, I clutched my bag, inching through the sitting men.

"Have you seen Ayaz Peermohammed?" I asked anyone who'd look at me. "He's tall ... a Mussalmaan. Six foot two, bushy 'brows, wearing a white kurta with a black waistcoat and a taqiyah."

Stones rained down on the troops. I stopped as one just missed the side of my head. Two men suddenly blocked my way. One, a bulk of a man with a massive chest and big brown arms, wearing a brown-colored kurta and a white turban. The other was quite the opposite – scrawny-looking with dark, black hair falling across the sides of his round, wire-rimmed spectacles.

"Memsahib," the bulky man said, "are you crazy?!"

I screamed as one grabbed me around the waist, pulling me from the crowd. He ran us to a small side street and glared at me.

"Memsahib?" he stated firmly, "are you okay? Why are you here?"

"I ... I ... yes, I'm fine."

The men stared at me.

Who are they? Where was Ayaz?

"Who sent you here?" the scrawny man asked.

"Nobody," I replied. "I'm looking for –"

Vermilion Harvest

"Are you out of your mind?" the big man asked. "This is *no* place for a woman!"

My thoughts felt bland, no longer was I in my body. Instead, I was just standing there watching. Maybe I was out of my mind. "This *is* a public railway station," I said.

"Not today!" the skinny man snapped. "Can't you see? This is now a war zone!"

"I have as much right to be here as you. I'm an Amritsari too."

The bulky man glanced at his friend, before glaring at me. "Memsahib, don't misunderstand us, but you just missed a stone hitting your head. You must leave."

The stress of the event was making me just as irrational as the stone-throwing rioters. I tilted my head and nodded. "I apologize. I meant to say *thank you* for moving me out of harm's way. You are kind, really. May I ask a question?"

The large man nodded.

"Why are they throwing stones at the officers?"

The skinny man thumped the heel of his palm on his forehead. "Memsahib, look at this scene! They are not allowing us to cross the lines. Who do these Britishers think they are to stop us? Bada sahibs ... think they are our superiors ... standing on the footbridge like that!"

"I agree," I replied. "It's despicable. What about *our* people? Why throw stones?"

"How else do we get them to move?" the large man asked. "All we want is to get to the Deputy Commissioner sahib's house. But they are blocking us and shamelessly beating us."

"Beating? What do you mean?" I asked, feeling the fear rising from my stomach.

"So many have been injured already," the large man replied.

"Did you not see what happened an hour ago?" the skinny one asked. He looked as though he was about to blow a gasket. "They had three magistrates on the footbridge along with a bunch of horsemen. All we did was climb three or four steps, and they went crazy!"

The large man placed his finger to his lips, glaring at his friend.

"First they started beating us with lathis," the skinny man stated.

Lathis? I winced at the thought of the soldiers using sticks on our locals.

"That's when we retaliated with the stones," the large man added, explaining with somewhat relative calm. "The soldiers opened fire on us!"

Then it had happened after all. The violence was real. *Oh my god, Ayaz!*

"For revenge, Bugga and a group of his cronies dragged Mr. Pinto, the telegraph master, from his house," the skinny man said.

A throbbing sensation pulsated through my head. I felt myself turning pale. Bugga was known to be a loudmouthed troublemaker in Amritsar. Ayaz had feared this kind of retaliation, and now it was all happening just like he predicted.

"Why would he do that?" I asked. "Mr. Pinto has done nothing wrong."

"Regardless!" the skinny man replied, his anger growing, "Mr. Pinto is a Britisher. If the Britishers treat us ill, we treat them ill."

But Mr. Pinto wasn't British. He was like me. His name and his privileged government job were granted by virtue of his Anglo-Indian status. The pain and humiliation of being kicked off Ram's tonga flashed through my thoughts. There was clearly a rising sentiment against Anglo-Indians. The realization hit – the locals thought of us as half-bloods – the British-half now offensive. Ayaz warned of this type of retaliation.

Obviously, these men couldn't tell that I had British blood flowing through my veins. The throbbing in my head was suddenly more pronounced. It felt as if the stone from a few moments ago had actually hit, puncturing my lungs.

The large man held my arm. "Memsahib, what's wrong?" He stepped back aware of the impropriety of his gesture.

I bit my lip and this time I tasted blood. As reality sunk in, everything spun, slowly at first but rapidly picking up speed. The men morphed into a hazy blur, and their voices faded.

"Memsahib!" someone was shaking my shoulders

"Ayaz?" I whispered.

It wasn't Ayaz. It was one of the men who had moved me to safety from the violent crowd.

"It will only get worse," the skinny man said. "You must leave immediately!"

"Sorry, memsahib …" the larger man added, "… but we cannot help you anymore. We need to get back to our people."

Their people? As though *they* were different from *my* people.

I was grateful for the help, suddenly conscious of making a fool of myself – first coming here and then mistaking these men for Ayaz. I smiled and cleared my throat. "Thank you for your kindness. I should be leaving now. Namaste."

The men bowed and disappeared into the mob, thrusting their fists into the sky. They were soon joining in with the angry cries. "Gandhi-ji ki jai!"

Gandhi was purported to be the purveyor of peace, yet he was ultimately responsible for this outbreak of violence. The irony.

My bag was missing. Oh goodness – my purse, my files. Where had they gone and where to begin searching? Perhaps it didn't matter. The value of holding my job had taken a sharp downturn these last few days. And now, I had no way to get home. Crossing the lines was out of the question, so was taking a tonga on the longer route around the city. Instead, I aimed for Amrita's, the only safe haven.

As I walked down the side streets, I didn't notice the people pushing, filling the sidewalks the way gas filled a jar. People avoided the main streets of the mall. The space in the smaller alleys of the Hall Bazaar was packed. It was as if the people were programmed to get as far from one another as possible. Make no eye contact and move fast. This was the city where I walked freely, a place I considered to be my safe zone. Yet today, every corner and shadow was potentially dangerous.

Vermilion Harvest

I was face to face with the stark reality of danger scattered to the four winds. I wanted Ayaz, for I could find safety in his arms.

⌘HAPTER 13

April 10, 1919

Amritsar - anarchy in the city

Amritsar was alive with anarchy, but the streets were much calmer inside the gates of Hall Bazaar. Word had spread like wildfire about the violence and many had stayed home – a choice – if one *was* home or one had a *way* home. It was just a matter of finding my way. I was a lost child – physically, emotionally, and spiritually.

My feet found their steps to Amrita's shop, an unconscious action. I stared at the silent and dark store. It was shuttered to the world outside. The Singhs had retreated to their apartment above. Not a single window was open, just a slight light bleeding through from the first-floor windows. The area outside was deserted.

Disturbing their family time did not seem like the right thing to do. I paced the area, my eyes sweeping the length of the shop.

"Jaan?"

Vermilion Harvest

Ayaz! My tears blinded my vision.

He ran to me, grabbing my waist, lifting me up and off the ground in a mad, passionate embrace. For the first time, I didn't stop to see who was near us. All I cared about was being safe in his arms. For a few moments, he simply held me tight, stroking my hair as I let loose a deluge of sobs like hiccups.

It took me a while to calm down.

Ayaz pulled away and looked deep into my eyes. His own, dark pools of fear. "By the time I arrived at Irving's bungalow, I heard what happened at the footbridge. I left to join the people there."

"I came looking for you!"

"I know."

He knew? My eyes searched his face for answers.

"They told me you were there. That you escaped the attack."

How could that be? Nobody knows who I am.

Ayaz read my mind. "There were no women there. When a man said a young mem was looking for me, I knew who it was."

Sadness filled me as I pondered the meaning. I believed in the ideal of the passive resistance, but now all I could think of was Mr. Pinto being dragged by his neck. I squeezed Ayaz's arms.

"You said it would be peaceful! You said the people of Amritsar believed in Gandhi-ji. I believed you! Look what they did to Mr. Pinto. Why frame him when he wasn't a participant? He was just doing his job!"

"It's clear that the people of Amritsar and elsewhere do not have the grit of Gandhi-ji. They are jealous of people like Pinto –"

"People like Pinto?" I glared at him. "You mean people like *me?* Because of our half-blood status? Because we're given jobs in the railways, the post office, and government services?"

Ayaz shook his head. "The thing is … those jobs are never given to the locals. They consider them to be examples of jobs stolen from them."

His words struck me like an arrow to the heart. However, he was making perfect sense. No wonder Ram, the tongawala, hated me once he got to know my true identity. And no wonder the staff of Saint Mary's couldn't stand my so-called *cavorting* with a local like Ayaz. At one level, I accepted the futility of his words, and then again, I needed to persist.

"There're plenty of locals with good government jobs," I stated. "Look at Mr. Kamra of Chartered Bank."

Ayaz nodded, his eyes casting down. "Alongside his British bank-manager colleagues, Mr. Kamra saved them even though they were on the edge of danger like the other British bankers."

A heaviness descended upon me once again. "What *other* British bankers?"

"That Stewart and Scott of National Bank … and that Thomson of Alliance Bank."

I had no idea what he was talking about. From the way he stared at me, it must have been obvious.

"You didn't hear? They were cornered in their offices, attacked, then dragged outside, doused with kerosene, and set on fire."

"What? When?"

My body felt numb. Had Ayaz been walking by the bank earlier? What if he had been caught in the violence? He could have been burned or worse, killed.

"Just a few hours ago I tried to warn you that things were unraveling. That's why I asked you to go home."

"Go home? While you risk your life?"

A wave of sadness crossed his face. His fingers curled over his thumbs in that tell-all fist of stress. He shot me a wan smile.

"Aruna, this is my life. Fighting for our purpose. I carry a dark weight in my belly. However, I'd never forgive myself if something happened to you."

Ugh! There it is again.

Ayaz – the inevitable ray of sunshine. He was radiating my world on one hand while beating down unbearably on the other. Looking out for me? What about looking out for us? What about our dreams of a future together? Or the home we were building in Bombay?

"If this is what your life has become, then where does that place our tomorrow?"

An awkward silence filled the space between us. He was trying to find a way to justify his actions. I now hated myself for falling in love with him. Why had I trusted a stranger? Why had I not listened to my inner voice when it warned me that nothing good would come from me falling for Ayaz Peermohammed?

He pursed his lips and rubbed the base of his neck. "How can we build tomorrow, jaan, when we have no freedom today?"

"Freedom? A Muslim and an Anglo-Indian ... that will forever be our present, our past, our future."

Ayaz wiped away the tears streaming down my cheeks. "Jaan ..."

"Don't call me jaan!" I stated firmly. Pulling away from his hold, I glared at him. "How can I be your life and love when my own jaan, the very life inside *me* is diminishing by the second? No one sees me as one of their own anymore."

Ayaz started to say something but remained quiet.

"Seriously! People see me as a Britisher. Every day, I curse my father, whoever that is, for raping my mother nineteen years ago."

The thought reminded me that we were standing outside the Singhs' shop. Our embrace was open to public view. By now, tongues would be wagging, and I would inevitably have to face my mother's wrath. If I made it home. Feeling embarrassed, I stepped back and sat on a small mooda placed in front of the shuttered shop. Crouching next to me, he placed his arm around my shoulders. I pushed him away.

"You must have faith," he whispered. "We are good people. They will see that. Look at Kamra."

"Kamra doesn't suffer the curse of being Anglo-Indian."

"No, but look at what he did today ... he saved the lives of two Britishers ... and how many people are cursing him for that? He actually rescued the bank managers. He prevented them from being burned alive, taking them to the kotwali."

Vermilion Harvest

The kotwali was the main police station in the center of town. Ayaz explained how the British bank managers had just sat for hours until Major MacDonald, who was stationed in Lahore some twenty-five miles to the west of Amritsar, ordered his soldiers to evacuate them.

"We've been negotiating with Major MacDonald for the last hour."

Ayaz tried to wrap his arm around my shoulders again but I pushed him away. His attitude appalled me. I just didn't know what to think or what to want. Major MacDonald was in Amritsar. Disturbing news, but to hear that Ayaz had been in contact with him set me on edge. He was falling deeper and deeper into this dark void.

"Negotiating what?"

"About disregarding the order. If he uses force to prevent us from gathering, it'll amount to no good."

I stared at him, my arms across my chest. "For heaven's sakes! Are you serious about gathering in groups after what happened today?"

He held my hands, caressing them. "Aruna, Baisakhi, the spring festival is on Sunday. People are arriving by the dozens for the horse-and-cattle fair. If there was ever a time for gathering, it is now. Plus, there's the issue of the funeral processions ..."

I had forgotten that Baisakhi was just three days away. But what funeral processions?

"... for all the people who died today ..." he continued, "... you know the custom ... dead bodies can't be left for more than twenty-four hours. Tomorrow, Amritsar will be full of mourners carrying their dead to the crematoriums and burial grounds."

I held my head with my free hand. My temples were pounding as though they would burst. "This is going from bad to worse."

"Have faith in God's good soldiers," Ayaz whispered. "MacDonald is a reasonable man."

"What are you talking about?" I eyed him for a moment. "At the station, the railway guards were firing at people who were pulling up the tracks, the line to Lahore and Jullundur. People were shaking their fists, shouting at the railway officers."

"These are acts of stupidity. MacDonald knows it. He'll stop this." He inched closer.

I frowned and turned away. "Will he? When … after they set fire to the post office?"

"He is reasonable, I tell you! Irving wants to issue a proclamation against gatherings. And use *all force* to control this. For the last hour, we have been convincing MacDonald that this is a foolhardy idea."

My brain spun in neutral, stunned and exhausted, trying to make sense of what Ayaz was saying. He tightened his grip but I just glared at him.

"And why would *he* listen to *you*?"

"Because proclamation or no proclamation, there is no time to get this information out to the public."

It was five o'clock. As far as I was concerned, there were plenty of daylight hours left to get the message out to everyone. But Ayaz was quick to remind me that I was not up to date with what was happening around Amritsar.

"Telegraph and telephone lines have been cut. MacDonald is aware of this. And … the burial grounds are on the outskirts of the city."

"What does that have to do with MacDonald being reasonable?" I asked.

"He understands how much time it takes for a procession to reach the borders."

"But that doesn't make sense. They have all day to do this."

"No, they don't. Irving set deadlines."

None of this was making any sense. Since when did the British care about local funerals or setting deadlines for Muslim burial rituals?

"Lawyers representing families of deceased Muslims have asked for time to have their funeral procession reach the outskirts," Ayaz replied. "They've been granted permission, but Irving has issued a deadline of two o'clock for the crowds to disperse."

"And if they don't?"

"Apparently, he's sending machine guns and planes with bombs."

I shifted my eyes to Ayaz, grabbing his arm. Perhaps a little too violently this time. "You said MacDonald was reasonable. That's not reasonable. If the funerals are not over by two, the funeral processions will be bombed? How on earth is *that* reasonable?"

"I didn't say he was playing ball. I said he's trying to reason with his superiors and ignore his orders."

Good on MacDonald for trying. Was he was on the streets, looking for the corpses of the three dead British bankers? Thinking about that stopped me. I sympathized with MacDonald and what he was enduring. It wasn't that I supported the acts of the administration, quite the opposite, but the idea of innocent people losing their lives due to a touch of madness brought me to the brink of collapse. It didn't matter if they were Britishers or Indians.

Ayaz pulled me toward him, and this time, I didn't resist. His arms moved to caress me, and all I could think about was how he was the rays of sunshine beaming right through me again. His lips moved slowly to mine, his kiss different – with unforgettable tenderness – like the action was a promise of a lasting love that was yet to unfold. It was incredibly romantic to understand the intention of that kiss, to know that in that alley outside the Singhs' shop, spending time with me *was* his priority. I took pride knowing that Ayaz wanted this moment and me. We morphed inside a silent symphony until I gasped.

As Ayaz walked me home, we witnessed the atrocities. The people of Amritsar had retaliated by bringing down the symbols of British power. We walked past the Town Hall, the telegraph office, telephone exchange, and railways all of which had fallen prey to destruction. Destroyed by the mobs in just a few hours. The properties were smoldering, many had broken windows.

On the streets, people stood frozen in mid-commute, gathering at corners, talking to strangers, or gazing at the blazing scars cut into the sides of the banks that had been ransacked. The steel had melted around the impact zone, reflecting the sunlight and giving the edges a quicksilver sheen like an overwrought special effect. Despite the horror, an assumption spread that the worst had passed. Although many believed that what was left standing would soon come down. It was a show of brutal violence, something Amritsar had never seen before.

There wasn't much conversation between us. Though physically together, our minds were miles apart, each in a quiet detached place. Ayaz seemed pre-occupied. Perhaps he was thinking about the funeral gatherings to take place tomorrow. I couldn't help but dwell on how close I came to danger. I shuddered at the thought of being ushered to safety by strangers. What might they say if they had known I was Anglo-Indian like Mr. Pinto? Or that I was a teacher at a local government school? Would they accuse me of stealing a job that should rightfully been given to one of their people?

Probably.

Here we were, clamoring at the fringe of a modern world. Yet it was still a world where we could not speak our minds.

Reenita M. Hora

Elliott & Fry
photo in public domain

Mahātmā Gandhi

(1869-1948)

Indian lawyer, anti-colonial nationalist, and political leader who urged peaceful resistance to British rule. He assumed the leadership of the Indian National Congress in 1921.

After being imprisoned for his political ideals, many in India followed his teaching for freedom.

Gandhi was married to Kasturba and they had five children, four who survived.

For more information, please visit:

https://www.jagranjosh.com/general-knowledge/mahatma-gandhi-1411387880-1

Gandhi as a young law
student in London
photo in public domain

Gandhi with wife, Kasturba, 1940
photo in public domain

Colonel Reginald Dyer

(1864-1927)

The man who ordered his men to shoot innocent civilians - a portrait of evil.

photo in public domain

photo in public domain

Sir Sidney Arthur Taylor Rowlatt

(1862–1945)

Appointed in 1918 by the British Indian Government to curtail Indian liberties, Sydney Rowlatt was the president of the Rowlatt Committee and creator of the Rowlatt Act, *Black Act*, which authorized the colonial British government to imprison any person living in British India suspected of terrorism for up to two years.

Vermilion Harvest

Sir Michael Francis O'Dwyer

(1864–1940)

An Irish colonial officer in the Indian Civil Service who served as Lieutenant Governor of Punjab, British India *(1913-1919)*, implementing martial law in Punjab to curtail his fears of an Indian rebellion.

photo in public domain

Sardar Udham Singh

(1899 – 1940)

History presumes that Sardar Singh was an eye-witness of the Jallianwala Bagh massacre, which spurred his actions to assassinate Michael O'Dwyer.

photo in public domain

photo in public domain

Dr. Saifuddin Kitchlew

(1888-1963)

An Indian activist and politician who lead the peace movement, and who protested the Rowlatt Act.

Where the Jallianwala Bagh massacre took place. 1919 News Punjabi

photo in public domain

CHAPTER 14

April 10, 1919

Amritsar - mob mentality

"I've been waiting for you to return, Aruna!" My mother's words welcomed and berated at the same time as I walked through the door. Her deep wrinkles showed she'd been worrying herself silly all afternoon. She rushed to me, smothering with bear hugs and complaints about the unruly mobs outside the cantonment.

"There was this schoolteacher who was apparently assaulted today. I was worried sick that it might be you –"

"What schoolteacher, Ma?" I pulled my dupatta closely around me. The mention of the word *'assaulted'* sent chills down my spine. I thought about my lost bag – and potentially my job.

"It was a Miss Sherwood. Turned out she wasn't a schoolteacher after all but a Christian missionary. They were protesting and shouting throughout these streets, surrounding the cantonment. I was worried you might get caught up in the mess."

I nodded, wanting so desperately to explain. But she never gave me a chance. Instead, she unleashed a laundry list of concerns, fidgeting while attempting to look calm.

She took a closer look at my swollen eyes. "Maybe now is not the best time to discuss this." She ran her fingers down my tear-stained cheeks before giving me a tight hug. I pulled back and studied her face. I felt terrible that I had made her worry. Feathered lines surrounded her eyes with dashes of salt and pepper hair spreading from her temples and behind her hairline. All this accentuated by the concern over me.

"Come ... I have fresh kulchas just off the stove." Her warm smile accentuated her high cheekbones as she beckoned me into the kitchen.

The most gratifying part of being at home with my mother was the ability to retreat into my inner child where words and meanings were replaced with food and love. Cooking was perhaps her only form of expression since she abandoned her communal knitting and embroidery. Once ostracized by the Punjabi community, she just didn't care anymore. As her only child, she graciously fed me parathas and kulcha, flatbreads stuffed with vegetables of all shapes and sizes, achar – fermented pickles handmade by Punjabi ladies in the community each winter, and lassi – the quintessential northern-Indian yogurt drink. It was her way of demonstrating her love and that no matter our disagreements, we would forever be fine. We would forgive.

The radio blared in the kitchen, belting out the day's statistics.

Vermilion Harvest

Seventy-three rounds fired by the army at the footbridge. Several more rounds were fired by the police. But the bullets proved to be a poor excuse for control. Witnessing each casualty only served to incense the crowd. The announcer recounted the story of Miss Sherwood, a Christian missionary, who was pulled off her bike and beaten.

> "The destruction of property, not much less sacrosanct than life itself, is deplorable, and the murder of several European men even more reprehensible, but nothing could be more intolerable than the assault upon the defenseless Englishwoman, Miss Marcella Sherwood. A Church of England missionary and a resident of Amritsar for fifteen years. She was unable to escape the wrath of the crowd. As she was bicycling, she was knocked down, receiving several blows to her head with sticks while she was still on the ground. Miss Sherwood stood and started running when she was again brought down. On the subsequent attempt, she reached a house, but the door was slammed in her face. She was again beaten and left on the street in a critical condition. The crowd left, and Miss Sherwood was eventually rescued, prompt medical attention saving her life ..."

I recoiled from the radio as though avoiding a blow from the instrument itself. The words of the story shattered my head into what felt like a million pieces.

That could have been me!

I dropped to the couch, wiping the sweat on my brow with my dupatta as a new wave of nausea clutched my stomach.

The announcer talked about the incident as if it was a normal day's activity. In total, five British men were killed, and two British women were brutally attacked. It was the worst confrontation between the British rulers and their Indian subjects in recent times.

Over the next twenty-four hours, six-hundred troops arrived from Lahore and Jullundur, all under the command of Major MacDonald. He had just been deputed from Lahore to take over for Captain Massey who the administration had labeled a *failure* given the day's events.

𝕮HAPTER 15

April 11, 1919

Amritsar - a deadline to drop bombs

Two days before the Baisakhi festival, the mood in Amritsar had become somewhat somber. The British administration in Punjab declared the city a war zone. People floated through the streets like ghosts, questioned by guards at practically every exit.

Irving issued a dire proclamation:

> The troops have instructions to restore order in Amritsar, and use all the force necessary. No gatherings of persons, no procession of any sort will be allowed. All gatherings will be fired at. Any person leaving the city, or persons gathering in groups of more than four, will be fired at. Respectable persons should keep indoors until order is restored.

But even though his intention was to deliver a strong and forceful message, Irving could not think of a suitable way of circulating his proclamation.

He was visited by a group of lawyers representing the families of the deceased. They sought permission to bury their dead outside the city. The administrators were less than sympathetic. Fearing a rebellion, they were reluctant to allow the families to openly grieve, at least not for as long as they wanted. Nonetheless, they granted the lawyers the permission they sought and increased the number of people at the funeral processions to eight.

Eight?

What good was eight going to do? Muslim families on average had ten to twelve, and even if the women were to stay home, it was customary for the men in the community to lead the processions to the funeral grounds. Ayaz would most definitely be a part of this, and I knew that the numbers in the processions would well exceed eight.

But Irving handed the lawyers his so-called *proclamation* – a simple note stating that although people would be allowed to bury their dead, there would be a bugle call at two o'clock. Fifteen minutes after that, firing would start.

The lawyers dutifully obeyed his command by reading Irving's note inside the city's gates.

Hundreds of innocent people were in the streets, scouring the damage of the day before. Black smoke filled the sky, providing evidence from just about anywhere in the city. Amritsar had transformed into something like what I had seen in pictures of The Great War-era of London, after falling prey to German air raids. Whole sections of the city were evacuated with a military presence on every corner. The acrid smell of smoke and ash lingered, and people walked around looking shell-shocked – a mixture of adrenaline and despair – as they waited for what many assumed was the inevitable next attack.

There was the question of local residents gathering for funerals. When Gerard Wathen, principal of Khalsa College, received word of Commissioner Kitchin's impending arrival and his intent to have troops march through the city firing at random, he realized the need to take action.

He pleaded with the authorities, but they remained resolute. The smoldering remains of the buildings had cast an ugly shadow over the British administration's ability to maintain respect and order. Irving and Kitchin feared another outbreak. Unwilling to take a risk, they issued an order for the streets to be lined with rifle-bearing soldiers, and prepared for the skies to be lined with aerial bombs.

Obviously, they learned nothing from the previous day's events.

With a combination of tenacity and the right skin color working in his favor, Wathen finally negotiated an arrangement with the authorities. The families of the dead would indeed be allowed to properly gather for their funeral processions, in reasonable numbers of not four or eight, but two thousand. However, all would return home before two o'clock. If they failed to disperse by then, military would be given the go to drop bombs on the city.

Wathen was also asked to spread the word through his staff and students that a state of war had been declared. Seeing the gravity of the situation, he dispatched a charter of students, professors, and a local maulvi to warn people about the two o'clock deadline.

𝟔HAPTER 16

April 11, 1919

Amritsar – a funeral procession

Gurcharan Singh, an administrator at Khalsa College, found himself caught between a rock and a hard place when two students arrived at his home with news from Wathen. I was at their shop just that morning. We were preparing for prayers to honor the memory of a fellow shopkeeper who fell prey to the events at the railway the day before. Gurcharan Singh was busy selecting verses to recite from the Guru Granth sahib, the holy book of the Sikh religion. Amrita and I were making the traditional poori-aloo for the langar meal following the prayer meeting at the Golden Temple just a mile from where the violence had taken place.

"The funeral procession must be finished by one o'clock. All prayers after that must be contained in the gurudwara," one of the students said.

"But that's impossible," Gurcharan Singh replied. "The funeral procession will bring the body to the cremation grounds by twelve, and only then can we head to the Golden Temple!"

"I'm sorry, Singh sahib," the other student stated, "You must change the order of ceremonies. The maulvi is doing the same for the Mussalmaan ceremonies."

"That is a ridiculous thing to say!" Gurcharan Singh grunted. "What does a Muslim priest know about the order of Sikh funeral ceremonies?"

"It's not that, Singh sahib," the first student replied. "It's just that the situation after two o'clock could be quite dire. You must arrive at the Golden Temple earlier. I can go now and speak to the bhaiji in advance."

It was an earnest suggestion, but to Gurcharan Singh, perhaps it sounded more like an accusation of incapacity. "No need for that." He looked mystified. "I am perfectly equipped to speak to the bhaiji. I don't need a student still wet behind the ears to act on my behalf."

The students exchanged glances, perhaps recognizing the need to walk softly.

"Sorry, Singh sahib, I didn't mean any offense," the first said.

I was minding my business, helping Amrita with the food prep. She was peeling potatoes and I was kneading the dough for the pooris. Inserting my opinions into a heated exchange, particularly one that involved Gurcharan Singh, was not the optimum move. I knew that from past experiences. However, I just couldn't resist jumping in to break the tension.

"What is the situation after two o'clock?" I asked.

Vermilion Harvest

The student leaned forward, resting his arms on the shop's platform. "Anything could happen, memsahib. They're asking that all crowds disperse."

Gurcharan Singh cast a skeptical eye on the student. "But they've been saying that for a while. At least for the last few days." He frowned.

"It is serious now," the second student replied. "Wathen sahib was negotiating with authorities all morning. He sent us to deliver this message to everyone we can."

"But what kind of danger does he anticipate?" I asked. My fingers hastened as I rolled and kneaded the dough.

"He is fearing damage to the city, and in particular, to the Golden Temple," the student replied.

A flicker of anger took shape in Gurcharan Singh's eyes. The trouble over the last several days had emerged on the heels of the First World War, when half a million Indians had volunteered to fight for the British. British rhetoric promised that these subjects would be looked after. There was talk among politicians of giving the Sikh, Gurkha, and Baluchi soldiers dominion status. But then to blatantly break these promises – to show the Indians they had to fight for their freedom. It was obvious now that the colony was never on our side. Instead, they were duplicitous, racist, and violent.

"If anything like that happens, then the Sikh soldiers would rise in rebellion against the Empire," Gurcharan Singh stated.

The first student yanked a piece of khadi cloth from the fruit baskets, unconsciously toppling a handful of apples. "Exactly, Singh sahib. That's why he has sent us to talk to the people."

Amrita was watching, her eyes wide, her face writ with fear. She glanced at me, turning to her husband. "Jeeo-ji, do you think Ayaz sahib knows about this?"

"Ayaz Peermohammed sahib?" the student asked. "Yes! He was with us when Wathen sahib issued the order just this morning. He is in the city with two of our students and the local maulvi to deliver this same message to the Muslim households."

What? I kneaded the dough with more deliberation.

Gurcharan Singh's ruddy complexion now paled. "Aruna-ji, did you know about this?"

A rush of adrenaline flooded my body. "No, I did not." I shook my head. "I haven't seen Ayaz since last night."

Gurcharan Singh patted the sides of his turban as if ironing it out. "I saw him briefly this morning, but he didn't mention anything about this."

"I hope he's not in any danger," Amrita whispered.

The dead air that followed spoke volumes about what was flashing through our minds, and the familiar heaviness returned to my chest, slowing down my kneading that had come to a stop.

"Ayaz is a sensible man," Gurcharan Singh stated. "If he is delivering the message, then I doubt he is in danger. But I'd like to talk to him about our prayer meeting tonight. I'd like to ask for his advice." He stood and grabbed his kalgi.

"Apologies, Singh sahib," the first student said. "There is no time for advice. There is no time for anything. It's running out even as we speak."

Gurcharan Singh nodded. "If we hold a body 'till later −"

"Jeeo-ji!" Amrita whispered loudly. "Unthinkable! How can you say such a thing?"

"What else do we do?" he asked.

"It's nine o'clock now," the second student added. "You must start the funeral procession. If you can finish with the cremation by eleven, you can finish with the ardas prayer meeting by one at the latest. After that, everyone must return home. The crowds must disperse by two."

We had heard rumors of a bomb threat at two. Perhaps this rumor could become a reality.

"It's still unclear ..." the student said, "... but this we know ... reinforcements were sent in from Lahore. There is danger they may drop aerial bombs on public gatherings in the city."

Aerial bombs? On people collecting for funeral prayers at the Golden Temple? Had I heard him correctly?

"The Golden Temple is our holy place!" Amrita sounded furious. She threw down the peeler, slapping her hands on her hips.

"Memsahib," the student gasped. "Please, please, listen to me. Wathen sahib has been at the station all morning with the authorities. What if they drop a bomb on Harmandir sahib?"

Gurcharan Singh shook his head. "He's right, Amrita. It's a real threat."

"But –"

"No time for buts," he interrupted. "I must gather the menfolk and get on with the funeral procession. You and Aruna-ji proceed to the gurudwara and speak to the bhaiji about bringing up the time for the prayer meeting."

"What about Gopal?" Amrita asked, her eyes wide with concern.

"Ask the neighbors to help," Gurcharan Singh replied. "Our prayer meeting must be brought forward to escape this threat."

I glared at Gurcharan Singh, feeling depleted yet anxious at the same time. Could this *really* be happening? Or was it just rumors built up from the last few days? Punjab was an army recruiting ground for the British since the early part of this century. The British invested in Amritsar both as a military district and as a garrison state. Why would they destroy everything by dropping a bomb on their recruitment camp? It didn't make sense.

I took a step. "Singh sahib, I know these rumors are spreading, but how real do you think they are? You yourself said there has been no violence here. The colony are so heavily invested in our people. They just can't risk allowing the Punjab to deteriorate like that."

Gurcharan Singh glared at me through narrowed squints. "Aruna-ji, it is not my position to think about things from the colony's point of view. You are correct that since the 1857 mutiny, Punjab has been quite loyal. But if anything happens to our Harbinder sahib, that loyalty will be gone in just a few seconds." He folded his hands.

"Jeeo-ji, be careful. Out in the streets ..." Amrita whispered.

I held my friend by the arm to reassure her. "It's alright, Amrita. We have time. The danger will be after two. Not before. But we are on a tight schedule. Let us proceed."

The student shot us a reassuring glance. "Don't worry, memsahib. Our brothers will be with Singh sahib. No harm will come to him. Not if we get things moving."

I gathered the remaining dough into a steel dish and motioned at the front door. "Amrita, let's go to the temple. We'll need to speed up preparations for the prayer meeting."

Gurcharan Singh stepped in front of us. "Wait, Aruna-ji. Let these students go with you."

"But, Jeeo-ji —" Amrita said.

"Amrita, no!" Gurcharan Singh stated firmly. "These are treacherous times for womenfolk to be out on their own."

And they were indeed. Something I had become quite aware of over the last few days.

☙HAPTER 17

April 11, 1919

Amritsar - a change

The streets were clear by two that afternoon as fear of a bomb threat spread across the city. Although it was never announced, the word was that Major MacDonald had succeeded in averting the plan to bomb the city.

Ensconced in the safety of our kitchen, I couldn't help but wonder whether it was just a vicious rumor or whether Ayaz had been right about Major MacDonald. Was he a reasonable man? When I read the papers, I realized the foolishness in doubting Ayaz and Gurcharan Singh for even a second. It was no rumor – just luck that Amritsar was under the control of the *reasonable* Major MacDonald. The news spoke of the administration's disappointment with MacDonald's mild reactions when it came to quelling the *so-called* rebellion. It definitely validated his position. By objecting to the means of the proclamation and attempt to force the military to interfere with the funerals, MacDonald was a key player in preventing an outbreak of violence.

As far as the administration was concerned, MacDonald had failed and was sent to Lahore, replaced by General William Beynon, another officer who they believed would not be *afraid to act* should the need arise.

Ma and I remained home as the situation grew tense. The continued hartal in the city meant a shortage of fresh food and daily supplies, leaving us feeling trapped. Like a good Indian housewife, Ma had a habit of stocking up on long-term rations. With a variety of daals, rice, spices, and grains, we had plenty to eat. I felt irked that censorship had taken hold of our society. Ma was not cognizant of this, but to me, it was obvious. With school closed for the third day in a row, we remained glued to the radio, still pining for news from the outside world. When it finally came through, it unleashed stories about violent clashes outside Punjab.

"Turmoil has engulfed the nation as Gandhi has pushed too far too fast. While traveling around India, he was arrested, provoking angry mobs to fill the streets of the cities ..."

As violence swept through our country, Gandhi ordered the mobs to return to their homes, calling off his campaign. "If Satyagraha could not be carried out without violence," he declared, "it would not be carried out at all." People were reminded of his insistence on a passive political resistance.

"How do you call this censorship when we are getting all this news about Gandhi-ji?" Ma asked. Her face looked tight and drawn.

Oh, Ma! Understanding the subtitles had never been her forte. Whether it was language or the inability to hone into the details. I couldn't tell.

"Look at the nature of the news, Ma," I replied. "They are happy to report about him being a menace, about the failure of Satyagraha, but do you hear anything about Irving and Kitchin being unnerved?"

"That is speculation, Aruna." Ma poured me another cup of warm elaichi-infused water. There was no milk for chai or lassi. We had to remain content with the flavor of cardamom easing our stomachs and hopefully our nerves.

"Speculation only because it hasn't been confirmed," I replied. "Why do you think Irving replaced MacDonald with General Beynon? Because he thinks the people of Amritsar are unrepentant, and that something more needs to be done to make them realize their stupidity."

Ma remained silent as the cardamom water in our cups cooled. The last few days had been difficult and exhausting. I was concerned about Ayaz and Ma being worried about me while the stress in the city grew. Ma knew I wanted to be out there with Ayaz, but of course, there would be far less for her to worry about if I simply stayed home. It was hard to look at her, but at the same time, it was hard to look away. I felt her watching me, resisting the urge to speak.

The doorbell rang, almost as if on cue, to break the silence. It was a British soldier from the barracks along the cantonment. It was a common sight, them marching through the streets in their khadi uniforms and knee-high black boots with a massive rifle behind their backs. Yet never did they show up at our doorstep. This one was carrying a piece of blue plastic in his arms. What could he possibly want?

"Is this the home of Miss Aruna Duggal, a teacher at Saint Mary's government school?" With a flat voice, he stared at me with skeptical eyes.

"Yes, I'm Aruna," I replied.

"We found this in a corner alley of the city." The soldier lifted the blue plastic to reveal my bag. The one I had lost in the scuffle at the railway lines.

I accepted it and checked the contents. Everything was still there - purse, papers, and files. I looked up at him.

He scowled at me. "You are under orders to stay away from the school this next week."

What? School was closed thanks to the hartal? And why was this soldier appointed to deliver this message to me? Just because he found my bag on the street?

"Will the school be closed next week?" I asked.

"By order of the administration," he replied.

"The school administration?" I repeated.

"The school administration and the Punjab administration. And you are ordered to remain home."

"Why? Because the school is closed?"

"Exactly, memsahib. There is danger in the streets, and you have been observed in the company of undesirable elements."

"Undesirable … what?"

"This letter should explain everything," he said, handing me an envelope.

I accepted the letter and opened it.

April 11, 1919

Dear Miss Duggal,

Considering our private conversation
and the unrest in the streets of
Amritsar, we hereby request you remain
home until normal operations resume at
St. Mary's School. The safety of our
staff and the reputation of our school
is of paramount importance.

Any deviation from this request shall
place us in a position where we have no
choice but to deal with the
consequences.

Thank you for your understanding.

Yours sincerely,

Col JS Lewis

Retired Colonel J.S. Lewis
Headmaster
St. Mary's Government School

This was no ordinary note from a school headmaster safeguarding his staff. It was a cold and dire warning.

"This is not an order," I said. "It's a request. What *undesirable elements* are you talking about? There is no reference to such a thing."

"Memsahib, you've been observed in the company of revolutionaries."

"What revolutionaries? Is this about you finding my bag near the railway lines?"

His icy demeaner conveyed a dangerous quality. "I am not at liberty to say more. Kindly respect the order."

"It's *not* an order!" I yelled. "And what about Baisakhi on the 13th?"

"The order does not preclude anyone from participating in public festivals," he replied. "We are expecting a change of command with far less tolerance for past behavior. I would be careful about who you are seen celebrating with."

"Or what?" I asked.

"That too, I am not at liberty to say."

Was this soldier at liberty to say anything? Or was my life about to be reduced to a mere guessing game? My anger grew as I stared at the letter. How dare Colonel Lewis write such a thing. I hated the school, the administration, the situation in the city. I hated everything, and most of all, I hated this soldier for willingly representing it.

"What change of command are you talking about and what do you mean who *I'm seen with?*" I asked.

The soldier looked at me with a bland expression. "Message delivered, memsahib. Good day." After a quick salute, he was gone.

Closing the door, I turned only to see my mother simmering.

"There you have it! They've seen you!" she screamed. "I *told* you *not* to go out with that Mussalmaan!"

"Do *not* call him that!" I screamed back. "This has nothing to do with Ayaz. It's just a note from the headmaster warning me about the hartal."

"It is too a warning!" she yelled. "If you disobey it, you will lose your job. And yes … it has *everything* to do with *him*. They've seen you together. You, a Hindu, and he, a Mussalmaan, with his activist mentality, and they've labeled you!"

"How would you know that?" I asked, feeling foolish because I understood she was right.

"Do you think the headmaster would send this letter through the hands of a soldier if they did not know?" Ma glared at me with her nose crinkled, fidgeting with her saree pallu. "It's obvious that *someone* from the administration saw you with a revolutionist, a Mussalmaan one at that. That's it, Aruna. I am putting my foot down. I forbid you to see that man again! What Hindu girl goes off with a Mussalmaan? Not permissible! I will *not* allow it!"

But I wanted to hear nothing from her. I didn't have the patience to listen or the will to fight. Covering my ears with my hands, I simply shut out her words. I thought only about Ayaz and how he was labeled. There was no way I was going to stay home while he was in danger. Grave danger, but how grave I just did not know.

The radio spoke of the violence in Amritsar. It seemed that the police firing at demonstrators on the railway lines provoked many to being destructive.

What we didn't hear, was that later that day, the city was handed over to a man, Colonel Dyer, from Jullundur. He claimed to have received a telegram from the Army's 16th

Vermilion Harvest

Division ordering him to proceed to Amritsar and take charge. First MacDonald and now this Dyer. Why was another from another city in Punjab required to order us around? Ironically, no record was ever found of any instruction given to Colonel Dyer and no evidence of a telegram ordering him to go to Amritsar. The circumstances around who had sent him remained unclear. From the analysis of the documented evidence, it appeared that this man had made a personal decision to invade Amritsar. Interesting development given that a more junior officer, Lieutenant Colonel Major Morgan, was also dispatched to Amritsar for the same reason, apparently on the heels of Colonel Dyer.

And thus, the colonel began his havoc through indiscriminate arrests and bans on meetings and gatherings.

CHAPTER 18

April 12, 1919

Amritsar - Colonel Dyer at Rambagh

Saint Mary's school was closed with no indication of when it would reopen. Ma and I had no choice but to remain within the four-walls of our home. On the upside, I enjoyed home-cooking even with our limited rations. Something about Ma's culinary skills could never be replicated in a dhaba. On the downside, our emotions were running high. Ma refused to say anything that didn't involve admonishing me about Ayaz, and of course, I refused to listen. We both understood how the situation was placing a strain on our relationship. Though the silence was deafening, we recognized it was better than succumbing to fiery explosions of in-built resentment. We simply felt tired, scared, and overwhelmed.

It was two days since I had seen Ayaz. No communication once he dropped me off in hushed quietude. To say that I missed him was an understatement. Every waking moment, I felt the pain of holding him in my heart and not my arms.

He would not leave my mind. A clear signal that I was supposed to be with him. I ached to see Ayaz more than I thought was possible.

His parting words, "Aruna, you and I … we have always lived by different rules. It's why our two worlds collided in the first place. But there is an unfolding trail that we must first follow."

"Trail?" I had asked. "How can you talk of trails when there's so much at stake in the city?"

"There is a trail, jaan, one that will lead us to a place in the sun. I am convinced. But while we traverse this trail, we must be ready to face the adversity."

I definitely could see the adversity. It was an unfolding trail of extreme danger. Ayaz had twisted his beard, looking straight into my eyes. It seemed like ages since we had spent a relaxing moment together. Our last meeting was wrought with worry and stress of political strategy. Perhaps a momentary lapse of propriety.

"There is a stubbornness about you …" he had said, "… that can never be frightened from the will of others."

But the charm of that night had long worn off. Although I relished the nostalgia of our early days of flirtation, I was not in the mood to be cajoled by our Jane Austen-isms.

"Enough, Ayaz," I had stated. "Where are you going with this idea of a trail?"

He sighed. "On our personal trail, there is no room for uncontrolled emotions."

Ayaz's tone was warning me to not be fooled by the tranquility of a summer's day. Initially, I loved the way he could read into me and my emotions, all part of the initial attraction. But now, I despised it. I didn't want him to be accurate about us. And ... I didn't want him to leave me out of it.

"I shall traverse this trail with you ..." I had whispered, "... devoid of emotion."

"No, jaan. Not now."

"What do you mean? You just talked of traversing it together."

"Together in our minds and spirits. Physically, we cannot be together. For now, you must remain here ... at home."

"While you are out there? Didn't you just use a reference to Elizabeth Bennett to describe me?"

"Only as a matter of —"

"A matter of what, Ayaz? Did you forget that the rest of the quote talks about how her courage rises at every intimidation?"

"My jaan —"

"No! You are too lenient with your words. What does *jaan* mean? You cannot risk your life and leave me at home for safekeeping. That story you read to me from the Indian Ladies Magazine ... that love and pain were linked. Isn't that what you read?"

Our relationship was increasingly complicated. Although, it started as flirtatious and romantic, my mind picturing Ayaz as the perfect lover faded, and a few cracks had developed. His desire for me to stay home rose from a deep caring. He was acting in my best interest. However, to me, it felt as if he was pushing me away in order to tackle this on his own. Not what I wanted.

Vermilion Harvest

He had left me alone to my own devices. Somewhere deep inside, he must have known I would not obey. If Ayaz was out there fighting a cause, I didn't want to be at home, cut off from the rest of the world. The visit from the soldier and his reference to a change of command concerned me. I decided I could use the letter from Colonel Lewis as my pre-text to look for Ayaz.

My mother was anything but thrilled to see me leave. "Might I remind you that you have been ordered to stay home?" Her arms were folded across her chest, her 'brows arching high into her forehead.

"It was a request, Ma, not an order," I replied. "And nobody has the right to stop me."

"What about your job?" The strain in her voice was apparent.

"What about it?" I clasped my hands, unclasped, and clasped them again. "If I must risk my job, then so be it. Nothing and no one can stop me from leaving this house!"

As I spoke the words, I knew they were untrue. Of course, I couldn't risk losing my position at the school. I needed the funds to care for my mother. We relied on my income. She did receive a small *pension* from her husband each month. But it was not enough to live on and enjoy life. Until I started working, Ma added to this income by working odd jobs for British memsahibs that lived in the cantonment – housekeeping, shopping, light tailoring. The last thing I wanted was for her to accept odd jobs again.

A headache pounded through my temples as I thought about the reality of choosing between my job and Ayaz. Had it actually come down to this? I couldn't shake Ayaz from my thoughts. The memory of his hands running through my hair, the aroma of his skin rising warmly against mine. The thought of losing him was unbearable.

"And how exactly will you ensure his safety?" Ma asked, fidgeting with her saree pallu. "If you should find him, you'll only make it worse for you both. Can't you see how endangered your job is? Our livelihood?"

Sensible as her advice was, I wasn't prepared to listen. "I don't care! He needs to know."

Ma glared at me. "You said there is barely a woman out on the streets. Why do you have to be so different?"

"This is *my* life at stake, it isn't a matter of child's play."

The words flew from my mouth like an involuntary reflex. I knew there was something about the term child's play that cornered Ma into a most vulnerable place. I never knew why, but the insecurity it generated felt real. It tied into the reason why she never allowed me to go outside as a young child. The look in Ma's eyes told me everything. The blood had drained from her cheeks, turning white as marble. Losing her balance, she tottered for a moment before grabbing the back of the kitchen chair.

Our relationship had just shattered into sharp, glassy shards. I had always wanted to press Ma for details about the mystery of child's play. I suspected it had something to do with my father, and the day he raped her, but I also knew that talking about it was out of bounds. Ma was unable to withstand the pain of that memory.

I took a step and whispered, "What I mean is … I just need to find Ayaz."

Vermilion Harvest

Ma was devastated. "If he wanted to make the time to see you, you would have heard from him by now."

She was right, but I didn't want to believe it. I had to lean on the hope that somehow, I was a part of Ayaz's mission. Or maybe, I just wanted to know what was going on in the city.

"What about the danger?" Ma threw her hands in the air. "Ayaz told you to stay home! You are pig-headed. Pig-headed to go out when your Ma forbids it!"

It was true. Everything she said made sense. Pig-headed only scratched the surface of the appropriate vocabulary to describe my attitude. But I didn't care. I was willing to risk everything. My persistence was leading me down a path of the nonsensical.

I slipped out the front door and aimed for the cantonment boundaries. Mrs. Wintertree, who was preoccupied with the contents of her shopping basket, hit me broadsided. I stumbled, sending three mangoes flying in the opposite direction.

"How did you buy mangoes during a hartal?" I quickly gathered the fruit before they could roll down the street.

"One must be resourceful during times like these," Mrs. Wintertree replied. She wrinkled her nose, averting more questions. "To be honest, I'd rather not be compelled to resort to such resourcefulness." She rubbed one of the coveted mangoes. "The sooner Colonel Dyer gets things under control, the better."

What? Colonel Dyer from Jullundur? "Have they set up a command outside Amritsar?"

She laughed. "Colonel Dyer arrived in Amritsar last night. He will regain control of the city." Her eyes strayed to the edge of the cantonment.

Regain control? It sounded like an anarchist's paradise. Aside from the violence at the footbridge, the citizens maintained a peaceful hartal.

"He's been at the kotwali all night, the police station. He said he will not stand for any Danda Fauj."

Danda Fauj? An army of soldiers carrying batons? This was news.

Mrs. Wintertree said that such an army of stick-bearing activists was rumored to be heading into the city with the sole purpose of driving the Britishers out. Major MacDonald was no longer in command, Colonel Dyer had taken the reigns.

I flinched at her words. None of this was reported on the radio or in the papers. The gossip through the cantonment was infinitely more reliable. The Britishers knew the administration's movements minute by minute. Listening through the official communication channels, one would think of the British Raj as a slow-moving energy, thoughtful and calculating. Truth be told, the tide of resentment against the government had forced its members to make decisions quickly, moving at a rapid pace, even if on the quiet.

Major MacDonald being relieved from duty was not a good thing. Based on news reports over the last few years, Colonel Dyer had a reputation for defining life as a set of black and whites with no subtle shades of color. Outwardly, he approved of free speech and a free press, but he also

believed they should be restricted to enlightened people –
excluding Indians.

A pre-judgmental frame of mind that didn't sit well with
me. Who was Colonel Dyer to opine on what Indians were
capable of or what they should or should not say? Who was
Colonel Dyer to pigeonhole us on our very own land? More
importantly, was Ayaz aware of the Danda Fauj or Colonel
Dyer? Given that the news was restricted to cantonment
circles, he couldn't possibly know. I needed to find him.

I escaped the clutches of Mrs. Wintertree and headed to
the shops situated closest to the banks on Hall Bazaar.
Amritsar was like a ghost town. The deserted streets were
littered with debris, and several of the buildings were
nothing more than gutted shells. A few were still
smoldering. British soldiers were disassembled around the
pickets, but the shops and bazaars were closed. It wasn't a
hartal as much as a moment of rest to allow for the sullen
and subdued to make preparations for the dead. My heart
drew cold. To me, this felt like a war.

I stopped outside the banks, feeling numb as I stared at a
flock of black crows. Did they signify that death had to
happen or that more was to come? A headache pounded at
my temples, reminding me of Ayaz's hands combing through
my hair.

Salim, a local durzee who owned a tailoring shop near the
banks, was clad in his usual tailor's uniform – a white kurta
buttoned up to the neck and a maroon turban wound tightly
on his head. He was seated cross-legged on a colorful sheet
spread out across his shop's platform, looking busy as he
threaded his needle through a yellow skirt, looking poetic in

a frenzy sort of way. Salim wasn't taking new orders but working on clothes that had piled up over the last several days.

His colleague stepped out from the back room. Salim glanced over the top of his round metal glasses perched at the edge of his hooked nose. His gaze fell to a band of British soldiers disassembled around the pickets. He probably had seen me eyeing them.

"There are a number of troops who have left the railway lines," he whispered, threading his needle through the skirt. "They are heading to Rambagh."

Rambagh? Did that mean the trouble was over and they were moving out of the city? This would be a good thing, no? Or was there more to it that I was missing?

"Excuse me, do you know where they are going?" I asked.

Salim, busy tying a knot, looked confused. "Memsahib, I don't understand." He sat the skirt down and picked up a dark, blue pair of trousers.

"What I meant was, earlier they were standing at the picket lines."

The tailor glared at me, still looking confused. He threaded his needle with a piece of dark, blue yarn. "And your question relates to …?"

"Are the picket duties being disbanded?" I asked.

"No, not at all. Just reduced," he replied.

"Okay …" I allowed the numbers to run through my mind. "That should be a good thing."

"Why would you say that?" Salim asked.

Wasn't it obvious? If picket duties were reduced, that would indicate a lower risk of violence.

"Just because they are being reduced in the main part of the city doesn't mean they are being reduced everywhere. Right now, they appear to be moving out."

But that didn't make sense either. It was the railway crossings and the surrounding areas the authorities wanted to guard. "What do you mean by moving out?'" I asked.

"The picket line, memsahib," he replied. "The trouble in the city has been curtailed. Our city is effectively a prison. They want to keep us inside our narrow lanes ... our neighborhoods. Far away from the rulers in their fancy cantonment housing."

I flinched at the reference to our neighborhood. My salwar kameez and parandi adorned braids somewhat hid the fact that I was a tenant of housing owned by our pugnacious rulers. "They want to keep us in the city. Why?" I asked. "Are they afraid of us congregating at the deputy commissioner's home to protest the arrests of Dr. Satyapal and Dr. Kitchlew?"

"Apparently so." Salim nodded.

I scratched my head. "Then why do they still guard the railway lines?"

"Arrey, memsahib. There are two issues here," he whispered. "First, they do not want us protesting. Second, as officers of His Majesty's Empire, they believe it is their duty to prevent rebellious communications from spreading to cities outside Amritsar." He frowned. "Who knows what tricks these people planned. Be cautious. The troops are setting up at Rambagh."

The words pierced through me like an arrow. Then it was true. Rambagh. My Rambagh. The one place that Ayaz and I shared as an escape from the world was now controlled by the British army. Salim would never understand my inner torment.

"Regardless," he whispered, glancing around as if being watched. "Rambagh is now their headquarters. That's where the troops will be stationed under the command of the new colonel from Jullundur."

A new colonel? Was he referring to Dyer? His words pulled a heavy sigh from my chest. I had already played out this scenario several times. Over the last several days since the footbridge incident, my inner voice kept warning me that it was only a matter of time before the tides rolled in. Hearing his words felt like a sharpened blade slicing through my heart. It was no longer a matter of speculation. It was real. A potential bloodbath was boiling just under the surface.

It took me a few moments to gather my composure. "This new colonel and his troops are they in Rambagh now?"

"I understand he is on his way to the northern part of the city. A crowd has gathered at Sultanwind Gate. Another gathering of funeral processions."

Sultanwind Gate – the city exit commonly used to enter the Muslim burial grounds. Ayaz was probably there too, mourning the loss of his people. Maybe this was the ideal opportunity for me to find him. Should I try and meet him there or wait at the shop for his return?

Salim remained quiet, sewing with savage ferocity. His colleague had returned to his work behind the curtain. Every few seconds, he would look over his spectacle at the soldiers.

The insanity of our city was bleeding into my reality somehow tainting it. Taking the sane route and returning home was tantamount, but would not allow me to understand the root of the problem. I felt helpless.

With a parting namaste, I walked toward the northern perimeter of the city, which housed the Sultanwind Gate.

𝕮HAPTER 19

April 12, 1919

Amritsar - Sultanwind Gate

By the time I arrived at Sultanwind Gate, Colonel Dyer and his men were approaching. It was apparent he wanted to arrive as quickly as possible. Deputy Commissioner Miles Irving and two senior-level officers, Captain Massey and Mr. Donald, were with him. There were also about a hundred British officers and three hundred or so Indian soldiers – and two armored cars.

The small crowd was acting openly hostile and belligerent, represented by taqiyah-capped Muslim men and wide turbaned Hindu men. I was one of three women, standing back several rows. My view lent an added sense of allusion. As if I were not a part, but just watching a silent movie, except this one had sound and was in color. I searched for Ayaz but could not see him.

As Dyer and his men approached, they were greeted by the insolent crowd. Several in the front spat on the ground.

"Hindu aur Mussalmaano ki jai," they yelled. *Praise be to Hindus and Muslims.*

By now, it was obvious to most that chanting slogans of Hindu-Muslim unity was a way to incense those in the administration. Dyer was no exception. He stood back while Irving and Donald yelled.

"Go home at once!" Irving shouted. "Go home, I say! How many warnings do you need?"

"Warnings? What kind of warnings, Mr. Irving?" a voice from the crowd called. "It is we who should be warning you about the impact of your behavior. You stopped our prayers after murdering our brothers!"

Another group was coming, their chants growing louder as their slogans filled the street.

"Arrest that man!" Colonel Dyer ordered to Mr. Donald and Captain Massey. He waved his baton in the direction of the insolent protestor.

"Chod do unko! Dafa karo!" the people shouted. *Leave them alone! Go away!*

The protests echoed the cries of the angry men. Yet they remained calm, without violence. Nor were they throwing stones.

The other group of mourners entered from a small gulley to the southeast of the gate. They carried a stretcher with a corpse covered with a white sheet, surrounded with gaudy marigolds.

"Where are they coming from?" Colonel Dyer asked Irving, his mustache twitching.

"It's another ruddy Muslim funeral," Irving replied. "They're coming from the direction of the Kahir-ud-din mosque." He was visibly irked by the sight of Hindus.

The procession stalled when it arrived at the junction of the gate.

Irving singled out a Hindu man in the front row of the procession and gestured to Captain Massey. "You!" Irving shouted at the Hindu man. "Down on your knees!"

Captain Massey pointed his rifle at the back of the man's head, forcing him into submission.

"You're Ratto, aren't you?" Irving asked.

A roar clamored through the crowds. I had no idea who Ratto was, but it was clear that everyone else did. Judging by their negative reaction, this Ratto, was an euphemism for trouble.

The man now on his knees tried to look up, but Captain Massey forced his head to the ground. "No, sahib," the man yelled. "My name is Somdatt."

But Irving and Massey proved to be a merciless combination of power and terror.

"Shut up, I say!" Irving yelled. "You are Ratto. Admit it!"

"No, sir," the man pleaded. "I am not. I am not Ratto."

That's when I spotted Ayaz stepping out from the crowd. He was behind the funeral procession. My heart sank upon seeing him.

"This man is Somdatt," Ayaz stated. "A respectable lawyer at the Superior Court of Amritsar."

Mr. Donald stepped up to Ayaz, pointing a handgun at his face. "And who are you?"

"I am Ayaz Peermohammed, a lawyer-in-training."

"Do you believe that is enough to stick up for your imposter friend?"

"He is not an imposter!" another voice yelled. "He is Somdatt!"

Mr. Donald pointed his handgun toward the voice. "Shut your mouth, or you'll be next."

The crowd was now stirred into a frenzy with uncoordinated shouting. My heart resembled a boulder weighing me down. Ayaz hadn't seen me, but perhaps it was better that he hadn't. I took a few steps back, my fingers finding their way to my dupatta tassels. Not that I needed to hide but now was not the time to be conspicuous.

"Ratto," Irving yelled. "You are a liar!"

"This won't be the only funeral you'll witness today," Mr. Plomer, the superintendent of the police, yelled.

Somdatt's head was still on the dirt. He cried but it sounded more like hiccups. "Hindu-Mussalmaan ki jai!"

The crowd went crazy, echoing his words.

Irving glanced over at Colonel Dyer, who nodded.

"Arrest him!" Irving ordered.

Two guards stepped forward and handcuffed Somdatt, leading him to the police car.

Ayaz looked enraged. He rolled his fingers over his thumbs into his signature style before shaking one at Irving. "You haven't proven anything!" Ayaz yelled. "Not with your false arrests or your insolence."

My body felt odd as if no longer mine. My hands found my ears, covering them, praying I could drown out the sound. I wanted to scream, make Ayaz hear me. Could he not remember his parting words of just two nights ago? "On this trail, there will be no room for emotions!" I was hemmed into this volatile situation.

"Gandhi-ji ki jai! Hindu-Mussalmaan ki jai!" the voices yelled.

Irving ordered his men to point their rifles at the crowd. "Quiet!" he yelled. "Or I'll shoot!"

Was that an empty threat?

The people stormed the entrance of the Sultanwind Gate, resembling a stampeding herd of cattle. The sound of Hindu-Muslim slogans filled the air, but a little more muted this time and with more disparaging tones. The guards ushered everyone away encouraging them to return home.

I lost sight of Ayaz but stood in the shadows of an arched doorway, determined not to move until I could see him again. I scanned the mass of faceless bodies, squirming every time someone brushed passed, fearing a hidden enemy with a gun.

"Memsahib," an unfamiliar voice echoed through my ears.

An enormous, uniformed officer stood silent, brandishing a rifle. I couldn't remove my eyes from his weapon.

"Why are you just standing here?"

"I am waiting for –"

"For who?" He stared at me through sensitive deep-set eyes under a pair of thick eyebrows. "Did you not hear our orders for dispersion?"

"I need to find someone."

The policeman peered at me. "Who are looking for?"

I stood, trying to think of something to say.

"Me," Ayaz stated. "She's waiting for me."

Ayaz stood tall against the arch, with his arms crossed. His bushy 'brows jutting out against his dark skin.

Vermilion Harvest

The policeman turned and faced Ayaz. "The troublemaker?" He brandished his foot long lathi.

"I am her mangetar," Ayaz replied. "She was waiting for me."

The heaviness in my heart melted like ice on a summer day.

The soldier looked at us, disbelievingly at Ayaz and then at me. I was flushing at Ayaz's reference to fiancé.

"Mangetar?" he repeated. Skepticism plastered across his face. "You expect me to believe that a Muslim man will marry this Hindu?"

"Believe it or don't believe it." Ayaz's expression tightening. "We are not afraid of speaking the truth. This is my fiancée, and I will take her home now."

"You'd better if you know what's good for you both." The policeman growled. "We don't want trouble."

Ayaz nodded, taking my arm and guiding me out of the archway. We hurried down a gulley heading to my home. So much was going through my mind, I didn't know what to say.

"Ayaz –" I whispered.

"Shh!" He glanced around "Wait till we are in the city."

The heat of his gaze hit as we slipped into a smooth rhythm, pacing the gulley with silent speed. The flames he emitted were less of passion and more of virulence. It wasn't until we arrived at the Hall Bazaar that he finally spoke, his expression tighter. He ushered me onto a side street, still holding my arm with a firm grip.

"You have not listened to my requests, Aruna!" he whispered loudly.

I gazed up at him, loving that he was so tall. His chest and shoulders made me feel protected and secure. But a new intensity in his eyes, one that I had never seen, frightened me. It was a face of war.

"That's a little hypocritical, don't you think? Expecting me to listen to the radio while you're here, face to face with danger?"

"I've told you, Aruna …" he said with a raw voice, "… respectable women –"

"Respectable women?" I repeated. "The phrase is getting old. I don't exactly fit the title. I am ostracized for being Anglo-Indian and an outcast. I apparently cavort with unsavory characters. Respectability is not part of my equation."

He tossed up his hands. "Aruna, don't make this about you."

His voice sounded distant. I couldn't tell whether he was talking to me or directing the comment at himself. A blend of anger and frustration blazed in his eyes. Did he want a justification as to why I wouldn't obey him? I was not about to quietly control my emotions. Could he not see the hypocrisy of his statement?

"It's never been about me," I stated. "It's always been about you!"

Ayaz's eyes narrowed. His expression was saying everything. "Unsavory characters?"

I nodded. "That's what a soldier told me last night. He delivered a note from Colonel Lewis, the headmaster, ordering me to stay home. Or … I could lose my position."

Ayaz's face darkened. "Then they've seen us together."

"Yes." I nodded. "And they've already judged us. But I don't care. It's not just that they're judging, but fellows like that Somdatt!"

"What do you mean?" he asked, his brow furrowed.

"Why were they trying to bully him into admitting he was Ratto? Who is Ratto?"

Ayaz let out a sigh, his eyes flickering into a distance thought. "Mahashe Rattan Chand. A respectable trader who's now wanted for crimes."

"Mahashe Rattan Chand?" I repeated slowly. "Is he the chap who organized the Ram Navami celebrations?"

Ayaz nodded "And the Hindus and Muslims showing unity that day has made him a criminal in the eyes of those mutton-shunters."

"Just as the Hindu-Muslim unity between you and me is making me a criminal in the eyes of the school!"

"The school doesn't see you as a criminal," Ayaz said.

"The administration then. Lord knows who from the administration has nothing else to do but to spy on us."

"It's complicated," he replied.

Ayaz turned away, crossing his arms over his stomach. He rocked back on his heels. Of course, it was complicated. Hindu-Muslim-Sikh unity was unprecedented. Something the locals never experienced before, nor the establishment. It was unnerving.

"We must stand together," Ayaz said.

"Standing together is fine, but this thing about the gatherings –"

"It's an infringement on our rights!" He shook his head. "Did you not hear them as we walked back here?"

"What?"

"Shh!" Ayaz placed his fingers to his lips.

Footsteps, marching to the beat of a drum, echoed between the shops. We stood silent and listened. When the marching stopped, the sound of a bugle echoed. "From here on! Any assembly over five will be considered illegal and punishable." The marching rhythm again filled the alley as the troop moved to another part of the city.

This was serious. I crossed my arms against my chest, staring at Ayaz. "This must stop. You can no longer take any part in gatherings."

Ayaz's look was total disbelief. "I will speak at just such a gathering tomorrow in Jallianwala Bagh."

How is that even possible. Tomorrow is Baisakhi!

"Lala Kanhaiya Bhatia, one of our local Congress heroes, is replacing Dr. Satyapal, and Dr. Kitchlew has asked us to draft a series of resolutions to debate."

"Debate? Like what?"

"Our disapproval against these despotic acts by the government and our disapproval of the Rowlatt Act."

"Disapproval?" I paced. "What about disapproving of these revolutionary activities? An inevitable result of these despotic acts?"

"Of course, Aruna, but ..." – he grabbed my shoulders – "... all the same."

Was it? Could Lala-ji not see that the meeting would be deemed political? "A political meeting will be seen as a revolutionary act."

"He is a Congress leader and should know what's best. He is calling this meeting to state what we reject."

I wanted to trust that it would turn out as Ayaz said. But I simply could not believe him. "Will it be a peaceful meeting?"

He released my shoulders and leaned his head back for a few seconds. "We only meet in peace," he replied. "We are soldiers, but unlike those in khadi uniforms, we are Gandhi-ji's soldiers of peace. We need to reassure the families of those who have been arrested that they have our support. That we will continue to protest the Rowlatt Act."

It was decided. The meeting would happen in Jallianwala Bagh the following day. The best place for a political meeting thanks to the success of previous ones held there before. But this one would be different. The people of Amritsar would already be gathering to celebrate Baisakhi.

But what about the proclamation stating that gatherings beyond five people were illegal? Were we to march to the beat of the British drums? The administration may have placed soldiers and pickets all over the city, but they had not forbidden its inhabitants to celebrate the harvest festival or had they?

"I'm sure even Irving understands he doesn't have the right to stop us from celebrating. But what about Colonel Dyer?" I asked.

Ayaz twisted his beard. "Does a British Colonel have more rights than the city commissioner?"

"I still don't like the sound of this. Why should you be the one drafting resolutions? Leave it to others. I don't want you ending up in the Andamans."

Ayaz's expression tightened again. "Direct your concern to your own fate, Aruna, and to that of your mother. Not me." He sighed. "My place is with the Congress Party."

His tone might have been sincere, but his words seemed callous, unfeeling, and heartless. Was that all that mattered to him? "You will choose the Congress Party over me?"

"That's not what I said!"

"You didn't have to say it, Ayaz!" I whispered.

"Aruna!" He threw up his hands again. "I have no choice."

"No choice? You have another choice. Choose me! Not your political ideals!"

Ayaz glared at me. "Listen … when we get out of this mess, we can move to Bombay as we planned. I can finish my studies there instead of Lahore. We can take your mother with us."

The ground beneath me tipped sideways as I listened to his words change the course of my life. Did he honestly believe it was that easy? That the fantasy of moving to Bombay was the answer? We would simply pluck up my mother and ship her to another city – just a snap of a finger. My position at Saint Mary's didn't matter?

How did I make such a grave mistake to fall in love with a man who valued his political ideals more than he valued me? Here we were, metaphorically hurtling toward each other, when everything in the world was trying to keep us apart. But the only way we could make it work was if we both played in this dangerous game – politics.

Feeling weak and defeated, I whispered, "And if you end up in the Andamans?"

"A chance I must take." He sighed.

Vermilion Harvest

His every word, every action displayed some kind of reckless hardihood. It was difficult to say what spoke louder, his savage desperation or his rejection of me. A heavy darkness passed through me like a shroud. The situation was starting to make sense. Here he was ready to go to the Andamans for a political cause just after promising me a life together in Bombay. Loving Ayaz was almost an impossible feat. Our relationship was under scrutiny, judged by others, but the deepest scrutiny needed to come from me. Loving Ayaz placed me in a difficult dilemma. On one hand, I wanted desperately to support his cause, but on the other, I wanted him home and safe. Either way, the world was conspiring against us, and if I didn't make the correct choice, I may have to relinquish him once and for all.

"Go take your chances, Ayaz," I stated. "Sadly, I cannot take them with you."

"Aruna!"

"I'm sorry." I held up my hand. "You think of me as a woman who says it like it is. The truth is, I've been resisting saying these words. I will not ... cannot ... wait for you in the hope that one day the Congress will achieve Home Rule, and you and I might end up in Bombay. It's a pipe dream. I must face reality. I have a responsibility to my mother ... and to myself."

Obviously, it wasn't what he wanted to hear. His expression betrayed a sudden wandering, perhaps uncontrollable thoughts. A restlessness for something undefined.

"Aruna, please ... listen ..."

I placed my palms together in an anjali, a prayer position. He enclosed my anjali with his own.

"Aruna!" He looked deeply into my eyes, understanding that I meant every word of what I just said. That holding on was a desperate, futile attempt at the impossible.

"I have something for you," he said. "Regardless of your decision, I want to give it to you."

My gaze penetrated the depth of his chocolate brown eyes. I didn't know what to say. Ayaz rummaged in his pocket, pulling out a small cloth.

"Vermilion and green," he said, opening it. "Two colors that depict Hinduism and Islam, surrounded by a border of gold … the color of sunshine … that which opens the darkness to light."

Sunshine! Another reference to the duality that was my life, my love, my Ayaz.

He unwrapped the bundle, revealing a golden pendant – the AUM symbol of Hinduism welded with the graceful crescent emblem of Islam. Nestled in a small sachet, lay sindoor, the vibrant vermilion powder – the sacred mark of a married Hindu woman.

A darkness shimmered from inside my heart, emptying that hidden place I never knew existed. Was this his way of showing true and lasting love?

"You've had doubts about whether society will permit us to be together," Ayaz whispered. "When two hearts beat as one, God and religion fuse. We can be free to live as who we are rather than what we're supposed to be. From this moment, I declare you as my bride."

The light in my veins glowed as time slowed. I wanted to say something, but I just stood there, feeling dumbstruck, unable to form words.

Vermilion Harvest

He placed the chain around my neck, reaching behind and gently moving my hair aside. He fastened the clasp. I focused on the sensuous quality of his fingers, caressing my skin, making my nerves tingle. A deep and meaningful connection materialized between us, a feeling of rightness, as though we were meant to be, as though we were joined on a level that transcended the physical. Ayaz stood quiet. His hand cupped around my neck.

"This pendant belonged to my grandmother," he whispered. "There's a history behind this. I've wanted to tell you but could never find the right moment."

My fingers touched the pendant. The proximity between us was too close. The aroma of Ayaz's spicy musk attar called out to me, making me want to lean in and bury my face in the curve of his neck. Our heat rose as he cradled my head in his arms, pulling me closer.

"Aruna, please reconsider?" Ayaz pleaded.

I became silent, melting into him as he kissed my temples, from there to the bridge of my nose, and then to my lips. A tingling spiraled down my spine, spreading through a hundred nerves. In another moment, I knew I would lose control, and this was not the place. It was not the time.

I gave myself a shake, both mentally and physically, pulling away to take a deep breath. No need to say anything about the pendant or my bridal mark. I didn't want words to ruin the feelings that were growing inside me. I shook my head, touching one hand to his as his other found its way to the exposed curve of my collarbone.

We parted ways.

Ayaz stopped and turned to look my way. I resisted not allowing my eyes to meet his. If I did, I'd run the risk of giving in and falling prey to his amor once again.

I spent the rest of the day walking the narrow streets behind Hall Gate. I read the news stating that the satyagrahis were maintaining hartal at their shops. I thought about the turn of events over the last few days and the angry faces of strangers. Punjabis were a hot-blooded people, and unwarranted agitation could easily lead to thug mentality. Desperation and hysteria burned from inside, I couldn't help it. I wanted to scream, but who would hear me? I ran my fingers over the pendant and thought about what I had said to Ayaz. I ran every word through my mind, repeatedly, as if there were some secrets I had missed the first time.

I felt numb. I could feel nothing - no hunger, no fatigue, no anger, no pain. It had all gone wrong and what was my role now? How could I have stopped him? What could I have said differently? How could I ever have believed that I would truly be happy the day Ayaz made me his bride? I couldn't breathe, it felt as if an invisible hand was strangling me. The feeling of water slowly filling my lungs hit. I was drowning inside my liquid pain. I wanted to scream but no sound escaped past my lips. It was horrible, the strongest feeling of helplessness. Our relationship was over.

My tears fell. Large, salty drips flowed down my cheeks. It was a moment of reckoning.

A few blocks behind me, Colonel Dyer was marching his troops to the city, where he would spend the rest of the afternoon making illegal arrests. The prisoners would be handcuffed and marched back to Rambagh Gardens where they would be chained to a tree in the center.

Colonel Dyer's aim was to occupy strategic sections of the city to issue his wretched proclamation. But a few drumbeats here and there didn't spread the message fast enough. Most of Amritsar were bracing to celebrate the Baisakhi festival tomorrow.

CHAPTER 20

April 12, 1919

Amritsar – a curfew

I hurried home through a back alley. My mind racing with thoughts of Ayaz and what life without him would be.

"Memsahib ..." a voice asked, "... may I ask where you are going?"

The question caught me off guard. It was a Gurkha soldier. He stood rigid in his starched khadi uniform. His hat tilted slightly to one side, held in place with a string below his chin. His rifle hung behind him suspended from a shoulder strap that attached to a belt with reserve bullets and other ammunition. The khadi threads marked him as a fighter, a protector, but in the dim light of the early evening, he was just a boy. Only a few years younger than me. Short and muscular with square shoulders and close-cropped hair, he had a handsome face, slightly uneven by his crooked nose. Perhaps it had been broken when he was younger.

"I'm going home," I replied.

Vermilion Harvest

Army soldiers wandered the cantonment on a regular basis and were used to the comings and goings of the neighborhood's inhabitants. If anything, I expected him to ask why I had been out instead of staying at home, but the conversation didn't go that way.

"Perhaps I should ask, where have you been?" the soldier stated.

"I was out near the Hall Gate," I replied.

"What was your purpose in visiting Hall Gate at this late hour?"

Late? It was barely seven in the evening! Why the interrogation? Did he know about the note from Colonel Lewis? Or had someone seen me with Ayaz? I cleared my throat. "Excuse me, but is this about the so-called order from Colonel Lewis?"

The soldier looked confused.

"Why are you asking such questions?"

"Memsahib, I am a British officer," came the rehearsed reply.

I could see that by the way he was dressed. But there was a slight difference. Those men were white, flown in from England or English raised in India. This boy was a local recruit, forced into the army at an unreasonably young age. I wondered how he had the courage to be plucked so early from the safe arms of his mother. Maybe it wasn't a matter of courage but a lack of choice. The British army was notorious for forcibly enlisting Gurkhas and Sikhs at a young age. Even though the great war was over, the army's recruiting protocol was not.

India was a seasoned colony, some one hundred and seventy years into the Empire. It had more than reached an age where it should be independent. We yearned for independence, although no one could accept the trauma of becoming independent at too young an age. I thought about what that meant for these young soldiers, uprooted from their nest before they were ready to fly. They were forced to grow up overnight, relying on their peers to learn how to shave, how to iron, shine boots, and run for hours over rocks and through rivers – learning to be independent, away from home and his mother.

As I studied his face, I thought he might have learned how to shoot a human, but he was nowhere near the age to kill.

"Memsahib?" His stern tone jolted me back to reality. "Under what circumstances were you visiting the Hall Gate?"

I glared at him. Why was he asking all these preposterous questions? "Under a circumstance of my own business," I replied.

"I will need an explanation."

"Why?"

"To make a report," he stated. "We are recording movements of everyone tonight." He whipped out a notebook and pen from one of his multiple pockets.

The thought of this young Gurkha making a report on me, ridiculous. My fingers searched for the ends of my dupatta.

I could tell he wanted to be a hero, a patriot. To serve with courage and dignity. He was everything his country would be proud of. He was completing his reports so that his superiors would look upon him with pride.

But what if one day, he returned home with disabling injuries? What good would this report do? Who would care for him? But here he stood, reporting on me for visiting the market.

"Oh, for god's sake, I refuse to listen to any more of this childish banana oil." I rolled my eyes. "Next, you'll want to arrest me for standing in the streets!"

"Memsahib, the markets are not open today. Shopkeepers are on strike. It is well within my orders to ask why you were walking the streets."

"Seriously?" I asked. "Why is anybody ever in the streets? The real question should be, why are you in the streets hassling innocent citizens?"

The Gurkha shot me a weak smile. He sighed. "Memsahib, may I assume that your activities today were not controversial?"

To be referred to as memsahib from someone who was barely a year or two younger than me felt odd. "Why would you assume that I'm a person who engages in controversy?"

He glanced up from his notebook and looked me in the eyes. "Assumptions, memsahib, are made entirely based on people's actions."

"I'm sorry ..." I whispered, "... what?"

A breeze swirled around my legs from the direction of the young Gurkha, bringing a faint whiff of dried sweat and talcum powder.

"You alone at this late hour," he said, sounding stern also ridiculous.

"It's seven o'clock," I stated.

"Yes, and in another hour, you will be breaking curfew." His hands were now clutched behind his back.

Curfew? What curfew? Pulling on the ends of my dupatta, strange thoughts of fear ran through my mind.

"A curfew has been ordered," he said.

"Now, how would I be aware of that?"

"It was issued this afternoon. No resident of Amritsar is permitted to be out of their house after eight."

It was not yet eight. I had been out all afternoon, and this was the first I'd heard of the new rule.

"Please, take heed and return home quickly," he said. "Consequences are dire in an hour. Anyone out after eight will be shot. Those are our orders." He glanced around apologetically.

"Ridiculous!" I stated. "Whose idea is this?"

The Gurkha fumbled a reserve supply of ammunition on the side of his belt. "Colonel Dyer."

Colonel Dyer? I yanked on my dupatta so hard that it caught my throat, making me cough. "Then Amritsar is now a police state?"

The Gurkha furrowed his brow. "I am not at liberty to say, memsahib."

"Well, I am at liberty to ask."

"Memsahib, a curfew has been established by our commanding officer Colonel Dyer. Meetings are prohibited. We must track revolutionary activities."

Revolutionary activities. How I had grown to detest the use of such terminology. I thought about Ayaz doing lord knows what. "What if I want to visit my friend after dinner?"

The soldier frowned. "What friend?

"My friend ... Amrita Singh?"

"Married to Gurcharan Singh sahib of Khalsa College?"

"You know of him?"

He nodded. "We are tracking his revolutionary activities."

His words sent chills up my spine. My mind fell back to what Colonel Lewis had said to me that day in his office. Had Gurcharan Singh been placed on their watchlist for revolutionary activities?

"He's a distinguished academic," I replied. Although I wasn't overly fond of Gurcharan Singh, I felt a particular need to defend him. He was, after all, married to my best friend.

"He's a revolutionist," the Gurkha said. "The evidence is clear."

How could the evidence be clear? The man simply helped to organize a few hartals. I searched the Gurkha's face for clues.

"It may be difficult to understand the nature of our investigations, but we have informers," he stated.

Informers? A neighbor had sold my friend's husband down the river. *Who?* My mind flew back to the day I had found the sugar cubes wrapped in a threatening note at their shop. A plant. I eyed this young Gurkha carefully. Beneath the brim of his hat, the sweat collected on his brow. He was nervous, perhaps because he feared he had said too much. So young, so naive, wet behind the ears. What was it that kept him going? Grit or bravery? Perhaps I could use his nervous disposition to my advantage. I loosened my dupatta, shooting the young soldier a faint smile.

"And what will you do with these so-called revolutionists once you have them?" I asked.

He straightened his stance, as if looking for a way to craft his next sentence. "Any hint of agitation against the Empire will be dealt with severe consequences."

I glared at my feet for a few moments, tight-lipped, blood rushing to my head. It was one thing to hear this nonsense from a British soldier but to be accosted by a Gurkha. For land's sake, we were the same people. The Indian soldiers were mere puppets manipulated by the British. Perhaps it was simply a job that supplied him with money to feed his family.

I clenched my fists to control my emotions. "Empire? Okay, but what about our citizens' needs? We, the people, who are bound by the shackles of this Empire? You Gurkhas, if you join the British for a little money, who will plow our fields? Who will care for our elders? Which of you will understand that our people are not criminals?"

The Gurkha's brow softened as a hint of despair crept over his face. He stepped back, took a deep breath, and fumbled with his belt. "Memsahib, these things do not escape us. We Gurkha, Pathan, and Punjabi soldiers are in a more difficult position than civilians."

I paused, trying to make sense of his words. If the Indian soldiers truly understood the plight of their people, then why would they support the proclamations and Rowlatt Act? "Are your family members among those participating in the peaceful meetings?"

The Gurkha paused. "I am adhering to orders." His tone was slow and deliberate. "My neck will be on the line if I do not obey." He hesitated, looking around, with big rabbit-like eyes. "It is almost eight. Please, return home quickly and stay there until curfew has lifted."

I nodded, there wasn't much else for me to do. "When is curfew lifted?"

"Tomorrow, at sun light."

That didn't seem too terrible. Perhaps things would be all right after all. "And then what? Everything back to normal?"

"Normal given that everyone understands the rules," he replied. "No illegal gatherings."

"What about Baisakhi?" Pilgrims had arrived from all over Punjab to visit the Golden Temple. Families were gathering to celebrate.

"Celebratory gatherings are not considered illegal. If the celebrations are just celebrations."

"I don't understand."

Whatever was going through his mind could not be good. He glared at me before flipping through his notebook. He pulled out a sheet of paper, handing it to me.

"Here. You should read this."

I accepted the paper.

```
PROCLAMATION #1

    The inhabitants of Amritsar are
hereby warned that if they will cause
damage to any property or will commit
any acts of violence in the environs of
```

Amritsar, it will be taken for granted
that such acts are due to incitement in
Amritsar City, and offenders will be
punished according to military law. All
meetings and gatherings are hereby
prohibited and will be dispersed at
once.

R.E. Dyer, Colonel
Commanding Jullundur Brigade

My mind flew to the political meeting planned at Jallianwala Bagh. There would be no way that Ayaz would know about this, or Gurcharan Singh, who was already labeled as a revolutionist. I felt an odd something burning in the pit of my stomach.

"You can keep that, memsahib. Feel free to show it to your friends and family. There is something else you should know."

"What?" I asked.

An uncomfortable, feeling quivered inside my belly, more powerful than any heaviness. It was as if my body knew something that my mind had not yet figured out.

The Gurkha whipped out another paper from his file and held it up to the streetlamp. "No person residing in Amritsar is permitted to leave his house after eight o'clock. Anyone in the streets after that time will be shot. No procession of any kind is permitted to parade the streets or any part of the city or outside of it at any time. Such processions or gatherings shall be considered as treason and an unlawful assembly and dispersed by force."

Vermilion Harvest

In print, but not in print. I couldn't take that rule and show it to others. Who would believe me?

The Gurkha snapped his file shut. His mannerisms agitated. "Memsahib? Please, go home and stay there."

Home. A safe harbor or a prison? Allowing my dupatta to flow freely, I dug my nails into my palms. I turned from the Gurkha and headed for home.

ℰHAPTER 21

April 12, 1919

Amritsar - longing for love

I could not get my mind off Ayaz. Although the soldier had referred to a list, the Gurkha had not mentioned Ayaz. Although, I was no longer obliged to worry about Ayaz, I still loved him. He was still in danger, and I was worried. It started with a mild emotion. *Where is he? What is he planning for tomorrow?* My emotions grew. I needed to talk to him. Could I get in touch with him? How could I pass the night without him?

I opened my bedside drawer and took out my copy of Pride & Prejudice. I opened it to the scene featuring Mr. Darcy. Even Jane Austen couldn't calm me down.

I thought about Gurcharan Singh. The Gurkha's words had unnerved me. The fact that he knew his name and where he worked, and that he'd labeled him in the category of revolutionary activities. I traced the problem back to its source – the wrapper. The rationwala. My thoughts fell to the tongawala. Were all these walas connected?

I needed to sleep, but my mind was plagued with worry. To believe that someone like Gurcharan Singh could be skating on thin ice. What did that mean for the rest of his family? For Amrita and Gopal? I learned about the psychology of home and family during my training as a government schoolteacher and was aware that fatherless children faced a myriad of maladies, everything from poor educational performance to drug and alcohol abuse – and criminality. It was especially prevalent in the Punjab. Gopal lived in a home where his father was physically present but emotionally absent. Not that it was any of my business, but given my closeness to the family, it felt that way.

The British culture espoused the concept of a godparent, something quite alien to Indians who lived in large families. But with the Singhs being far from their nuclear home in rural Punjab, I was closer to Gopal than his blood relatives – something of a godparent, in the Indian sense.

The Singhs had no idea that Gurcharan Singh had been branded a revolutionary. My inner voice urged me to warn them somehow. With no way to leave at this late hour, there might be a possibility of a telephone message. However, neither we nor the Singhs owned telephones – a luxury more than a necessity. That said, I could visit the local provisions shop and telephone a message to one of Amrita's neighboring shopkeepers. But then again – the curfew. That was if the telephones were working. Most lines had been cut, rendering the exchange useless.

I needed Ayaz. I wanted him. As much for his comforting touch as for anything else. But I couldn't have him. I missed his warmth, his aroma, his embrace. We were supposed to meet at Rambagh yesterday, the day before, and the day before that. But it didn't happen. I touched the parting of my hair where he applied the sindoor. It was as if our love had been ripped from my heart like a bandage off an open wound, beating whimsically, bleeding as though life would slowly drip into a painful oblivion.

Stop pitying yourself.

These next few hours would either pass as a blip on the course of my life, or they would be the final trauma that would break me. I needed to occupy myself. Clutching the edges of my dupatta, I paced the floor, thinking of how Irving's actions had been responsible for bringing Colonel Dyer to Amritsar. What would happen tomorrow?

Irving!

My mind fell to Ayaz's snake reference just a few days ago. I had questioned him. Snakes were considered auspicious in India, symbolic of material wealth. This was also true of Punjab where people were ready to matha-teko, to bow before a snake and offer milk. But wasn't that the crux? Asking the snake politely to leave? The reason we worshipped snakes was because we were afraid of them. We wanted protection from them. We wanted to remain out of harm's way, harm caused by a snake. Perhaps the Western reference to a snake was more apropos than I understood. Irving was indeed a treacherous, deceitful individual. As for Colonel Dyer, he appeared harmless. However, he could be the kind of fellow that Emily Dickinson had referred to in her poetry – a snake in the grass.

As the daylight dwindled, my tension grew. I entered the kitchen and filled a saucepan with water to boil for chai. I actually had no intention of drinking it. My eyes darted to the door as if it would open and I would see him standing there. I turned on the radio and sat, only to turn it off a few minutes later. I couldn't risk hearing bad news. When the water boiled, I stood an inch from the door, praying it would open. It did not. Instead, Ma walked in.

"Aruna, what is it?" she asked.

"Nothing."

"Then why are you –"

"Nothing!" I snapped before she had a chance to finish her question. "I wanted some chai, but now I don't want any."

A stiffening of Ma's face was replaced with a weak smile. "Should I make you some –"

"No! No, Ma." I lowered my tone. "Sorry. Tired. I'm going to bed."

I left her alone, making my way to my room. I closed the door.

I could not stop thinking of Ayaz. Maybe I needed to see him again. Just once more to bring closure to our relationship. I curled my knees to my chest, wishing I had a way to reach him. It was strange to know that he was out there in this besieged city where anything could happen.

The fan whirred, interrupting my thoughts, sending a thousand more flinging through my mind. I needed to relax, to sleep.

I missed Ayaz. His aroma, his warmth, his physical presence. I ran my fingers through my hair, and each time my fingertips grazed my scalp, I imagined that the touch belonged to Ayaz. The thought sent tingles floating through my body, making me ache. Had I been wrong to abandon him? To walk away after he had taken me as his bride?

What if they took him? No, they couldn't do that, could they? I refused to give them that power. My fingers found their way to the pendant he gave me earlier. And from there, my fingers moved slowly, ever so slowly, to the exposed curvature of my cleavage. Even fully clothed, thinking about him was enough to awaken sensations profound enough to send waves of electricity undulating into my soul. Ayaz had said many times that the only way to bring something into action was to manifest it into being. I decided to spend the night with him. If not in his presence, then telepathically, through my imagination.

I closed my eyes and meditated on his tall, never-ending, silhouette. His broad male chest, perfectly defining his lean musculature. As his shape took form, I watched him step carefully toward me, close enough to inhale the woodsy fragrance of his musk and sandalwood laced ittar.

He stood at the threshold, smiling. His eyes glinting in the moonlight. No more did they have that faraway gaze, but rather one that was strong, purposeful and on me.

In one fell swoop, he lifted me off my feet, making his way to the bed. He placed me down, head between the pillows before climbing on top, pausing for just a moment until I nodded. Our interlude more than a lust. He treasured me. Evident from the way he caressed my body, encasing my emotions with the simplest of touches. He used his finger to lift my chin, ensuring my gaze was locked into his. He wove his fingers through the loose strands of my hair, pulling my mouth to his, slipping in his tongue as our lips met. He devoured every inch with his lips, my neck, my breasts, my belly.

I could feel his head between my legs, nuzzling and setting off a series of sensations that were exhilarating, exciting, and forbidden. His beard, a little rough, felt wonderful on the inside of my thighs. I tried to hold it together. I wanted to keep these feelings forever.

With his lips, then his tongue, he struck the spot. I cried out, almost in astonishment that, through Ayaz, I learned to touch myself in the right area. That special spot I hadn't known existed until he showed me.

I floated through the sensations pretending it was him. Like a flower bud tracking its way to spreading its petals in the early hours of sunlight, it was only me and him. Something I was seeking, something I was trying to achieve with the risk of losing it. I kept going, recognizing I was in a place of desperation. I needed more, and I would not lose him now. My petals opened wide, catching the early morning dew, and I sighed.

ᘓHAPTER 22

April 13, 1919

Amritsar - Baisakhi Day

In what seemed like only moments, the bed shook. The legs that supported the footboard snapped, rolling me to the floor, hitting my knees.

Hare Ram, what is happening?

The spasm seized my room, growing stronger, faster. The walls groaned, the window cracked and flipped open. I felt suffocated by a thin strand of something around my face. It was the mosquito netting that had fallen from the hooks. The shelves crashed, scattering books and papers. The violence multiplied, fivefold, tenfold. I imagined my skull smashed under the beams of the ceiling that would soon crash down.

Don't let me die here!

My prayers were answered by the shattering of glass, glistening in front of me like finely cut diamonds. A spilled water jug splashed a sea of liquid into my face. The undulating floorboards, the chest of drawers toppled.

I had heard about the anger with which Shiva the Destroyer disrupted the stability on Earth but never had I faced this kind of angry torment. I closed my eyes, forming a mental picture of Lord Shiva. All I could make out was a snake around his neck. A king cobra hissed as if I were the enemy. I chanted what my mother had taught me to hold in reserve for difficult times.

Om Namah Shivaya. Perhaps taking the name of the Lord would underscore my appeal for peace.

I opened my eyes to find my room normal and calm. I sat up too fast, and my head filled with panic. Everything was in its proper place. No damage. No earthquake. It had been nothing but a dream.

But why?

Why such a life-shattering quake? Could it have been a premonition? The anxiety spread like a raging fever. A series of images formed, one after the other. Today was Baisakhi. The residents of Amritsar would be celebrating the harvest festival, including me. Nothing would stop me from attending. No soldier with so-called orders from Colonel Lewis, the headmaster. The curfew of last night and the Gurkha soldier had me worried. Gurcharan Singh was branded as a revolutionist, but his family didn't know.

Ayaz was out there, planning a meeting in Jallianwala Bagh, which could be lethal. Or could it? My mind absorbed by an interrupted flow of worrisome thoughts filled me with dread. I tried to control them but couldn't.

Just a figment of my uncontrollable imagination, inviting trouble before it could form its objective. The disturbance to my peace was a fly settling on my footboard. I would not manifest this illusion into a reality. I grabbed the flyswatter from my bedside table and with perfect aim, thrashed it on the unknowing victim, crushing it into a ball, before flicking it in the direction of the waste-paper basket.

The reality of the situation had hit. I already doubted the severity a few days ago when Major MacDonald miraculously prevented things from getting out of hand by disobeying Irving's orders. The Gurkha soldier of last night wasn't a random meeting. That boy had read me the proclamation. The situation was real. I could no longer sweep things under the rug as a rumor. Not anymore. I needed to get to the Singhs first and let them know what I had learned. Then, I needed to find Ayaz. Even if I had called off our romance, I had to stop that meeting in the bagh.

I glanced over at the clock on my bedside table. It was seven-thirty. The curfew would soon lift, but shops were still closed. After all, it was a public holiday. Ma would not want me to leave. Therefore, I'd better leave now. I jumped off the bed, threw on some clothes, and left before Ma noticed I was awake.

I raced to their shop at the speed of a racehorse. I arrived sweaty, finding Amrita busy scraping her brassware with a half-cut lemon. Gurcharan Singh had already left. Gopal was nowhere to be seen.

"Left for where?" I asked.

"I don't know," Amrita replied. "To college perhaps."

"It's Sunday."

Amrita continued with her chores without so much as a glance. As far as she was concerned, my behavior that day was no different from any other. I arrived with my usual paranoia fostered by a long string of conspiracy theories.

"Yes it is," she said. "He has many things in the works today."

I all but jumped at that strange premonition feeling taking shape again. It started with a dark heaviness from somewhere inside my soul. What did Gurcharan Singh have in the works? Feeling overly suspicious, I shrugged. The Gurkha soldier had very accurate knowledge of Gurcharan Singh's life.

"What kinds of *things* are you talking about?" I asked.

"I don't know. Their Satyagraha activities, I suppose," Amrita replied, scrubbing the saucepan harder. "Why so many questions?"

"I don't think it's safe to go out today."

"What do you mean?" Amrita asked. "It's Baisakhi." She stared into her pan, non-plussed, as though it were a hand mirror throwing back her reflection.

"Amrita!" I grabbed her arm. "Stop fidgeting with that pan."

She stopped and looked at me as if I was a half-wit. "Do you know what it means to take care of a household? To have responsibilities that go beyond chasing after the details of your husband's minute-to-minute activities?"

I had no right to pounce on her like that, and honestly, it was the very last thing I wanted to do. "I'm sorry, Amrita! That did not come out the right way."

Amrita just looked at me and then back at her pan. "You are quite animated today. I don't understand what you are all worked up about."

I held my stomach, as if the action could curb what I was feeling. "Last night, on my way home, I was stopped by a Gurkha soldier. He asked me all sorts of personal questions."

"What kind of questions?"

"About who I was, where I had been, why I had been there. He knew Singh sahib's name."

The way Amrita was staring at me, I could sense this was going to be a rough road to reality. "Everyone knows Jeeo-ji's name. He's a popular professor at Khalsa College."

My gaze met my friend's puzzled look. I bit my lip, consciously this time. "I know ... I know. Listen, that's not what I'm saying."

"Then what are you saying?" Amrita asked.

My mind formed the image of wild grass waving gently in the breeze, before picking up cadence with a brisk gust. It wasn't the wind. The wild grass unbraided to reveal the spotted shaft of a cobra rearing its head with its hood spread, ready to strike. The uneasy feeling in my stomach morphed into a slow burning sensation. I pushed the picture away.

"This Gurkha ..." I said, "... he hinted that there could be trouble if people gathered today."

Amrita peered intently at her brassware.

"Today is Baisakhi. People *will* gather. That's what we do during the festival."

"As long as it's kept to a celebration, it should be fine," I whispered.

"What else could possibly happen during Baisakhi?" Amrita asked. She glared at me. "I will head to Jallianwala Bagh with Gopal to join Jeeo-ji later this afternoon."

The burning feeling deep in my stomach grew hotter and more intense. It was my turn to fidget now. I grabbed the end of my dupatta, closed my fingers in a ring around it, and moved it up and down like a long pipe.

"I know what I'm saying," I stated. "They're planning a political meeting at four-thirty. They want to discuss what they object to. I think it's a bad idea."

"Why?" Amrita asked.

"Because of what the Gurkha said. And that brings me to my second point. The time is ripe for our men being labeled as revolutionaries. And they think Singh sahib is a part of it."

Amrita shot me a disapproving look. "Jeeo-ji is no such thing."

"I know that, but *they* don't."

"Who are they?"

"The British administration. The Gurkha soldier ... last night ... he said so about Singh sahib."

Amrita's facial expression morphed from disapproval to anguish. "Jeeo-ji? Have you talked to Ayaz sahib about this?"

The mention of his name radiated a shooting pain into my heart. I felt numb. "About the meeting, yes. In fact, it was he who told me about it. But I didn't know about Singh sahib being branded a revolutionary yet. Maybe Ayaz knows this already ... he's on a list too. I found out through Colonel Lewis." I shrugged.

"The headmaster?"

"Yes, he knows about me and Ayaz, and he ordered me to stop seeing him. Saying I would lose my job if I didn't listen."

"What does a school administrator have to –"

"Oh my goodness, Amrita!" I stated. "He's ex military. He lives inside the cantonment with the privileged Britishers. He's friends with Mr. Plomer, the deputy police superintendent, and with Commander Wintertree. These people are all together and gossip spreads. I live on the outskirts and hear this kind of stuff all the time."

Amrita looked like she had seen a ghost.

"I just know that Singh sahib must be involved," I said. "Has to be."

Amrita glanced into the distance, her furrowed brow deepening. "We must find Jeeo-ji and Ayaz sahib."

My heart pounded as I prepared to tell her what had transpired the day before. I couldn't believe how hard it was pumping, like I had just run a mile.

"Well I don't know if I should go ..." I whispered. "What I have not told you is that I broke up with Ayaz. I couldn't hold to a relationship insisting on these political meetings time and again. Between that and the fact that my job is at stake ..."

My personal woes were far from the focus of Amrita's mind. She was more concerned about her husband and rightly so. Her distraught features showed her pain. I squirmed at the idea of being the bearer of bad news.

"I need you to help me try and stop that meeting," she stated. "Help me warn Jeeo-ji. Please, Aruna. I don't know where he is. I planned on seeing him at four this afternoon at the bagh with Gopal."

Vermilion Harvest

Four o'clock. Close to the witching hour.

I winced as the burning sensation engulfed my pounding heart.

"Aruna, is there any chance you could be overreacting?" Amrita asked, a blush of innocence coloring her already rosy complexion.

"I might be, but it's worth the drama if something is about to happen."

"What *is* about to happen?" Amrita asked.

"He showed me a proclamation issued by Colonel Dyer. It threatens to shoot offenders according to military law."

"But there is no military law in Amritsar," she said.

I nodded. "What if all that has changed? It's been two days since Colonel Dyer arrived."

The image of a cobra rearing its head between the wild grass blocked my vision. It flicked its tongue.

"He is not the Deputy Commissioner."

"He is not, but he is here to *take control of things*, whatever that means," I replied.

"Take control?" Amrita asked. "What does that mean?"

"Who knows? The Gurkha talked about a change in command, and that was before anyone knew about Colonel Dyer. You heard about what happened on the footbridge. What if things turn violent in the bagh?"

"But it's Baisakhi. The harvest celebration. It's playtime at the bagh for the people of Amritsar."

Playtime at the bagh. A phrase that had such a nice ring. Why did it intensify the burning and pounding that was wrecking my insides? Was this just about me and my paranoia? Perhaps it would be fine, and people would go on with their celebrations.

"The notice said all meetings would be dispersed under military law," I whispered.

"That simply means they want *meetings* dispersed. Like they dispersed the funeral crowds yesterday and the day before that. It doesn't mean they are going to stop Baisakhi."

"And what about this four-thirty meeting?"

Fear was written all over Amrita's face. She was now making sense of what I was trying to say. Her expression changed from wide-eyed to determined. "There's only one thing to do. I must get there before the meeting starts and find them." Her eyes met mine with an expression that pierced my insides. "I will ask you one more time Aruna, will you come with me?"

I thought back to my last exchange with Ayaz. None of it made sense. What was wrong with me? How could I be so heartless, so cruel as to discard him when he had taken me as his bride, when he was counting on my support? I loathed myself for sabotaging my future with Ayaz by giving in to my mother's reprimands. Just because he was a Muslim or a political activist, I needed to stay away from him?

I had given in to weakness and wronged us both. Today was different, today I understood that nothing was more important than me loving Ayaz. But understanding this was not good enough. I needed Ayaz to understand it too. I needed to tell him that I had accepted my new journey as his bride. I was with him for life.

I nodded at Amrita, my chin in sync with my pounding heart. Although my body felt like it was going to explode, there was nothing that would hold me back from going with her.

Ꮎ HAPTER 23

April 13, 1919

Amritsar - playtime at the bagh

The alley leading up to the bagh spilled over with people and families scrambling to get inside for the Baisakhi festival. Carefree and joyous, they were ready to fill the harvest air with gidda-dancing and unassuming cups of tea and parathas. It was obvious that no one had heard of Colonel Dyer's proclamation, and the politicians speaking at one end of the garden were only part of the picture.

As the city was under joint military and civilian control, Dyer had combed his way through the streets with Deputy Commissioner Miles Irving and Deputy Superintendent of Police Plomer. Together, they claimed to have advertised the proclamation that there should be no gatherings, which proved to be ineffective. However, they took only a partial route through the city.

Vermilion Harvest

Jallianwala Bagh itself was not much more than a barren piece of land where families gathered for respite from their busy week or rest after praying at the Golden Temple. An irregular quadrangle surrounded by aging houses – three trees and a well on one side and a small shrine on the other. It was surrounded by a five or six-foot wall on all sides with just one narrow opening that served as both an entrance and exit. The only way to get to this opening was through a narrow alley flanked by equally high walls. Tho other gates, no larger than a door, were locked shut.

It was four o'clock by the time Amrita, Gopal, and I arrived at the mouth of the alleyway leading to the narrow entrance of the bagh. The crowds were milling at the entrance, many at the behest of street vendors luring children with treats and trinkets. Channa sellers, balloon sellers, and oversized pathans were crying, "Punjabi dieting di maa di." The aroma of hot chole bhature, the classic Amritsari chickpeas and puffed breads cooked on open-air tavas, drifted through the crowd. The perfect snack for the harvest festival.

We waited at the mouth of the alleyway, watching the families pass. We were hoping for a glimpse of our men. Gopal became restless at the sight of the goodies.

"Mumma, Mumma, can I have a phugga?" His mouth and eyes widened with fascination at a balloon seller showing off his collection of red, yellow, blue, and more to mimic the colors of spring.

"Hmm," Amrita whispered. "Let's get inside," she said. "There'll be plenty more to choose from in there."

We jostled our way through the crowd with Gopal. Inside the bagh, families were strewn around the grounds picnicking, playing games, or relaxing. I couldn't tell how many were there, but it was well in the thousands. Never had I seen the bagh this crowded.

I scanned the crowds, noticing a group of elderly men gathered together playing rummy in the northwest corner. A group of housewives was belting out Punjabi harvest songs to the beat of a dholki. A woman hit the side with a large stirring spoon. Somewhere else a group of pre-teen children played pitthu, a local game combining hopscotch, tag, and langdi tang. I glanced around the periphery, my eyes resting at the scene playing out in the southeast corner. Several groups of kurta pajama clad satyagrahis were tracking Gandhi-ji's movements and retracing the course of events in the city over the last few days.

Amrita and I scoured the grounds for Ayaz and Gurcharan Singh. Amrita heard her name.

"Amrita, Gopal, why are you here so early? I thought you weren't coming till later." It was Gurcharan Singh.

Amrita faced him, tears welled in her eyes.

Gopal made a beeline for his father's legs, wrapping his arms around them. Gurcharan Singh lifted Gopal, staring into his small face with almost hypnotic fascination.

"Ki gall hai, mera sher?" *What's happening my little tiger?*

"Jeeo-ji, where have you been?" Amrita stated. Her fear-stricken eyes scanned the area. "We've been looking for you."

"I've just arrived from college. We were going over the agenda for the four-thirty meeting," he replied.

"Jeeo-ji, that's what we wanted to talk to you about," Amrita said, casting a rabbit-eyed glance at me.

"What is it?" Gurcharan Singh asked.

"They are threatening to take action on our gatherings," Amrita said. "You have to call off the meeting." She said it louder than she intended, and a few turned to glance in our direction.

"Don't be foolish, Amrita," Gurcharan Singh frowned. "We are just about to begin."

"Please, Jeeo-ji," Amrita said, the alarm ringing through her voice. "There is trouble brewing. They are threatening action."

"Who is threatening?"

"The Britishers," she said, lowering her voice.

But Gurcharan Singh was not one to have his vision blinded by clouds of despair. He waved her off. "They've been threatening us for awhile now. Nothing has happened and nothing will."

Amrita cast her eyes my way, imploring for advice. "But, Jeeo-ji, it can happen. They listed you as a revolutionary."

Gurcharan Singh studied us. He was speechless for a long moment.

"Aruna was stopped by a soldier last night who confirmed it." Amrita looked at me. "Aruna, tell him."

I nodded to support her words. I was willing to step into the conversation to stand by my friend in what looked like a streak of hopelessness. "He told me last night when I was walking home. Colonel Dyer set up camp at Rambagh, and he has issued a proclamation calling for no gatherings of a political nature."

Gurcharan Singh brushed us off as though we were flies buzzing in the way of his mental peace. "Yes, yes, we are aware of that."

Did he mean the accusation of being revolutionist or Colonel Dyer's plans? I wasn't sure which one, but he didn't give me the opportunity to ask.

"As long as we do not agitate, we are fine. We've been hearing that all day. But anything that is peaceful, they will not have a problem with. It is Baisakhi after all."

"No, Singh sahib," I replied. "This is something new. Something issued just yesterday. Last night, I think. Under these circumstances, it will be hard for him to see what is peaceful or not."

I glanced at the narrow alley of the bagh. As I dreaded the thought of seeing a soldier in uniform, a small part of me wanted to see one so I could say so. Recognizing the perverse duality of my thoughts, I sighed.

Gurcharan Singh had little tolerance for what the British were or were not thinking. He glared at me. Ayaz was overly thoughtful sometimes, Gurcharan Singh was the opposite. "Are you speaking for *them* now?"

His words hit like an arrow of ice. I lost my stance, but only for a moment. I knew that this would one day arrive. The moment that my friends would doubt me.

"Singh sahib, please –" I began.

But Gurcharan Singh was not listening to reason. "No, seriously, Aruna. Your attitude has been nothing but negative. As though you are ardently against everything that Gandhi-ji is saying."

"Jeeo-ji!" Amrita's dupatta fell from her head, but she looked too shocked to do anything about it.

I bit my lip. How I wished Ayaz were here. Though equally adamant in his views, he was far less reactionary than his friend Gurcharan Singh.

"No, Singh sahib," I stated. "You know that's not true."

"Well, that's what it seems like," he said. "Ours is a peaceful cause. Your own Ayaz Peermohammed is taking the lead."

My own Ayaz? A shooting star took life and then died somewhere in the open space of my mind. "That's why I am here. Where is he? I need to find him. To stop him. To stop all of you."

Gurcharan Singh's wince confirmed that I had said the wrong thing. Not that my intent was wrong but I had conveyed it incorrectly – using the wrong words.

"All of us?" he asked slowly. "Are we now a different breed of humanity?"

The alarm flashed through Amrita's eyes. She had heard these words before. If not these very words, then others very much like them – ever since the tongawala pigeon-holed me into an *us versus them* situation.

"Jeeo-ji, please!" she begged. "How can you talk like that?"

"No, that's enough, Amrita," Gurcharan Singh said firmly. "I'm sorry, but it's tiring to do your damnedest to fight for a cause only to be knocked down by those you thought were your people. Maybe it's true what they say about Anglos. That eventually you walk to the other side."

Amrita raised her hands to her ears. A sigh of punctured anguish escaping her reddening face. "Jeeo-ji! Stop it, have you forgotten who you are talking to?"

I wasn't offended. I just didn't care anymore. I felt no heaviness in my chest, no pit in stomach, no more burning. My hands hung free of my dupatta or fist-clenching. It was as if I had built up the mettle to deal with the onslaught of racism hurled at me on a regular basis and by the people I thought were my own. I was acutely aware of the fact that my Anglo-Indian identity would inevitably come home to roost. I had no choice but to brave the storm.

The afternoon breeze hovered over the aroma of hot chole. A group of cows lowed from somewhere in the bagh. It was a standard holiday thoroughfare.

"No, Amrita. I have not forgotten, but I would urge Aruna to remember whose side she is on," Gurcharan Singh stated. "Or, if that has changed, then perhaps it is time to be honest about it."

He glared at his wife, his grim face softening just a little. "Take care of Gopal, please, and yourself." He looked me directly in the eyes. "Excuse me. Like Peermohammed sahib, I have places to go."

Gurcharan Singh stomped into the crowd without further words, somewhere in the direction of the satyagrahis.

My mind was on Ayaz again. A series of sensations filling my body with fear. Sweat ran down my cheeks, which had nothing to do with the heat of the afternoon sun. I was desperate to find him.

"I can't wait anymore," I said to Amrita. "You and Gopal stay here. I'm going to look for him." I scanned the grounds of the bagh. People were moving around like shoals of fish – chattering between buyers and sellers, old friends catching up, new friends introduced. I rotated three hundred and sixty degrees, ensuring I didn't miss a fraction of the full-spectral of chaos.

"Maybe we should come with you," Amrita said.

"No," I replied. "It's better you find a safe spot near the entrance. Should there be any need to escape, you'll be right where you need to be."

"Escape?" Amrita repeated. "You saw Jeeo-ji disappear into the thick of the bagh. There's no question of us going anywhere without him."

I grabbed her hands. "Listen, Amrita. I say this only because you matter too much to me. Gurcharan Singh is your husband, your family, and I understand where we come from. There is nothing more important than keeping our family together. But sometimes, and believe me, I hate to put it like this ..."

My iron tear ducts were a thing of the past. I felt the tears welling in my eye, but I couldn't let go of Amrita's hands. I squeezed them as if to lend her strength in her weakened, insecure state.

"We need to break family down into its core units. As much as Gurcharan Singh is your husband, you have to remember that Gopal is your son. And as much as you owe it to your family to keep them together, you owe it more to the individual members to keep them safe."

"But Jeeo-ji —"

"We fell in love, you and I, with people who promised they would help make us whole. Part of that wholeness comes with an understanding and respect for their ideals, their passions, their invigorating habit of rebelling against this despotic officialdom. But we need to understand that sometimes they get caught up in their ideals. Too much perhaps. Their melancholy and sensitive nature puts them in touch with their deeper currents of thoughts and feelings. These currents may not be in sync with what's best for their immediate family … their children."

Amrita glanced at Gopal who was watching the balloonwala. Her eyes moist.

"Sometimes, you have to make a choice between being a wife and a mother. Should anything happen to Gurcharan Singh today …"

Amrita's fists tightened in my grip.

"I am not saying that it will. But just in case, you need to think about Gopal and what you can do to make sure he has at least one parent."

A tear rolled down Amrita's cheek as she nodded.

"Because, my dearest Amrita, that is entirely in your hands."

I squeezed her hands in acknowledgment, before planting a kiss on Gopal's forehead. Slipping into the crowd, I elbowed my way through the multitudes flowing past.

"Ayaz!" I called his name, but no answer. I could not see him anywhere.

Vermilion Harvest

After much bumping and jostling, I edged toward the area of the bagh where the satyagrahis had gathered. Many had stopped to listen. It was the afternoon meeting quietly getting underway even as the bagh filled with more people. About two hundred had gathered around a makeshift stage created from a raised mound, and one by one, various speakers addressed the audience. Most were well-known Amritsar personalities. Those sitting listened intently, while children played on the greens beyond.

That's when I saw him. It was only for a moment, but for me, it seemed like hours. He stepped out from the same group that Gurcharan Singh had disappeared into. It was difficult to distinguish one from the other.

No sooner had I caught sight of him, he climbed onto the mound of grass. How would I get his attention now? I waved from the sides. He did not see me. He was already absorbed in a heated political discussion. I instantly felt on edge. The last thing we needed was for him to be checked off the so-called *list.*

"Gandhi-ji says that it only requires a small body of determined spirits fired by an unquenchable faith in their mission to alter our country's history." Ayaz folded his hands into a namaste.

Passion streamed from his words and movements. The memory of the first time I had experienced his passion hit. It was in the dhaba, just a few months ago. How did we ever arrive at this place? How could everything change in such a short time? A sense of remorse filled my heart as I recalled my practical mind telling my passionate one that no good could possibly come out of becoming involved with this man.

I willed my eyes to remain dry and my mind focused. There were too many people in the bagh who were watching him with as much fervor as he was addressing them. I needed to show strength and embody the way forward, not allow my fears to become a public spectacle.

"England is so powerful," Ayaz stated. "So powerful with its colonial web cast over the world. But when a power removes the rights of defenseless people, it shows their brutality. That is why the Mahatma begs us to take the course of peaceful resistance."

It was late in the afternoon, the sun dipping into the horizon. The brighter rays spread across the crowd just like Ayaz spread his words. Straining to avoid the orange glow from blinding me, I waved from the edge of the crowd, trying to catch his attention. But Ayaz was too focused.

I remembered his token of love. Surely, he would recognize it. I pulled out the red and green handkerchief from my sling bag and stretched out my arm. I waved it in circles, slowly. Its golden border glinting in the late afternoon sunshine caught Ayaz's eyes. He acknowledged my presence with a slight nod before returning to his speech.

"They consider *us* the terrorists. But if we fight, then we become the vandals and they become the law."

Ayaz glanced at me again, but with a faraway look, somewhat sad or disbelieving. As if he knew what I had come to say and that I was desperately looking for a way to say it. Maybe a figment of my imagination, but it appeared that way. I waited for an opportune to speak with him alone – a female in the crowd of male satyagrahis. Through his words to the crowds, it seemed that he was speaking directly to my soul.

"It's not only about the steps we take that mark our journey through life, but overcoming the obstacles we encounter along the way." Ayaz dropped his tone into a meditative thoughtfulness. "The Quran says that God gives us only as much trouble as we can handle. The Bhagavad Gita says we're kept from our goals not by obstacles, but by a clear path to a lesser goal. Our religions speak about this great obstacle course that we call life, and how each step marks a new victory in our ultimate journey."

It was the perfect soul-stirring invocation for the already impassioned crowd.

"Hindu-Mussalmaan ki jai," they roared in unison.

A strange buzzing echoed over our head. It grew louder, turning into a deafening whirl, drowning the shouts and cheers. A spotter plane was flying low. A wave of restlessness spread through the crowd.

"Haraamzaade! *Those bastards!*" someone yelled. "Are they sending warplanes now?"

"Oh my lord, it's an airstrike?!" another voice screamed.

I froze, my inner voice churning through the possibilities. Did the plane have bombs? If so, how many? Where could I hide? Where could anyone hide? What about Ayaz and these families? The ramblings of my inner voice was not making sense. People stood to leave. My chest tightened.

"My children!"

"My family!"

The plane gained height, disappearing into the clouds.

The audience was still yelling with a mixture of fear and amazement. Several had gathered their families, heading to the gate. Others stood rooted, wondering which way to run or to run at all. Ayaz paused for only a moment before commanding the attention of the audience.

"And so, in this journey to Home Rule, we must identify our obstacles," he said, raising his voice. "Recognize them. Analyze them and plan how we can *together* overcome them. Only then can we chart our course."

"Jai Hind!" the crowd rumbled in a delightful fury.

"Nothing can stop those who are resolute in their mission. No guns, no bombs, no warplanes."

"Jai Hind!" the audience repeated. Their zeal increasing with each cheer.

"Remember, Hindustan is not a nation-state. It is a civilization, a historical state, the land of our identity. In a world of democratic nations, of scientific advancement and modern political states, why should ours be left behind? Hindustan may not be a nation-state, but it is an idea for one."

"A nation-state where we are masters of our destiny!" someone in the crowd shouted.

"Indeed. For better or worse," Ayaz yelled. "We may not yet understand the best way to govern our people, but as with every obstacle, we learn to overcome."

"Let us falter," another voice stated. "Let us learn. Let us discover the best way forward."

Ayaz clasped his hands, rolling them in a descriptive gesture. "A talented runner will jump and cover more ground than you and I alone." He broke his clasp and held up an index finger. "But if we are to cover the vast terrain of life, then it takes not one runner to finish the race but an entire team."

"We are the relay team!" a voice stated.

"Yes!" Ayaz waved his finger. "Let us not look to one Gandhi-ji alone or the two Congress leaders who were taken away. Let us collect as a team. We need to chart this course together." He clasped his hands to signify unison.

"We shall overcome!" a man in the crowd shouted.

"We shall," Ayaz yelled. "But to do so, we need our sprinters back. Back from Dharamshala where they have been taken."

The crowd bellowed praises for the two Congress leaders. "Dr. Satyapal ki jai! Dr. Kitchlew ki jai!"

Thunderous applause followed, filling the air of Jallianwala Bagh with intrepid desire. The crowd becoming more and more obsessed by Ayaz's words. Although he saw the cheers as positive, I knew I needed to speak up before it was too late.

In the openness of that massive space, I felt confined. Not by the people but by their ideals. I glanced up at the sky. The blue between the white clouds gave me strength to keep pace with the crowd's emotions. A bottled-up claustrophobia throbbed from my chest.

"But even now, as we are gathering our sprinters, Colonel Dyer is gathering his own." I felt suddenly conscious of projecting my voice into a male congregation. "Purportedly, to stop us in our tracks."

Ayaz was obviously not expecting me to speak. He cast a slack-jawed look my way with an air of sadness and a resolute purpose. "Purportedly? Are we to act on rumors and suppositions? If so, we might not take our steps in the journey that lay ahead."

"But Dyer has issued a proclamation threatening to disperse agitators!"

Ayaz tossed up his hands, twisting his beard in that characteristic style. "How do you define an agitator? One who is simply agitated or one who agitates in peace for progress? This cause is not a cause if it is just one person's journey. Unity is known to be strength, my friends."

"Jai Hind!" the crowd roared.

I had to try again. I couldn't succumb to the whim of the people. "Dyer could be planning his attack right now. Even as we speak. Wouldn't it not be better if we dispersed immediately –"

"To hell with Colonel Dyer!" he yelled. "Who is *he* to plan anything? He is but a visitor just like the others you see in the bagh who have come to celebrate Baisakhi."

Ayaz's words felt like arrows shot directly into my heart. His hatred for Dyer and the Britishers, and for anything anti-Home Rule, trumped anything I had to say. He had the support of the people. Maybe I should have remained quiet. Perhaps it was better to be a *no-one*.

"They do not have the guts to fire on us," a man yelled. "And if they do, they will use only blanks. Just like what happened at Chandini Chowk in Delhi last month!"

Ayaz made fists and raised them to his shoulders. "Be it blanks or bullets, we must remain resolute."

His body had said it all. Any scope of negotiation was gone – finished – over. There was no way to stop him. Nor could anyone else. All his promises of love and freedom and a life together in Bombay, nothing more than lip service. I felt betrayed, as if Ayaz loved his cause more than he loved me. It was as if he had just chosen a different lover. A bitter sting of betrayal.

My advice to Amrita about choosing motherhood over wifehood to protect her son focused before me. I needed to do the same. To prioritize my responsibilities as a daughter over my love as a fiancée. Should anything happen to me, my mother would never survive on her own. Not after everything she had endured. I should not have come here in search of Ayaz. It was time for me to step back.

Where was Amrita and Gopal? I last saw them near the entrance. I looked around, hoping to lay my eyes on them.

But the pounding of heavy boots filled the air. A multitude of men marched forward two by two through the narrow entrance of the bagh and onto the field.

𝕮HAPTER 24

April 13, 1919

Amritsar - Colonel Dyer

Colonel Dyer had planned his attack down to the smallest detail. Months later during the countless times when I looked back to analyze the events of those moments, I often wondered whether he had a map of the bagh or had sent a scout on a quiet reconnaissance. So many had said so many things that no one actually knew.

Not a single soldier in his coterie was British. Later we would learn that the colonel avoided the use of British soldiers as he wanted to avoid blame. He also avoided using Punjabi soldiers to lessen the risk of self-reproach. An interestingly disingenuous strategy.

Twenty-five Gurkha soldiers and twenty-five Baluchis armed with rifles and another forty Gurkhas armed with khukries, were there to deal with the crowd. Two armored cars along with pickets waited outside the gate. The people seeking escape would not be able to pass even if they had wanted to. We were trapped.

"Aa gaye! Aa gaye!" I heard the people chant. "They have arrived."

Many stood as if wanting to leave.

"The British will never fire," a man stated. "Their rifles are only filled with blanks."

Colonel Dyer lined up his men in two firing parties, one on each side of the narrow entrance. An entrance that he now blocked. Twenty-five Gurkhas to the right and twenty-five Baluchis to the left, barely a hundred yards from the people.

"Gurkhas right, 59th left ... fire!"

The order was repeated by a British subaltern, Dyer's second-in-command.

The foot soldiers knelt, raised their rifles, took aim, and fired. A volley of bullets sped into the heart of the crowd gathered near the platform. One thousand, six-hundred and fifty bullets – thirty-three rounds per man were released within a matter of minutes. Without pause.

Against the backdrop of the sound, the bagh filled with a din – children cried, mothers screamed, fathers shouted desperately for help. The crowd dispersed, and everyone scattered as bullets exploded into the grass, the mud, and the people. My mind told me to run but my body tensed. I crouched on the ground, counting down the seconds, praying that the metal shower would stop. The rat-tat-tat pounded through my ears.

The people fell as the bullets hit. I didn't recognize anyone, just a deluge of humanity desperately seeking an escape to safety.

Those closer to the meeting stood, but had no means of escape. They perished instantly.

A group on the outskirts ran, desperate to flee. Three men raced to the walls to push their way through the few narrow exits. Many dashed helter-skelter across the yard. A smaller group gathered at the corners, hoisting each other up to scale the bricks. The family that had been sitting only a few feet away, now flung themselves into the well – children included – only to be hit with flying bullets. Others surged at the only entrance. The entrance where the troops stood. But they too fell and rolled as the bullets hit.

Claustrophobia rose fast and furious inside my tightening chest. Panic pounded throughout my veins. As the people moved, I did too. If my feet failed to keep up, I risked being trampled. The faces that surrounded me looked gaunt and serious. There was nothing for me to do but move with the crowd. The stench of fear saturated the air. I could smell it, smell it all – an unholy agglomeration of coconut oil, body sweat, and over-applied attar.

The crowd was moving too fast and many could not keep up, everyone unruly and panicking.

Which way do I go?

We were packed together, creating a river of human fluid. We were now a molecule, a flowing crowd, moving at a collective pace. Any space created by a discordant move instantly filled with the human liquid.

Where is Ayaz? Amrita and Gopal?

Falling rays from the incandescent sun whirled across my eyes. The walls of the bagh rotated around me. The ground slammed against my ribs, and my nails dug into the hardened soil. Something unfamiliar and metallic-tasting filled my mouth. Blood, I had bitten my lip for real. I glanced up as a wave of bullets pulverized a small group clustered in the center. Loud screams and wails filled my ears before growing silent.

A human wave pushed me to one side. I gasped, I was now standing on someone who was dead. Feeling helpless and frustrated, a flood of panic soared. I screamed. A hard blow shoved me to the ground, and again the air escaped my lungs. My vision blurred and a dark smoke burnt my eyes. Each time I tried to see, my head was slammed onto the hard dirt as others tried to escape. The painful tread of sandals trampling across my face sizzled. With daylight gone, the area felt superheated from the hysterical cries. I tried to take in a deep breath, but the pain running through my head held firm. Blood filled my eyes, my nose, and dirt gritted against my teeth.

Voices screamed, calling for help. Death never visited me like this before. I was living as others died. I lay quiet, watching as feet darted past, praying that no one would land on me. The guns continued to fire.

The people in the bagh were trapped.

Bodies piled up near the entrance. Others rushed over them in a desperate attempt to escape. Many slipped before being trampled. Skulls cracked. I closed my eyes and prayed, not wanting to see the liquid ooze and pool in the dirt. Most were killed instantly by the bullets. A few suffered before fading away. Many suffocated from the dead piling on top. Only a few survived, owing our lives to the protective shields of the fallen.

I screamed as the sound of bullets tore through the human flesh, only to claim another on the other side. I waited for my bullets to come. I prayed it would be quick and painless. Blood splattered my face and I closed my eyes. A body fell and rolled across my chest. He was heavy, so very heavy. I concentrated on the firing, that constant rat-tat-tat. A white haze spread, hovering over the field of the dead.

The kneeling soldiers fired with uncanny accuracy until their ammunition ran out. A deadly silence now floated just under the white haze. Colonel Dyer ordered them to withdraw. The men stood for only a moment before marching out the way they had come in. The sound of a car engine roared. Colonel Dyer was leaving the scene and the carnage behind.

These innocent people had arrived to celebrate Baisakhi – *playtime at the bagh* – just an afternoon with family and friends. A child crying grabbed my attention. Now pinned under a heavy man, I stared into the sky and watched as the clouds passed.

Playtime had an interesting connotation in India. It was the time to escape the stress of daily life. A time that was critical to personal freedom. The locals who had gathered in the bagh that day, *playtime* meant hopscotch or chess, dancing to the tunes of the dholki, celebrating Baisakhi with songs of the harvest, and marking the importance of personal freedoms. For Colonel Dyer, *playtime* was an opportunity to seize control with a game of live bullets.

Vermilion Harvest

Not once over the following years did the colonel consider his actions to be a murderous attack on defenseless people. Even though he had no idea who they were, he had convinced himself that those assembled were guilty of treason to the crown.

To Colonel Dyer it was a war – not to mention, he wanted to teach *them* a lesson.

CHAPTER 25

April 13, 1919

Amritsar - the massacre

The mud walls of Jallianwala Bagh towered around me, but the walls of my world had tumbled.

I was partially buried under a blanket of the dead. It felt like an eternity. Pressure on all sides gave me reason to pause. An elbow or knee or fingers or a back or a head. I concentrated on what was digging into my sides, my hips. My arms and legs were pinned. No one but me was moving. My chest heaved – the air stale, almost rust-like.

I closed my eyes, taking short quick breaths. The air felt thick with the rusty bite of blood, a murky wetness filling my eyes that I couldn't wipe away. I was teetering on a razor's edge between life and death. Unprepared to die, I prayed. So many unfinished things. My position at the school, my responsibilities to Ma, Amrita –

Where are Amrita and Gopal?

My life with Ayaz –

Vermilion Harvest

Oh my god … no … Ayaz!

I never planned to fall in love with him. That first day we met, all I wanted was to find a dry place out of the rain. But that was him, my relief from the storm. Life never turned out as we planned. Things we were meant to do – the things we did do when our hearts led us astray. Life presented me with Ayaz. Life presented me with the chaos of Jallianwala Bagh.

My body jolted, as if my heart was in my throat, beating faster and faster. Now, it skipped a beat. My breathing labored. My fingers and toes felt tingly, weird random pain shot through my insides.

Is this death?

I gasped for air. For more light. A soft whiff of fresh air. A hole, a gap between the bodies that were piled on top. I wiggled toward the gap and toward those white puffy clouds. More and more, I pushed myself to those clouds. One arm broke free, then the other. I wriggled and wiggled and inched to the top. The people were heavy – a dead weight, but soft at the same time. Blood, blood everywhere and sticky. I stared into the eyes of a satyagrahis who was now dead. A large hole in his chest. Our eyes locked in a magnetic embrace for he was gone, his eyes searching after the trail his soul had taken into those white puffy clouds. My stomach churned with the foul and unpleasant stench of human blood.

The bodies lay lifeless around me. Heads cracked open, eyes missing, blood and brains staining their clothes – broken arms and legs, bodies with their chests missing. A rush of nausea hit and I held my breath. My heart raced with the pressure that was building.

I pulled and pulled, inching myself out from under the bodies. Crawling across the dead, I sighed when my hands touched the Earth, warm with an eerie feeling of being safe. Slowly, I stood, my legs wobbly and unsteady.

Jallianwala Bagh reminded me of a deserted battlefield. Bodies everywhere, blood now creating thick rivers, flowing into ponds that reflected the moonlight.

The rat-tat-tat still echoed through my ears, sending chills down my spine. Taking in a deep breath, I grabbed my chest. The stench of freshly slaughtered humans filled me with an ungodly feeling of dread.

My eyes locked onto a man who had tried to jump into the well. His body now dangled, his feet still touching the dirt. I glanced inside and his head was missing.

"My god! Can anyone hear me?" I yelled.

All remained quiet.

"Anyone need help?" I screamed. "Anyone alive?"

My eyes followed a shallow river of red to a pile taller than me. Those who had tried to climb the wall. All men, their arms and legs entwined as if hugging before their spirits left this world.

More and more I counted. A few were breathing but just barely. Most lay lifeless. Arms and legs ripped by the bullets, their bones shining in the haze-lit night.

So many humans – all in pieces. A lung over here, a piece of intestine over there, part of an arm with the hand attached, a jaw, eyes, body parts now spread out as if set up for a display – a demonic display.

I walked through the piles of human flesh, following the thin bloody rivers that flowed freely into pools. My eyes scanned across the crowd that now remained silent, quiet as Colonel Dyer had ordered. A body of a man with his black cap to the side grabbed my attention. He was wearing a white kurta now stained crimson, his arm reaching out to me. The undeniable fist clutching his fingers with his thumb curled.

Ayaz? Ayaz!

I touched the gold aum and crescent moon pendant hanging from my neck. It pressed hot against my skin. Each breath seared as if the world was on fire. My mind blank.

Ayaz was fine just a few moments ago. He was standing here on the Earth-made podium talking with fervid passion. He was fine just a day ago when he gave me this chain as a promise of our future in Bombay. He was fine just weeks ago, making love to me in the shadowy glen of Rambagh. The pendant from his grandmother, he was supposed to tell me the rest of the story. He promised to tell me the history behind it.

"No! No!"

I fell to my knees beside him, locking my eyes to his.

He promised he would fight. He promised!

I pounded on the dry dirt with a tightened fist. My teeth clenched. My hand reached for his. I tried to release his strong grip, but the fingers refused to move.

"Ayaz!" I whispered and my tears fell.

With the help of the dim moon, my eyes slowly followed the contours of his lifeless form. His gaze staring directly into my soul, penetrating deep, cutting deep. His soul had been ripped from his mortal remains. My heart pounded violently. I wanted to scream, but couldn't. As if watching a bad dream, I inched closer to his lifeless body. My hands and body shook.

I studied his wounds. He had been shot in the legs and chest. An ear was missing, but his eyes were wide, staring into the sky. I massaged his feet and his hands, over and over again, praying that by some twist of fate, he would respond.

My thoughts flew back to when I saw Ayaz at Pritam Da Dhaba, and when our eyes first locked. Within one swoop, my meaning for life had come full circle. Ayaz could not look away. He smiled at me, curling his fingers around his thumb.

Two days ago, Ayaz had said, "You can survive, Aruna. That is all I want for you. You do not need me. You can find your own way, with your own strength. My jaan, be brave."

I allowed jealousy to guide, sealing my decision to leave him. But for what reason? Because he stood for a cause? Why did I allow my self-esteem to be wrecked by an imaginary rival of his desire for a better world?

"I am, Ayaz," I whispered. I raised his head, tenderly, resting it on my knees, the pendant waving through the moonlight. "I was about me ... not a better world."

I waited for a response from his soul. Anything that would signify he was still there. All remained quiet before a glimmer of moonlight burst through the moving clouds. The colors resembled the chariot of the Hindu Lord Indra breaking through the horizon on his journey across the skies. Or maybe it was Ayaz on his journey home to the heavens.

Yes, it is you, Ayaz. You are answering my call.

It was what I needed to understand that this was his *namaste*. His soul illuminating across the horizon as a sign for me to be strong. He was gone. Never to return. I screamed as my soul bled, ripping through my heart. The tears fell. I bent over and kissed his forehead, softly, as I closed his eyes.

"Sleep, my love, sleep," I whispered.

Who knows how long I sat there, rocking Ayaz in my lap, begging his soul to touch mine. I whispered my devotion to him through my tears. The shock and grief grew from somewhere deep inside. No pain, my body and soul now numb. My tears were all I had left of him.

It was strange to think of my tears as a companion, yet how else would I refer to something that had helped me walk past this difficult moment? A companionship that would follow me for the rest of my life. My tears keeping my soul alive as I traversed through the hell the Britishers just provided.

"Maaa!" a young boy's voice yelled out. He sounded about twelve years old, maybe thirteen. He was hunched over the body of a woman, pounding his fist against her chest and wailing into her spiritless face.

My mind flew to Amrita. Where was she? What had become of Gurcharan Singh and Gopal? As if by divine intervention and through the maze of cries and confused voices, I heard a softer voice.

"Aruna, Aruna!"

I stared in the direction of the sound.

"Aruna! I am here …"

Amrita's voice! Her small body looked crushed and crumpled. She was covered in blood not far from the well.

I crawled to her, mustering the will to stop crying. Our fingers touched, she sighed, loudly.

Amrita drifted in and out of consciousness. Her eyes fluttering as if dreaming. "Jeeo-ji ..." she whispered, "... into the darkness. I must not leave him in the bagh." She was badly injured from trampling feet. Each breath brought another wave of pain.

"Amrita, shh ... where is Gopal?"

She pointed a shaking finger at the well. "There." Her voice trembled. "G...G...Gopal ..."

"In the well?!"

"Gopal ..." Amrita breathed out his name as her spirit followed the others into the clouds. Her arm dropped and her eyes fluttered once before closing.

A deep silence drenched the static that sizzled inside my head. My friend had just left this world. The warmth of her life stolen by the cold embrace of death.

The bagh twirled around me, my soul feeling the emptiness. I stared at Amrita repeating his name – "Gopal?"

I stared at the well, dreading to find his little body. Doubt ran through my mind and my vision blurred as a teary-eyed little boy peeped around the bullet-riddled bricks, and my heart gave a long, lasting sigh.

𝕮HAPTER 26

April 13, 1919

Amritsar - unofficial figures

According to the official figures, three hundred, seventy-nine were killed that day, and some twelve thousand wounded. The Congress tally placed the final numbers at a thousand. The unofficial tally set the number of casualties well over ten thousand. I bought into the unofficial tally, as did anyone who had been at the bagh. How could I not? I had seen twenty to thirty thousand gather that day. I had seen the Baluchis and Gurkhas open fire for over ten-minutes. I heard the rat-tat-tat of the bullets.

In November that same year, the British government established the Hunter Commission to inquire into the events of the massacre. In the days, months, and years that followed, I spent countless hours poring over the reports in a futile attempt to make sense of Colonel Dyer's orders. Despite the evidence, they were nothing short of puzzling.

```
Hunter Commission:
When you got into the bagh, what did you
do?

Colonel Dyer:
I opened fire.

Hunter Commission:
At once?

Colonel Dyer:
Immediately. I had thought about the
matter and doubt it took me more than
thirty seconds to make up my mind as to
what my duty was.
```

Thirty seconds? Was this the amount of time it took a colonel to make the decision to open fire on a crowd of thousands gathered for *playtime at the bagh* during their harvest festival? Without any warning? Or was this a premeditated strategy that he had conveniently omitted to mention during the Hunter Commission inquiry?

```
Hunter Commission:
As regard to the crowd, what was it
doing?

Colonel Dyer:
They were holding a meeting. There was a
man in the center standing on something
that was raised. His hands were moving
about. He was addressing the gathering.
He was in the center of the square, as
far as I could judge. I should say some
fifty or sixty yards from where my
troops were drawn.
```

Vermilion Harvest

Barely fifty or sixty yards. *Ayaz!* It had to have been Ayaz he was talking about. My Ayaz, who I had given up on those last few moments before I heard the sound of soldiers' boots marching in unison through the bagh. My Ayaz was Colonel Dyer's bullseye.

As contentious as the firing was, it was the fact that Colonel Dyer did not attend to the wounded but left them to suffer. Those who were unable to escape lay in the open for nearly two days, gradually dying. Most of the survivors kept their presence in the bagh a secret as they feared arrest should the truth be told.

Nonchalantly, Colonel Dyer explained to the Hunter Committee that hospitals were open to the wounded as long as they made the effort to get there.

```
Colonel Dyer:
The wounded only had to apply for help.
But they did not do this because they
themselves would be in custody for being
in the assembly.
```

Colonel Dyer never considered his act that afternoon as murder on the vulnerable. He explained to the Hunter Commission that he considered his actions as a matter of duty.

```
Hunter Commission:
I take it that your idea in taking
action was to strike terror?

Colonel Dyer:
Call it what you like, I was going to
punish them. My idea from the military
point of view was to make a wide
impression.
```

```
Hunter Commission:
To strike terror not only in the city of
Amritsar but throughout the Punjab?

Colonel Dyer:
Yes, throughout the Punjab. I wanted to
reduce their morale … the morale of the
rebels.

Hunter Commission:
Did it occur to you that by adopting
this method of frightfulness, you were
doing a great disservice to the British
Raj by driving discontent deep?

Colonel Dyer:
No. It was my duty to fire, and any man,
any reasonable man with a sense of
justice, would understand that I was
conducting a merciful act. They ought to
be thankful for me doing it. I thought
it would do a jolly lot of good to the
British people. My purpose was to strike
terror into the whole of the Punjab.
```

And he did strike terror into the whole of the Punjab. He proved to us how easy it was to kill. If you were Punjabi – to be killed – and how fast one could die.

Colonel Dyer was ultimately forced to resign from the British military, but despicable irony rests in the fact that he became a hero to many Britishers for his actions of that afternoon.

CHAPTER 27

April 16, 1919

Amritsar - chappals

The bullets fired on the people in the bagh that day, some suffered wounds that would never show, yet left deep scars. Wounds that cut so deep that in a moment of wakefulness, one felt like they were disappearing only to realize they didn't want to be alive anymore. Every hour of each day after the incident, I was living a nightmare from which I would never awake. My only solace, my only escape was to sleep, a dream state where my pain would disappear and I could spent time with Ayaz.

I was a wandering lost soul. Lost in a bleak wasteland where I couldn't recognize life. I had convinced myself that finding my way back to normalcy was just a matter of time. Then night would fall and I had no idea where I was or where I was going. I had bewildered myself into a world where the sun never rose.

The events of April 13, 1919 changed my life. In the days leading up to it, I often wondered how I would respond to an incident should one actually take place. One part of me was relieved I didn't shy away. I stepped up to the front lines to help. The other part of me was left wondering what would have happened had I gotten to them earlier. Would I have been able to stop Ayaz? Would he have listened to me? I couldn't help but think that in some way, even though I'd been with Ayaz, he was never truly mine. That eventually, I would have lost him anyway.

I didn't emerge from my bedroom for several days after the massacre. Seeing people seemed grimmer than a death curse. I just wanted to lie under the covers, shrouded by my misery.

"Don't give in to it," Ma pleaded from outside my door. "Social isolation will only trigger sadness. You have to shake yourself out before you get too deep. Because that's the thing about depression. When you feel it most, you won't want to let go. It becomes a comfort."

She should know, she'd suffered enough in her life. She was right, I wanted to cloak under the heavy weight of depression. I wanted to nurture it, cultivate it, and drift asleep in its arms.

"Keep the faith, Aruna ..." Ma stated, "... there are others to think about."

Gopal.

The thought of what that young boy was experiencing pulled me from my sadness. It was not just my life that had changed. He had lost family members, friends, and loved ones.

Vermilion Harvest

Even though we never saw Gurcharan Singh again, he was identified as a casualty when an official count was taken. Eventually, they would find his body at the bottom of a heap of other bodies. No bullets, he'd died of suffocation.

Amrita – Gurcharan Singh – Ayaz. Three different funerals to organize, arrange, and invite extended families.

There was still the question of Gopal, an orphaned child. It was clear when Gurcharan Singh's aged mother arrived in Amritsar for the cremation that the burden of another child was not something she was prepared to deal with. Gopal would remain with me – become a member of my family.

And although this four-year-old cried for his mother, he adapted to his new life almost instantly. The old ways soon became a component of his memories, sinking into the quicksand of his subconscious mind.

Gopal was curious about his parents. After the incident, his innocent mind could not compute they were gone for good. To him, it was as though they had disappeared for an afternoon outing, only to return shortly.

We walked through Jallianwala Bagh together a week or so after the massacre. I expected the area to be cordoned off, but we could come and go like any other day. Except on this one, our entry was marked with the complex aroma of blood and suffering. It was strange to be back in a place that had been so ravaged just days earlier. I hadn't been fearful as a child, but I couldn't help thinking that this place would remain the basis of my future nightmares. The dead were gone, but their slippers were strewn across the open ground.

"Oh my gosh, itne saare chappal!" Gopal said, clutching my hand as he eyed the thousands of ownerless slippers.

"Yes, Gopal, it's hard to believe there were this many people here." I smiled.

We wound our way through the bagh, and I thought about how different things had been just a few days ago when I fell over the dead, scores of dead. I stumbled at the thought, hit by a creepy sensation. Sadness pulsated through my veins. I clutched Gopal's hand as we made it to the well where he had hidden. Its walls were lined with slippers – red ones, blue ones, and green ones – rubber flip-flops, brown kolhapuris, gold threaded mojris.

"I remember the people," he whispered. "We came here to celebrate Baisakhi. But, Aunty Aruna, I don't remember all these chappals."

"It's true, Gopal. When you look at people, you remember their clothes, their hairstyles, their jewelry. You never look to see what they are wearing on their feet."

"I do now," Gopal replied. "That's how I can tell who they are."

"I don't understand?"

"My mumma always wears green chappals when she goes out, and my papa wears brown mojris."

I thought about it. Yes, indeed they did. Gopal was correct. "Perhaps people are defined by their footwear?"

"Why did they leave their chappals here?" he asked.

I thought about how to explain to the mind of a four-year-old. "These people have all gone to Bhagavan-ji's home. They don't need chappals there."

Gopal cocked his head to one side at the mention of God's home. It was a concept he was familiar with, conversations with his parents. "But they still need chappals to walk to Bhagavan-ji's house. It's a long way away, isn't it?"

I sighed. "Perhaps long for some but short for others."

"But not long for everyone?"

"Who told you that, Gopal?"

"Mumma. She said that from the moment you are born, you start your journey to Bhagavan-ji ka ghar. Such a long journey can take all your life. So ... how are all these people going to get there without their chappals?"

"They are already there, Gopal. In Bhagavan-ji's house, we do not wear chappals." I smiled.

"Is it like the gurudwara where you are not allowed to wear shoes?"

"Exactly, Gopal, exactly." I sighed. "But with a slight difference. God's home is about roaming free. Ayaz, Mumma, and Pappa are walking barefoot in the divine gardens, the Earth undulating under their feet."

Gopal's eyes lit at the thought of the gurudwara. "Mumma and Papa must be very happy. They love the kada prasad served at the langar on Sundays. Do you think Bhagavan-ji will give them their favorite kada prasad?"

"I'm sure he will." I smiled again. The innocence of the four-year-old warmed my heart. "In fact, I'm positive he will."

"It's not fair. I like kada prasad too."

Oh, my dear Gopal, you will have plenty of kada prasad. I allowed the thought to run through my mind. Ma and I would make sure of that.

As the afternoon sun shone through a rift in the clouds, its rays illuminated the young boy's smile. Gopal looked as if a divine angel was holding him with invisible hands. It was Amrita, his mother, accompanied by Gurcharan Singh no doubt. The thought sent a chill of energy through my veins. I glanced up at the sun and couldn't help noticing how its rays blinded my vision like Ayaz – *where did he go?* It had only been a few weeks, but it seemed like forever since he left.

Gopal's high-pitched voice broke my train of thought. "When will Mumma and Papa come visit?"

How was I to break the truth to this dear little boy? "My dear little Gopal, they will not visit us."

"Yes, they will. Even if they are happy up there, I am sure they'll come to visit. In fact, I am certain. I'll show you."

Gopal ran to the wall and stopped in front of a pile of slippers. He walked around the pile, scrutinizing each pair. He ran his fingers along the heap, searching intently as though on a mission.

"What are you doing, Gopal?" I asked.

"I'm looking."

"For what?"

"For Mumma and Papa's chappals."

"Gopal …"

But he refused to listen. And I understood that in his four-year-old mind, this was his way of having closure. I stepped back and allowed him to search. Not finding what he wanted, Gopal ran into the open area of the bagh to scrutinize the scores of the slippers that were scattered across the grass.

"What did you find?" I finally asked.

"Nothing. They're gone."

"Their chappals?"

He nodded. He lifted a finger to his chin and tilted his head. "That means Mumma and Papa really did go to Bhagavan-ji's house! They obviously had to wear them during the journey."

My head felt heavy, and my heart sunk deeper into my chest. I forced a smile. "Yes, Gopal, it does."

"And it means they will come back to visit!"

"How do you figure that?"

"Because they can't walk barefoot on dirty, dusty roads. They took their chappals because they knew they would need to wear them to come and visit me. I'm sure of it!"

I looked up and noticed a young woman sitting on a stack of bricks by the well. She was attired in a pink salwar kameez, her dupatta covering her head. My body did a double take as I watched her clutch a pair of chappals to her breasts.

Amrita?!

Of course it was not her. It could have been anyone – a wife or sister lamenting the loss of a loved one. The woman sat silently, crouching with profound sadness, a dark fatigue engraved on her face. Her eyes devoid of expression, her persona lacked energy, and though I could see her sitting there, she really was somewhere else.

She could have been another kind of mourner on a different day in history. She could have been my mother moments after her rape many years ago in Jallianwala Bagh.

Sadness inched through me, deadening my thoughts. My other emotions fought for space. A black mist settled upon me and refused to shift. No matter how bright the sun, I could not feel its warmth. I could not hear the birds. My world had lost that luster, that flicker of hope. I had to leave this morbid place.

"Gopal, do you think we should go home now?" I asked.

"Okay …" His childlike simplicity was refreshing. "I have a question."

"Yes?" I asked.

"Is there playtime in Bhagavan-ji's house?"

"Playtime?"

"Yes, playtime. Mumma and Papa always say that playtime is important for health and happiness. That's why we come to the bagh."

"Gopal, your Mumma and Papa are right. Playtime is important. I have no doubt they will have their share of it in Bhagavan-ji's house."

"In a bagh?"

"I'm sorry?"

"Is there a bagh? Because if there is no bagh in Bhagavan-ji's house, then where will they play?"

"There is one, there is one indeed. A big bagh, a beautiful bagh. So much more beautiful than this one. It's filled with flowers and green trees and happy people playing langdi and hopscotch and all sorts of games. And no one wears chappals."

"When do they play?"

"Throughout the day."

"All day?"

"That's right, because in Bhagavan-ji's house, it's always playtime at the bagh."

ᎧHAPTER 28

later in 1919

Amritsar – life after

The incident that took place on April 13, 1919 in Jallianwala Bagh inflamed the anger of all Indians. Of those killed, roughly half were Hindu, a third Sikh, and a fifth Muslim.

The survivors tell of the pain they endured as they experienced the loss – their way of life, their feelings of abandonment. Many thought of the massacre as a systematic process that was designed to dehumanize and kill.

"Why?" A question asked many times, including today.

After the incident, Colonel Dyer said he ordered his troops to fire to teach Indians a lesson, adding fuel to the fire. There were widespread protests throughout the country.

Rabindranath Tagore wrote a letter to the British administration, renouncing his knighthood in protest. Nationalist leaders condemned this shameful act.

Martial law was declared in Punjab for about two months after the shooting. It was Colonel Dyer's reign of terror inflicting inhuman cruelties that stemmed the rising tide of protest. People were tortured and newspapers banned. Individual punishment orders included flogging, making prisoners rub their noses in the dirt, forced marches, and bomb threats. People were housed in cages or evicted from their homes – all with no reason given.

However, this only strengthened the Indian people's determination to fight against the oppression.

In November of 1919, the hearings of the Hunter Commission took place in Lahore. Although Colonel Dyer appeared in person to defend himself, the commission's conclusions were damning. Colonel Dyer's actions were condemned on two counts – that he had opened fire without warning and that he continued to fire even after the crowd tried to disperse.

However, the British members of the Hunter Commission thought it was *'distinctly improbable that the crowd would have dispersed without being fired on.'* The Indians disagreed with this opinion, describing Colonel Dyer's conduct *'as inhuman and un-British and as having caused great disservice to British rule in India.'* The British members of the Hunter Commission rejected the official stand that his action had *'saved the situation in the Punjab and averted a rebellion on a scale similar to the mutiny of 1857.'*

Faced with both reports, the Viceroy of India, Frederic Thesiger, 1st Viscount Chelmsford, conceded that Colonel

Dyer had '*acted beyond the necessity of the case, beyond what any reasonable man should have thought to be necessary, and that he did not act with as much humanity as the case permitted.*'

In March 1922, the Rowlatt Act and twenty-two other acts were repealed by the government. Colonel Dyer was strongly censured and forced to resign from the military and return to England in disgrace.

In England, however, opinions were divided between those who agreed with the verdict and those who lauded Colonel Dyer's actions. Some held the view that Colonel Dyer was a hero and his *bloody firing* had saved the British Raj in India.

The episode soured relations between British and Indian politicians for years. It became a turning point in the history of India's struggle for freedom, helping to gather recruits to Mahatma Gandhi's policy of non-violent resistance to British rule.

Colonel Dyer died in England in 1927.

Michael O'Dwyer, former Lieutenant-Governor of Punjab, was assassinated in 1940 by Shaheed Udham Singh, a Punjabi revolutionary who, as a young child, was an eyewitness to the Jallianwala Bagh massacre.

Just over a hundred years later, the Jallianwala Bagh massacre remained one of the most horrific and heartbreaking episodes in the history of the Indian struggle for freedom.

CHAPTER 29

August 14, 1947

Bombay — just a memory

I run my fingers over the ivory-white envelope in my hands, desperate to uncover its contents, petrified of what the words might reveal. There was a reason she kept this envelope from me all these years, hidden under the newspaper lining of the third compartment of the almirah. The newspaper protected the clothes from insects, hiding inside, she had said so just days before.

I have always wondered why she talked about newspapers lining the compartments of the armoire. I passed off her words as old-age senility. Today, however, it makes perfect sense. The paper served as a cover for the secrets that were hidden underneath. In an Indian household, the most treasured possessions are usually found under old newspapers.

The time has come to discover why – hours after she was freed from the bondage of her failing human body and only hours before India is born to freedom.

Vermilion Harvest

India – on the eve of independence – and on the eve of the partition into two nations, into two Punjab's – one Hindu – the other Muslim. Outside my window, the careless whispers of those on the street – partly of fury, partly of sadness.

"I come from Hamid's home," one voice says. "He was listening to his radio. The news ... it is too much to take in."

"I received a letter from my village yesterday," the other voice replies. "The words I read have left me shattered. I worry about my people there."

"Our village has people who want to cross the border. They heard of the act. They knew they were on the wrong side," the first voice states. "One of the women, she lived around the corner from us ... only parts of her body were found. She was a fixture of my childhood, giving me lassi every day when I came home from school. I called her KHaala-zaad-bahan. I haven't been able to sleep since I heard of this incident."

"What has this country done to itself?" the second voice asks.

What has this country done to itself?

The Partition of India Act of 1947 has triggered the most unspeakable communal riots, and one of the most massive migrations that mankind has ever experienced. Millions have found themselves living in the wrong country. With the events that followed, it has made one think, was this a genocide on a scale not found in the history books?

Every day, the radio delivers a new narration of the line of division – properties burned, people evicted from their homes they were born in, or murdered in the most brutal of ways, train compartments after train compartments arriving from Punjab with nothing but dead bodies. Not Punjab – I cannot refer to it so loosely anymore. What I mean is – that part of Punjab, which just this morning was introduced to the world as Pakistan.

Here in Bombay, we are away from the division, yet on the streets just outside my window, Hindus and Muslims are declaring war on each other. One set of people with two sets of gods clawing each other in the name of freedom. Such is the price we pay for the freedom that Ayaz Peermohammed, my twin flame, gave his life for. A blessing he did not live to see.

Ayaz Peermohammed – gone some twenty-eight years. Ma – gone for barely twenty-eight hours. Once again, I'm trapped by a sense of loneliness. The irony hits and I laugh.

I grab the edge of the wooden bedpost, and the ivory-envelope floats to the floor. I sit at the edge of the neatly folded sheets, near the footrest. My legs dangle over the side almost a foot above the floor. The mirror reflects the evening sunlight, shining a halo around my mother's comb and cosmetics. A message from her soul, reminding me to open the secret she had left.

Tears blur my vision as I step down and pick up the envelope still resplendent with the aroma of her perfume. As if she had only just finished writing it moments ago, I trace the spelling of my name in the distinct cursive of my mother. Turning it over, I lift the flap and remove the letter.

She is in the room now. Firm yet loving, speaking to me as though she never left. I hold her letter, my fingers tremble and tears fall.

Vermilion Harvest

My dearest Aruna,

It is with much apprehension that I write this letter, perhaps more that you read it. There are things about my past you must know. My intention was to tell you, but I never found the courage. I am still tortured from the memory. But it is time you know the truth.

Assault is hostile, but for us, it proved to be bittersweet. You were the result of an assault on me all those years ago. And though the event stripped me of my dignity and respect, it brought you to me. You were the gift I yearned for. What a Hindu marriage could not bring, an untoward encounter with a British officer provided.

You too were blessed with a child who was the victim of an assault. Gopal lost his parents, but he gained a mother who loves and cares for him.

Assault is a funny thing. With one hand, it strips and with the other it gives.

We witnessed our great nation surrendering to an assault by colonial masters. They despoiled our people and *pillaged our lands. You have a sixth sense about these assaults, and it wrecks me to think how you were out there before the event trying to warn everyone.*

All these years, I held back from telling you the truth about your father. Truth can be hard to accept, and I could not cause you more pain. From a young age, you were living a nightmare, constrained by the thought of where society might place you should they learn the truth about your Anglo-Indian identity. You were unable to be free. Free to love.

My attention is broken by the sound of Pandit Jawaharlal Nehru's elocution-perfect voice blaring through the static of my Murphy radio. Moments before he had taken the oath of the first Prime Minister of independent India, his Cambridge schooled accent sounding more British than that of the average Britisher.

"Long years ago, we made a Tryst with Destiny."

The moment to enact that tryst has finally arrived. But did we truly choose to make this tryst? Freedom from the British rule is supposed to be a new ray of hope, yet what kind of tryst leads to a destiny of mass murder, rape, and arson?

Vermilion Harvest

As Pandit-ji's speech draws to a close, the muffled sounds of people walking the streets of Bombay shouting "Swaraj!" flow through my window.

Swaraj ... freedom.

Our freedom will finally become a reality. All thanks to the choices that people like Ayaz made all those years ago.

Ayaz Peermohammed! My twin flame.

The day he walked into my life was the day I discovered the value of freedom. Back then, though constricted by the rules of society while in Ayaz's arms, I was freer than ever before. Yet, today, I am still imprisoned by grief and loneliness.

When it comes to impending danger, indeed as my mother said, I have a sixth sense about these things. Even twenty-eight years ago, even if I was just a voice lost in the crowd.

As the speech draws to a close, the radio commentator analyzes Pandit Nehru's words. "To understand the horrendous events of this year, leading up to this impending moment of freedom, we must look back to 1942 when Mahatma Gandhi gave the call for *Quit India* and do or die.'"

But I think it goes farther back than that. Back to 1919, when Mahatma Gandhi gave the call for Satyagraha. I was just eighteen when we decided that freedom was a choice.

Our choice.

As the sunlight fades, my mind wanders to that fateful day in March of 1919 when the Rowlatt Act was alive and choice was but a distant dream.

An aspiration.

It was March 10th to be precise. The Defence of India Act, also known as the Defence of India Regulations Act or DORA, was an emergency criminal law enacted by the Governor-General of India in 1915. The intention was to curtail the nationalist and revolutionary activities during and in the aftermath of the First World War.

Similar to the British Defence of the Realm Acts, it granted the Executive very wide powers of preventive detention, internment without trial, and restrictions on writing, speech, and movement. However, unlike the English law, which was limited to persons of hostile associations or origin, the Defence of India Act could be applied to any subject of the King.

But from the time it had become a bill earlier that year, it was used to an overwhelming extent against us, the people of India. Anything a person said, did, or read could be taken out of context and deemed to be hostile against the Empire, which meant plotting against the King.

On March 10th, 1919, the Imperial Legislative Council in Delhi extended DORA into the Anarchical and Revolutionary Crimes Act, popularly known as the Rowlatt Act. However, we referred to it as the Black Act. Although the act was introduced as the Empire's method of responding to the agitation, we locals regarded it with alarm, bordering on panic. Indeed, the war was over, but peace was nowhere in sight.

Outside my window, the scene shifts from harrowed locals worried about riots in their village to re-sellers on the streets of Bombay, celebrating the freedom that would be theirs at the stroke of midnight.

Vermilion Harvest

That gruesome day in Jallianwala Bagh back in 1919 was a day on which our communities stood together – Hindu, Sikh, and Muslim – united as they single-mindedly dreamt of a free India. Not just on the day of April 13th, but on all the days leading up to it, including the cast of characters in my own life – Ayaz Peermohammed, Amrita and Gurcharan Singh. Tonight, India will be born to freedom, but it will also be divided, despite the sacrifices of those who stood united in that dream of freedom. Will they be happy today, celebrating the realization of that dream? Or will they say we were let down by everything that freedom promised?

I clutch the pendant that still hangs around my neck since the day that Ayaz fastened its clasp all those years ago. I later learned of its history from Ayaz's mother – how it belonged to her mother, also a Hindu who eloped as a young girl with a Mussalmaan, breaking the boundaries of societal norms. The couple had a jeweler craft the pendant as a symbol of their love and as their mangalsutra, the sacred thread symbolizing marriage worn by a Hindu bride until her husband's death. In our story, the mangalsutra was worn by a bride only after her betrothed's death. How ironic was the course of human history?

In many ways, I am glad that Ayaz did not live to see this day. The day that Lahore, his birthplace and home, is ripped from Amritsar, my birthplace and home. Two pieces of the Punjab, born from a common motherland, yet doomed to stay apart forever.

With a heavy sigh, I turn my attention back to the ivory-white letter.

Winston Churchill had said it was an appalling act and berated Colonel Dyer as a monster. You asked me if people suffer for the sins they commit. Colonel Dyer had a stroke and died in 1927. I heard that as he lay on his death bed, he said he wanted to meet his Maker to see if He approved of his actions. Maybe he suffered.

I look up from the letter. Why is she referring to all *his* actions? Or is it just the one pertaining to Jallianwala Bagh?

This brings me to the main point of this letter, and why I kept a secret all these years.

Your life was spent without a father. Fathers are a fundamental pillar to a young child. Growing up without a father was not easy for you. And I am sorry.

Perhaps holding the truth was not the right thing to do. Perhaps I should have said something earlier. In a parallel universe, you would have known, and who knows what action you might have taken. Knowing your personality, you may have charted a different course. Or maybe you would have resented me. I do not know. I thought long and hard, wondering how to make the right decision. It is difficult to be a good parent. So much is figuring out what is right and surviving the times we fail.

The bitter truth I must share with you now is that your father was that self-same perpetrator of the assault. It was another day at the same Jallianwala Bagh nineteen years before the incident. I remember the torment he placed upon me, and his scornful accusation of my unwillingness to play.

As I said, my child, assault proved to be bittersweet.

I cursed myself that I could not find the courage to speak about this. How could I? You were the one flower that bloomed in my life of adversity.

You faced so much adversity that I wanted to protect you from this secret for as long as I could. But this burden I must now share. This truth, although it might hurt, it will set you free. For it is the flower that blooms in adversity, that is the most rare and beautiful of all that survives.

The sounds outside resemble parrots set free from their cages. The bugles and shrill tones of whistling, the fireworks, and street illuminations give me hope. People hand out sweets and wave tricolor flags. For generations, we were a subjugated people, and now, we are being thrown off the yoke.

I look at my mother's letter. I had always known that my biological father was somehow connected to the British army. It was why he had taken pity on my mother, giving her lodgings on the outskirts of Amritsar's cantonment. But when she referred to my father as *that self-same perpetrator of the assault*, is this a metaphor for all British soldiers or could she be referring to Colonel Dyer?

No, it couldn't be. Or could it? Why had she kept the truth from me all of these years? I think back to those days leading up to that horrible afternoon in Jallianwala Bagh. About all those who dreamed of a free India – Ayaz, Gurcharan Singh, Amrita, and the thousands gunned down. The massacre proved to be an important breaking point. The younger generation had lost its faith in the Raj, and the freedom movement was born.

My brain stutters for a moment and my eyes take in more light from the window. I pause while my thoughts catch up. I understand, nearly thirty years later, why my mother had a problem with the concept of *play*. Why she never allowed me out as a child, and why the reference to *playtime* undeniably made her flinch.

Yes, the assault had been bittersweet.

Vermilion Harvest

And Colonel Dyer, the man at the center, had always been the bogeyman of my young life. Now, he will forever become engrained as the bogeyman of my existence.

Colonel Dyer?

For a moment, I am unable to think, sitting stunned as the name bounces inside my head. For a moment my mind paints a picture I have not seen in twenty-eight years. Two blades of wild grass separated by a cobra, rearing its spread hood, ready to strike. But then, in a matter of moments, the vision is altered. The cobra retreats, the slithering dissipates. What remains are blades of wild grass swaying innocently in a gentle breeze.

The life I have built in Bombay over the last twenty-eight years is living proof that we do not inherit the sins of our fathers. A gentle peace pervades my soul that comes from learning that to give is to receive. Love has shown me the way to stability and beauty. It has come when those who were traumatized were given a chance to breathe and heal, to regain their culture and rebuild their families.

I glance into the mirror and study the reflection. I see nothing more than a forty-seven-year-old Bombay schoolteacher wearing a white, cotton saree with a pale blue border. Her forehead is wrinkled from time, her unusually pale skin now darkened by the India sun. Her black hair grayed like that of any other. Her feisty nature long replaced by a fatigue she has gathered year after year, painting a muted cry of helplessness, rounding her shoulders on this late day of the Hindu month of Shravan.

Who is this woman looking back at me? A ghost of Colonial India?

No.

There is nothing left of that ghost. Nothing particularly Anglo about her. Not anymore. Any trace of that physicality or insecurity has long since dissipated. This is a Bombay schoolteacher far from the boundaries that divide Punjab along religious lines. As I study her now, this middle-aged woman could be Hindu or Muslim or Sikh. Or for that matter, she could be Parsi, Jewish, or Catholic. She could even be a representative of a free India. My mother's revelation has just recast my life, but it also validates this moment in history. Indeed, I can finally find peace. I look again at her letter and its very last sentences.

You now understand that freedom is a spirit that must be given a voice. And give thanks to people like Ryaz. It has become our choice now.

Please forgive me, my daughter, and live in peace.

Your Loving Ma

The streets are alive with euphoric jubilation. India has finally arrived at her destiny – after a long slumber and harsh struggle. She awakes now, vital and free. History begins on a new page, open for us to live, act, and write about. I can hear the resonance of excited voices opening a blossom of hope inside of me.

"Jai Hind!"

Reenita brings life to her stories from her South Asian experiences, featuring quirky characters who navigate a rollercoaster of imperfect scenarios – but who refuse to sell out.

She's an editor, writer, and script supervisor for notable publications and platforms such as National Geographic Kids, Disney India, Cartoon Network Asia, the New York Times, and CNN. Reenita garnered numerous awards, including the Eric Hoffer Book Award, the IndieReader Discovery Award, Santa Barbara International Screenplay Award, Script2Comic, Launchpad, and Emerging Screenwriters awards.

She produces two podcasts: the True Fiction Project (unscripted to scripted), and Shadow Realm (narrative fiction). Recently, LA Weekly dubbed her a 'top indie author' bringing Indian culture and humor to America.

Screenwriter & top indie author Reenita reinvents Indian humor in America – LA Weekly.

Reenita inked a Production Development agreement for her young adult romcom screenplay, *Operation Mom*. She also optioned her unpublished book, *Shadow Realm*, and a literary memoir, *Ace of Blades*. Anticipate her upcoming literary work, *Festival of Lights* with Harper Collins and her newest work, *Vermilion Harvest: Playtime at the Bagh* with Indignor House Publishing.

http://www.reenita.com

Reenita M. Hora

Vermilion Harvest

Author's Thoughts

From the echoes of my childhood, whispered from tales of my grandfather, Gopal Krishan Vij, the tragedy of Jallianwala Bagh seared deeply into my heart. He, a boy of eight or nine, bore witness to the aftermath, his memory of chappals piled high at the entrance – a stark, haunting reminder of the lives lost, ignited my obsession with this pivotal moment in time.

At sixteen and under the arches of Cathedral & John Connon Senior School, I stepped into the shoes of those affected by the massacre through a role in a savage house play written by Erna Vachha Gandhi that lit the flame of my curiosity. This wasn't just an act – it was an awakening to the tragedy's profound impact on India's quest for independence.

In crafting my story, the plight of the Anglo-Indian community had always captivated me – caught me between two worlds and belonging to neither. A duality that led to broader struggles for identity and acceptance and which led to my protagonist, Aruna Duggal, who emerged from this liminal space, navigating a world that offered no rest.

Aruna's love story with Ayaz Peermohammed, a young Muslim student, added conflict that delved into the complexities of interfaith relationships, a theme that still resonates with the power to challenge societal norms.

Reenita M. Hora

Vermilion Harvest

Acknowledgments

✓ To my grandfather, Gopal Krishan Vij, for kindling the storyteller in me with his vivid memories. His legacy is the cornerstone of my journey into writing.

✓ To Nikhil Rao, Associate Professor of History, a beacon of knowledge and dear friend since Cathedral days, whose generosity opened the doors to Colonel Dyer's court briefings, enriching my story with authenticity and depth.

✓ To Erna Vachha Gandi, whose play 'Playtime at the Bagh' not only inspired the subtitle of this book but deepened my connection to Jallianwala Bagh's haunting legacy and to a stage where I experienced history and my soul intertwine.

✓ To Lynn Yvonne Moon of Indignor House, my editor and publisher, whose belief in this story transformed it from manuscript to masterpiece. Lynn took a leap of faith with this narrative, embracing it with a passion that rivaled and perhaps surpassed my own. Her meticulous editing, iteration after iteration, elevated this story to its finest form.

✓ And to the indomitable spirits of Amritsar and Punjab, whose resilience and stories infuse this book with life. This narrative is a tribute to their legacy, weaving a love story not just with the characters but with India itself – as profound, complicated, and deep as the saga of the Titanic.

Reenita M. Hora

Vermilion Harvest

Glossary

almirah	a wardrobe
Andaman Islands	India activists were sent to the Andaman Islands for solitary confinement
Babaji	Great Avatar - Revered Father
bartan	a metal utensil used for cooking
Bhagavan-ji	a general acceptance of the Lord or God
bhaiji	brother, with respect
bindi	a pinch of vermilion power placed over the sixth chakra (above the nose/between the eyes) to retain energy and strength of concentration
chole bhature	a food dish of garbanzo bean and curry with puffed bread popular in the northern areas of the Indian subcontinent
dal fry	an Indian lentil dish
Danda Fauj	baton carrying army
dastar	an item of headwear associated with Sikhism (culture)
Dhaba	a roadside restaurant in the Indian subcontinent
dupatta	a long shawl-like scarf
gidda-dancing	a popular folk dance of women in the Punjab region
highfalutin	pretentious, fancy - expressed in or marked by the use of language that is elaborated or heightened by artificial or empty means – pompous
Imam	the person who leads prayers in a mosque
Imperial Legislative Council	the legislature of British India from 1861 to 1947
jaan	widely used term of endearment, the direct translation is *life*
Jalandhar	ancient city and third largest in Punjab
kadha prasad	a super delicious halwa our pudding that is served in gurudwaras as prasad
kalgi	plume or crest to adorn the front of a turban
kameez	traditional long tunic combination dress
karma	a cosmic law of cause and effect
KHaala-zaad-bahan	daughter of mother's sister
Khatri Punjabi	a traditional mercantile class of Punjab

kurta	tunic like kameez, collarless and a set of pajama pants
lachha paratha	a flaky and crisp layered whole wheat flatbread
lassi	an Indian yogurt-based beverage with a smoothie-like consistency
lathi	long, heavy bamboo stick used a baton
mangalsutra	an auspicious thread – a groom ties it around a bride's neck in India
mangetar	male fiancé
maulvi	a Muslim doctor of law; an imam
memsahib	a white foreign woman of high social status living in India
Mussalmaan	a common equivalent for Muslim - slang
pagdi	the term for turban
pallu	the loose end of a sari that hangs over the shoulder or the head
Provence	a region in southeastern France
Punjabi	an Indo-Aryan language
punkah	slow-moving fan
Rambagh Palace, Jaipur	the former residence of the Maharaja of Jaipur located a few miles outside the walls of the city of Jaipur on Bhawani Singh road
rationwala	a person in charge of a rations
sabha	'assembly' – important unit of self-government in Hindu society
Satyagraha	a phrase coined by Mahatma Gandi – a passive political resistance
satyagrahi	a person who practices Satyagraha
shikar	hunting, as a sport
Sikh	an ethnoreligious group who adheres to Sikhism or Dharmic religion from the late 15th century in the Punjab region of India
Swadeshi Movement	a self-sufficiency movement that was part of the Indian independence crusade and contributed to the development of Indian nationalism (1903)
talwar	a type of curved sword or sabre from India
tonga	tonga or tanga is a light carriage or curricle drawn by one horse used for transportation in the Indian subcontinent
Waheguru	a term used to refer to God
wala	person who is associated with a particular work or performs a specific duty or service
waqt	an Urdu word that has several meanings, such as an opportunity

Vermilion Harvest

Reenita M. Hora

Printed in the USA
CPSIA information can be obtained
at www.ICGtesting.com
LVHW041544290724
786663LV00006B/543